FORTUNE

FAVORS

THE

DEAD

FORTUNE
FAVORS
THE
DEAD

A NOVEL

STEPHEN
SPOTSWOOD

DOUBLEDAY   New York

Copyright © 2020 by Stephen Spotswood

All rights reserved. Published in the United States by Doubleday,
a division of Penguin Random House LLC, New York, and distributed
in Canada by Penguin Random House Canada Limited, Toronto.

www.doubleday.com

DOUBLEDAY and the portrayal of an anchor with a dolphin
are registered trademarks of Penguin Random House LLC.

Book design by Maria Carella
Jacket illustration by Rui Ricardo / Folio Art
Jacket design by Michael J. Windsor

Library of Congress Cataloging-in-Publication Data
Names: Spotswood, Stephen, author.
Title: Fortune favors the dead : a novel / by Stephen Spotswood.
Description: First edition. | New York : Doubleday, [2020]
Identifiers: LCCN 2020003428 (print) | LCCN 2020003429 (ebook) |
ISBN 9780385546553 (hardcover) | ISBN 9780385546560 (epub) |
ISBN 9780385547239 (export edition)
Subjects: GSAFD: Mystery fiction.
Classification: LCC PS3619.P68 F67 2020 (print) | LCC PS3619.P68 (ebook) |
DDC 813/.6—dc23
LC record available at https://lccn.loc.gov/2020003428
LC ebook record available at https://lccn.loc.gov/2020003429

MANUFACTURED IN THE UNITED STATES OF AMERICA

10   9   8   7   6   5   4   3   2   1

First Edition

To my father, Bob Spotswood,
who taught me to love a good mystery

Very few of us are what we seem to be.

—Agatha Christie, *The Man in the Mist*

WILLOWJEAN PARKER: The circus-trained right-hand woman of Lillian Pentecost. Learning the highs and lows of being a working detective.

LILLIAN PENTECOST: New York City's preeminent lady gumshoe. Not as steady on her feet as she used to be, but it's her steel trap of a mind you need to watch out for.

ALISTAIR COLLINS: Steel magnate and coldhearted patriarch. A little over a year ago he picked up a gun and put the final punctuation on his own life.

ABIGAIL COLLINS: Matriarch of the Collins family. Somebody ruined her Halloween party by bludgeoning her to death with a crystal ball.

REBECCA COLLINS: Daughter of Al and Abigail. Bold, beautiful, and more than just your average society girl.

RANDOLPH COLLINS: Rebecca's twin brother. Looking to take over where his father left off, and he figures that includes keeping his sister in line.

HARRISON WALLACE: Godfather to Rebecca and Randolph and acting CEO of Collins Steelworks and Manufacturing. Says he wants justice for Abigail, but that might just be lip service.

ARIEL BELESTRADE: Medium and spiritual advisor to the Upper East Side. Says she can speak with the dead, but is she leaving bodies in her wake?

NEAL WATKINS: Former university wunderkind turned Ariel Belestrade's assistant. How close is he following in his employer's footsteps?

OLIVIA WATERHOUSE: Mild-mannered professor with a passion for the occult. Her obsession with Ariel Belestrade might go beyond the academic.

JOHN MEREDITH: Longtime plant manager and brawl-scarred bruiser. He has a chip on his shoulder and strong feelings about the Collins clan.

DORA SANFORD: The Collinses' longtime cook. More than willing to spill the beans.

JEREMY SANFORD: The Collinses' butler. Practicing the perfect poker face, he keeps the family secrets locked up tight.

ELEANOR CAMPBELL: Lillian Pentecost's cook and housekeeper. Loving, loyal, and not to be trifled with.

LIEUTENANT NATHAN LAZENBY: One of the NYPD's sharpest. Underestimate him at your own risk. Willing to give Pentecost and Parker just enough rope to hang the killer. Or themselves.

FORTUNE

FAVORS

THE

DEAD

CHAPTER 1

The first time I met Lillian Pentecost, I nearly caved her skull in with a piece of lead pipe.

I had scored a few shifts working guard duty at a building site on West Forty-second. A lot of the crew on Hart and Halloway's Traveling Circus and Sideshow picked up gigs like that whenever we rolled into a big city. Late-night and off-day gigs where we could clock in after a performance and get paid cash on the barrel.

There were more jobs like that available in those years. A lot of the men who'd usually have taken them were overseas hoping for a shot at Hitler. When you're desperate to fill a post, even a twenty-year-old cirky girl starts to look good.

Not that it required much of a résumé. It was a knuckle-head job. Walk the fenced-in perimeter from eleven until dawn and keep an eye out for anyone slipping through the fence. If anyone did, I was supposed to ring a bell and shout and make a ruckus to drive them away. If they refused, I ran and found a cop.

At least that was what I was *supposed* to do. McCloskey—the site foreman, who was paying me—had other thoughts.

"You catch anyone slipping in, you give them a good clobber with this," he said, tugging at his greasy moustache. *This* was a two-foot length of lead pipe. "You do that, you get an extra dollar bonus. Gotta set an example."

Who I was setting an example for, I didn't know. I also didn't know what was around the site that would be worth stealing. Construction had just started, so it was basically a giant hole in the ground half the size of a city block. Some lumber, some pipe, a few tools, but nothing really worth pinching. This close to Times Square, I was more likely to get drunks looking for a place to sleep it off.

I expected to spend a handful of uneventful nights, collect a few bucks, and be done with my shift in time to run back to Brooklyn and help with the circus's matinee. I was also hoping to find some quiet time to devour the detective novel I'd picked up at the newsstand down the street. Maybe catch a few hours' sleep in some corner of the yard. On the road, solitary sleep—especially sleep without the rumble of trucks or the roar of the tigers prowling in their cage across the yard—was a rarity.

The first two nights, that was exactly how it went. It was actually kind of lonely. New York might be the city that never sleeps, but even those few blocks in the heart of Midtown took a catnap between two and five. Not much in the way of foot traffic, or at least little that could be heard through the seven-foot-high wooden fence surrounding the construction site. That half-block hole in the ground was eerily quiet.

So on the third night the creak of a board being pried away from the fence rang out like a bell.

Heart racing, I grabbed the piece of lead pipe and made my way around the edge of the pit. I was wearing dungarees and a denim shirt—soft fabrics that didn't make a sound. My boots had worn-thin soles, which didn't do any favors for my arches

but meant I was able to slip like a shadow. I crept up on the figure crouched on its haunches at the edge of the pit.

Whoever it was picked up a handful of dirt and let it
sift through their fingers. I thought about yelling and trying to drive them off, but they were bigger than me. In their
other hand they were brandishing what looked like a stick or
cudgel—something heftier than my length of pipe at any rate.
If I yelled and got rushed, I wasn't sure I'd be able to stay on my
feet long enough to hit back.

I took one slow step after another. When I was only a short
stride away I lifted the pipe above my head. I wondered what
it would feel like when I brought it down. Could I finesse it so
I just knocked them out? Detectives were always managing to
do that in the dime novels. More likely, I'd crack their skull
open like an egg. My stomach did the same kind of slow flip it
performed when I watched the trapeze artists.

I still had the pipe raised above my head when the figure
turned and looked at me.

"I'd prefer not to end my day with a concussion," she said
with a voice even as a tightrope. The hefty guy I had been
afraid would rush me was a woman. She was around the age
my mother would have been with her hair done up tight in an
intricate bun.

"You're not supposed to be here," I told her, managing to
keep my vibrating heart out of my voice.

"That remains to be seen," she said. "Have you worked
here long?"

"A few nights."

"Hmmm." There was disappointment in that murmur.

By all rights, I should have told her to scram. But for some
reason, call it fate or boredom or an inborn pernicious streak,

I kept talking. "I think McCloskey—that's the site manager—only just started hiring night guards. I think he used to spend the night here sleeping in his shack so he could double dip. That's what some of the morning shift guys told me anyway."

"Better," she declared.

She stood slowly, using the cane in her left hand for leverage. She was tall and solidly built, wearing a tailored houndstooth suit that looked expensive and an ankle-length coat like the kind Blackheart Bart wore when he did his sharpshooter act.

"Is that his shack?" she asked, looking over at the small wooden structure a quarter turn around the pit.

I nodded.

"Show me, please."

By that point, it was clear to both of us there would be no clobbering, so I figured why not. Maybe it was because the alternative would have been ringing up the police, and I have a cultivated dislike of anyone with a badge.

I headed over to the shack in the corner of the yard. She followed a little behind, using the cane as she went. She wasn't limping so much as wobbling a little. I wasn't sure what was up with her, but the cane obviously wasn't for show.

McCloskey had called the shack his office, but I'd seen chicken coops built sturdier. We were never supposed to go inside, and besides, the door was locked. The mysterious woman took something from an inner pocket of her coat—a thin, bent piece of wire—and went to work on the padlock. After a minute of fumbling, I piped up, "You need to go at it from the bottom."

"How do you mean?"

I took the wire out of her hand and had the job done in ten seconds flat. I'd picked harder locks blindfolded. Literally.

"You should get yourself some real picks if you're going to do this kind of thing regular," I told her.

In all the years after, I only ever saw her smile about three dozen times. She graced me with one then.

"I'll keep that in mind," she said.

The inside of the shack matched the outside. Dirty and jerry-built. There was a desk fashioned out of a couple discarded boards and some sawhorses. Papers were scattered haphazardly across it. On it were also a lantern and an army-issue field phone that someone had rigged so McCloskey could make calls without leaving to find a pay phone. The rest of the space was taken up by a narrow cot and a pile of dirty rags that on second glance were clothes.

My companion lit the lantern. The addition of light didn't do the cramped room any favors. I've seen monkey cages less filthy.

"Describe Mr. McCloskey," she said, fixing me with eyes the gray-blue of a winter sky.

"I don't know. Forty or so. Average, I guess."

She gave me a look I have come to refer to as her disappointed schoolmarm. "Average doesn't exist. Not when it comes to human beings. And don't guess unless circumstances force you to."

I was starting to regret not using the lead pipe.

"Okay," I said with a bit of a sneer. "About a foot taller than me, so figure six feet, give or take. About two hundred pounds—a lot of it fat, but there's some muscle under there. Like a roustabout who's taken to the bottle. From the patches on his trousers, I'd say he has two sets of clothes, neither of them more than three bucks combined. He's cheap but wants people to think he has flash."

"What made you determine that?" she asked.

"From how much he's paying me. Also, he wouldn't spend two bits for a shave but dropped at least five for a gaff watch."

"A gaff?"

"A fake, a phony."

"How do you know it's fake?"

"No way is this guy buying gold."

There was something in her eyes then. The same look Mysterio got right before he sawed his lovely assistant in half.

"Do you have his phone number in case of emergencies?" she asked.

"Yeah, sure. But he said not to use it unless something's really gone sideways."

"Something has indeed gone sideways, Miss . . ."

"No Miss. Just Parker," I told her. "Willowjean Parker. Everyone calls me Will."

"Please call Mr. McCloskey, Will. Tell him there's an intruder and she won't leave. Tell him she's asking about a gold watch."

It was an easy call to make, since it was the truth. After I hung up, the woman—who still hadn't introduced herself, and don't think I wasn't a little annoyed at that lapse in basic manners—asked me how he'd sounded.

I told her he'd sounded normal at first—sleep drugged and annoyed. But when I mentioned the watch, a thread of something like panic had come into his voice. He said he'd be right over and not to let this woman go anywhere in the meantime.

She gave a small, satisfied nod, then sat down on the cot, back straight, gloved hands holding her cane across her lap. She closed her eyes, calm as my great-aunt Ida praying in church. She reminded me of pictures of Okie wives I'd seen in issues of *Life,* a weatherworn face waiting patiently for the coming storm.

I thought about asking her what this was all about. Or at least her name. She had mine, after all. But I decided I didn't want to give her the satisfaction. So I stood there and waited with her.

After ten minutes of silence she suddenly opened her eyes and said, "I think it would be best, Will, if you were to leave out the Eighth Avenue exit. There is a station house about twelve blocks south."

"You want me to get the cops?"

"Ask them to call Lieutenant Nathan Lazenby. Tell them there's been a murder and that Lillian Pentecost says to come at once. Unless they wish to read about it in the *Times.*"

I opened my mouth, but she flashed me a look that said it was no use arguing, so I dashed out and toward Eighth Avenue but stopped before I reached the gate.

Like I said, there's no love lost between me and authority figures, especially those who carry guns and billy clubs and aren't afraid to do some judicious clobbering of their own. Besides, what did this woman think would happen? I drop her name and a whole squad of dicks come running?

Lillian Pentecost. Who the hell did she think she was, anyway?

Instead, I quietly retraced my steps around the pit. Before I'd gotten back to the shack the shriek of old brakes on Forty-second Street announced McCloskey's arrival.

I hurried to the rear of the rickety structure and crouched down. The walls were thin and I could hear everything. I figured that worked in reverse, so I kept still and quiet.

There was the sound of footsteps double-timing it across hard dirt, then of the door creaking open.

"Hey. Who are you? Where's the little carny?"

"I've sent Will away, Mr. McCloskey. I thought it best if we had this conversation in private."

"What conversation? What's the deal? Who are you?"

"I am Lillian Pentecost." There was a little inhale there. Apparently he recognized the name and wasn't too happy about it. "And the deal is that you are wearing a murdered man's watch."

"What are you talking about? That's a lie. I bought this watch. From a guy at a bar. Twenty bucks, it cost."

I shook my head. Apparently nobody'd taught him that adding too many details was the quickest way to foul a grift.

"The police will, of course, ask you which bar and the name of the man who supposedly sold you the watch and so forth and so on," Ms. Pentecost said. "But I think we can dispense with that. If for no other reason than no one would sell a Patek Philippe for twenty dollars."

"I don't know a Patty Phillip from nothing. This guy said he was hard up. Needed the cash." The whine that had crept into his voice advertised his guilt better than any Broadway marquee.

"Jonathan Markel was indeed in need of money, Mr. McCloskey. But not so badly as to barter with you."

"Who's Jonathan Markel?"

"The man you bludgeoned to death and from whose wrist you slipped that watch."

"Lady, you're crazy."

"Debatable. I've been accused of rampant narcissism, hysteria, deviancy, and a variety of delusional psychoses. But the dirt covering the back of Mr. Markel's suit coat was no delusion. Dirt that certainly did not come from the alley where his body was found. Nor were the grooves in his skull a delusion. Grooves that I feel confident will match the kind of lead pipe you instructed Will to employ on trespassers."

Even through the wall of the shack, I could hear McCloskey breathing. Heavy and panicked.

As Ms. Pentecost continued, she developed a hitch in her voice. Like her words were catching on something in her throat. I started to wonder just how calm this woman really was.

"I would have come upon you sooner, but . . . it was not until yesterday that I was able to examine the clothes Mr. Markel . . . was wearing that night. This construction site is one of only a . . . handful between his club and the alley where he was found. Perhaps there was no initial malevolence. Perhaps . . . after an evening of drinking, Mr. Markel sought a private spot to relieve himself and slipped through the gap in your fence. Mistaking him for a thief, you . . . hit him. A little . . . too hard, perhaps? An accident?"

"Yeah. . . . Yeah, an accident." It came out in a croaked whisper, like McCloskey was being squeezed. And the squeezer wasn't finished.

"But the second and . . . third strikes were certainly not accidents. Nor was it an accident that you stole his wallet and . . . watch. Or the subsequent covering up of the crime. These . . . were not accidents."

One of my legs took that moment to cramp. I shifted my crouch, careful to avoid crunching on loose gravel. When I got situated again, there was only silence inside the building. Then the hard click of a gun being cocked.

"Don't move, lady." The thread of panic in McCloskey's voice had swollen. I could practically hear the pistol shaking in his hand.

"Mr. McCloskey, this pit you . . . find yourself in cannot be escaped by . . . digging deeper. The police have been notified. They are on their way . . . even as we speak."

This was delivered in a slightly chiding tenor, like she was informing a waitress that she'd ordered the tomato soup, not the minestrone.

Except she was wrong. The cavalry had definitely not been called.

I don't know what was said next, because I was busy slipping around to the front of the shack, every muscle tense as I waited for the impending crack of a gunshot. The door to the shack was open. I peered inside.

McCloskey had his back to me. He had a gun—an ugly, snub-nosed thing—pointed right at her head. I caught him midsentence.

"—supposed to be here. I come in, find this strange woman snooping around. Maybe you leap at me holding that pipe there. The one you say killed that guy."

Ms. Pentecost was sitting just as I'd left her, gloved hands still primly folded across the cane in her lap. I'd have been sweating buckets, but she didn't betray an ounce of fear. In fact, her eyes were bright with something not too far from joy.

She gave a brisk shake of the head. "I don't believe the police will accept that theory, Mr. McCloskey. They are frequently . . . obstinate, but rarely . . . stupid."

The cane looked sturdy enough—smooth black wood topped with a heavy brass handle. I thought maybe she was thinking of lashing out and surprising him with it. Except I'd had a cousin who got that kind of hitch in her voice. Had a limp, too, though hers was a lot worse. I suspected that leaping up and clubbing a man wasn't in Lillian Pentecost's repertoire.

"Yeah, well—it'll be your word against mine," McCloskey sneered. "And you won't be doing any talking."

When I was questioned later—and boy did I get questioned—I said that I didn't think. I just reacted.

Except I did think. The circus kept me on because I had quick hands and an even quicker head. So I had a split-second, lightning-flash inner debate.

The voice in my head arguing the side of running away and letting what happened happen sounded a lot like Darla Delight. Dee-Dee was a former showgirl who did the books for the circus. Very practical woman. When Big Bob Halloway, the owner, would have his semiweekly brilliant idea for a new act, Darla was the one who would calculate the cost and put the kibosh on nine out of every ten brainstorms.

"Have to think about the costs," she'd say. "Especially the invisible ones. All those things that might not be on the bill but you end up paying in the long run. They'll come back and bite your ass."

The voice on the other side of my inner debate sounded a lot like my father. He never counted any cost. He just did what he wanted and damned who got hurt. That I listen to his voice more often than not is something I still wrestle with.

McCloskey muttered something I couldn't catch. Whatever it was caused Ms. Pentecost to lean forward on the cot, like a dog testing its leash.

"Who?" she said. "Who told you that?"

"Ah well," he muttered, more to himself than her. "In for a penny and all that." His arm straightened and his finger tightened on the trigger.

No more debate. I'd made my choice. I was already kneeling down, pulling up the leg of my trousers, and grabbing hold of the hilt of the knife I kept fastened to my calf in a leather sheath.

Long hours spent with Kalishenko in a hundred dust-choked fields between Boise and Brooklyn made what happened next almost too easy. I stood, and in the same motion brought the knife up and over my head in a long arc.

I remembered Kalishenko's words, delivered in a perpetually slurred Russian accent. "You do not throw the blade. You do not throw your arm. You throw your entire body forward. The trick is learning to let go at the precise moment."

I threw myself forward and let go at the precise moment.

The weighted blade hit home with a sickening thud. But instead of a pockmarked wooden target, it buried itself a full three inches into McCloskey's back. I'd learn later that only the very tip of the blade pierced his heart. It wasn't much. But it was enough.

The gun fell from his hand. Ms. Pentecost reached out with her cane and knocked it out of reach. McCloskey stumbled, clawing at the hilt sticking out of his back. Then he collapsed forward, his head clipping the edge of the cot. He gave a last, ugly gurgle before going still and silent.

Ms. Pentecost knelt by his body. I expected her to check for a pulse. Instead, her hands went to the watch. A few quick twists and the watch face popped open, revealing a small, hidden compartment. Whatever was inside disappeared into her hand, then the inner pocket of her coat, before she clicked the watch face closed.

"How do you feel?" she asked, standing.

"I don't know," I said. My hands were shaking and my breath was coming quick and shallow. It was a coin flip as to whether I was going to pass out.

"Can you walk?" she asked.

I nodded.

"Good. I fear we will both . . . need to go to the station house."

"Do we have to?" I asked. "It's just I'm not too fond of cops."

She *almost* smiled again.

"They have their purposes. And they do . . . frown on the casual littering of bodies. But I will be with you."

We began the twelve-block walk through dead-of-night New York City, me keeping my pace slow, both to accommodate my new companion and because I was still feeling a little shaky. The buildings seemed taller, the streets narrower. Everything felt higher and darker and more dangerous.

Ms. Pentecost laid a hand on my shoulder. She kept it there most of the way to the station house. For some inexplicable reason, it made me feel better. Like she was passing on a little of whatever had kept her even and calm while staring down the barrel of a gun.

She didn't thank me for saving her life. Come to think of it, she never has. Though it could be argued she paid me back a hundredfold.

It wasn't until years later when somebody suggested I start writing all this down that I was reminded about those invisible costs. They ended up being higher than I would ever have thought possible. I've never really tallied them up, though. I guess in writing this I'll be forced to. I don't rightly know how the balance sheet will come out. In the red? Or in the black?

CHAPTER 2

Ms. Pentecost's promise to stay by my side lasted all of about ten minutes after we got to the station. We were separated and I was taken to a windowless interview room, where I spent the next several hours being grilled by a rotating cast of intense, florid-faced men in cheap suits.

I thought about trying out some girlish charm, but I've never quite gotten the hang of it. Flirting was also out. I wasn't dressed for the part, and besides, I had no illusions about my looks. I inherited my father's puggish nose and muddy brown eyes, and the freckles I got from my mother tend to clump awkwardly across the tops of my cheeks.

So I opted for the almost-straight truth.

It started with a pair of sergeants who had me go through the events of the evening forward, backward, and inside-out. I gave them the lot, save for the trick watch, and that wasn't a load-bearing detail so it was easy enough to subtract.

Eventually the set of sergeants was replaced by a detective who looked so wet behind the ears I'm surprised they let him carry a gun. He had me go through the night's events again, this time with a little more focus on everything Ms. Pentecost said about this Jonathan Markel.

Again, I gave him the lot minus one.

After an hour, I got promoted again. Another detective—

this one sporting a face as hard and cold as a chunk of granite, with a gray and black beard that tumbled wildly down to his Windsor knot. He was a veteran cop, or at least I assumed as much from his age, his demeanor, and the way the baby detective scraped and bowed on his way out of the door. It turns out this bearded giant—he easily cracked six feet—was Lieutenant Lazenby, the detective Ms. Pentecost had name-dropped. If I was under the impression they were friends, he quickly disabused me of that.

"How much is Pentecost paying you?"

"When did she set you up with that job?"

"Did Pentecost plant the gun, or did she make you do it?"

"Who's her client?"

"Did she tell you who really murdered Markel? You let us in on that, and we'll get the district attorney to cut you a deal."

And a lot more along those lines.

I imagine for anyone who hasn't had a nose-to-nose with the law this could all seem terrifying. As it happens, being part of a traveling circus that on occasion skirted if not outright trampled civil ordinances, I had long experience sitting in police stations, being pushed around by a grab bag of state troopers and small-town sheriffs. To be honest, those hick sheriffs scared me a lot more than any of these city dicks.

If Lazenby was expecting to knock me off my story, he was out of luck. Eventually he realized as much, and I was given a statement to sign. After reading through it and making sure nothing had been inserted, I did.

"Willowjean Parker? That a real name?" he asked after I added my John Hancock.

"You think if I'm going to forge a moniker I'd stick myself with Willowjean?" I said, trying a charming grin on for size. Apparently it didn't fit.

"I don't know if I believe a word of this," he said, holding up the statement. "I don't know if the DA will either. My men and I will be confirming the details. In the meantime, if you think of anything you want to add, you let me know."

"Sure," I said. "What number can I reach you at?"

It was his turn to grin. Then he promptly ordered me taken down to the holding cells.

At first the guard was going to put me in the men's section, but I popped off my cap to reveal my mop of red curls and he quickly hustled me to the other side of the building and the smaller, and fractionally cleaner, women's section.

I spent the next three days in that cell with little contact other than the guards. The only exception was early that first morning when I was joined by a trio of girls who got busted at a Chinatown whorehouse. Apparently the owner had missed a payment to a judge and the girls were paying the price. They mistook me for someone in the same line and gave me the name and number of their employer. They explained to me that there was a market for girls who can pass as boys and vice versa. Nothing I hadn't long ago learned.

Anyhow, I spent a handful of hours learning the ins and outs of the world's oldest profession as it's practiced on the higher end in New York City. By lunchtime, the girls had gotten bailed and I was left alone, save for the bedbugs, which were present in unseen thousands. I scored an old newspaper off a guard and put it down on top of the mattress, hoping to put a barrier between me and the vermin. Still, I figured everything I was wearing would have to be scrubbed, scoured, or outright burned when I got back to Hart and Halloway.

If I got back.

The circus was set to leave in three days and I hadn't heard word one about what was going to happen to me.

Funny thing, it wasn't the possibility of getting pegged for murder that preyed most on my mind. It was the look in Lazenby's eyes when I told him Willowjean Parker was my real name. Because it wasn't.

Willowjean was legit enough. Yeah, it wasn't the most common name, but my mother had given it to me and I couldn't bring myself to throw it away. But I'd tossed my last name as soon as I joined the circus. Parker had been stolen from a character in an issue of *Black Mask*.

I kept telling myself that tracking down my kin was a hundred-to-one shot. And, besides, what harm could it do? I was a grown woman now. Not the scared little girl who ran away from home all those years ago.

But sitting in that cell, my anxieties bred fast, and like with the bedbugs, scratching only made it worse. I spent the second night alone. The only light was from a dim bulb far down the corridor. The bravado I'd managed to conjure up and wear like a shield drained away. I pictured the cell door opening and my father stepping in, his face red, leather belt wrapped tight around his fist.

Found you.

I squeezed my eyes tight until I was finally able to toss myself into a fitful sleep.

A little before noon on the third day, the cell door slid open. But no one stepped in. Instead, I was ushered out and escorted upstairs to a different interview room. This one was their deluxe model. It had a window and chairs that didn't wobble. I was only left alone there for half an hour this time before the door burst open and Dee-Dee barreled in, an avalanche of red-dyed bouffant and jacked-up bosom.

"Will, baby, I've been so worried." She rushed to hug me but I held her off.

"Better not," I told her. "Not before I've been deloused."

She settled for blowing me a kiss and took a seat across from me at the little interview table.

"What's going on, Dee-Dee? I've been flying blind for three days."

"I'm not sure, honey. I gather the cops have been nailing down details on this Markel murder. But it looks like a sure thing McCloskey killed him. At least that's what it says in the papers."

"It's in the papers?"

"Front page for two days running," Dee-Dee said, smiling. "All about how McCloskey might have done things like this before and nobody suspected. How this Pentecost woman did what the police couldn't. Anyhow, they're springing you later this afternoon."

"Yes!" I pounded the table with a triumphant fist. "I have never been more happy to go back to my lumpy little cot next to the tiger cage."

Dee-Dee frowned. It was a look she usually reserved for Big Bob when he had a particularly expensive brainstorm.

"That's what I wanted to talk to you about," she said. "This Pentecost lady came by the grounds yesterday. Sat in Big Bob's trailer for an hour lobbing questions at him."

"About what?"

"About you. Seems she has a business proposition."

I leaned back in my chair, suddenly wary. "What kind of proposition?"

"Some kind of job. Something long-term. Bob said she wasn't specific. She convinced him she's on the level, though. He said you should listen to her."

"Bob wants me out?"

She reached across the table and took my hand.

"It's not like that. He just thinks it's in your best interests. I gotta say I agree."

"What are you talking about, Dee?" The circus was the be-all, end-all, alpha and omega for Bob and Dee-Dee. I couldn't imagine either of them siding against life under the big top.

"Here's the deal, sweetie. Traveling shows are on their way out. Audiences are thin on the ground. More competition from amusement parks. The smaller circuses are getting gobbled up by the big ones. You know the story. And it's only gonna get worse. Better to go out on your own terms than get handed a pink slip."

I'd spent the last five years eating, sleeping, breathing the circus. Leaving would be like giving up oxygen.

"I'm not saying you have to take the offer," Dee-Dee told me. "I'm just saying listen to her. Weigh the pros and cons with as clear an eye as you can."

She stood up.

"Now, I don't care what you're infested with, I want a hug."

She wrapped her arms around me and did her best to crack a rib.

"You end up saying yes, and it turns out this Pentecost broad has a screw loose or maybe she's one of those types with a secret twist, you come running back. Got it?"

"Got it, Dee."

"Love you, Will. You watch yourself." With that, she walked out.

A few minutes later, a guard I hadn't seen before escorted me from the interview room, down a maze of halls, and out a back door. A jet-black Cadillac sedan was waiting for me. The driver was an older woman whose bulk barely fit behind the wheel. She looked like the love child of a sideshow strongman and a warden at a women's prison.

"You the one calls herself Will Parker?" she asked, her Scottish accent scouring off a layer of skin.

"I'm the one calls myself that."

"I'm to take you to Ms. Pentecost," she brogued. "In the back with you. I've put down a sheet. No telling what you picked up after three days in that hellhole."

I got in the back, careful to keep from touching any uncovered surface. I was taken on a bumpy, swerving course, with my driver slamming on the brakes whenever a pedestrian even glanced her way. We headed across the Brooklyn Bridge and into one of the nicer neighborhoods of that particular borough.

The car stopped in front of a three-story brownstone separated on either side from its neighbors by narrow, gated alleys. The woman escorted me inside, then down a short hallway lined with padded benches. I went past what looked like a well-apportioned office and up a flight of stairs to the second floor, where she took me to a small bedroom with an attached bath. A pile of clothes I recognized as my own was sitting folded on the bed.

"Ms. Pentecost took the liberty of retrieving some of your things. There's soap and whatnot in the bathroom. Wash up good and when you're done Ms. Pentecost will see you down in her office. You leave what you're wearing in the bathroom and I'll see everything gets a good washing."

"I think your best bet is a good burning."

She gave a snort I figured for her version of a chuckle, then left me to my bathing.

This was the first time I'd ever had use of a proper shower. I turned the spigots to scalding and stayed under there until the hot water finally gave up the ghost. I spent a few minutes brushing out my hair, which had gotten marvelously knotted after three days tucked under my cap. Then I slipped into my clean clothes—another blue denim work shirt, my second-best boots, and a pair of brown corduroy overalls I'd bought off the rack in the boys' section and that fit like a glove. Not exactly attire for a job interview if that was what this was, but it would have to do.

I made my way downstairs and into the office I'd passed on my way in. It was surprisingly large and must have taken up half of the first floor. Massive bookshelves ran the length of two of the walls. They were packed to bursting with the kinds of books that tended toward leather-bound and likely boring. I preferred the kind that came with paper covers and lurid pictures of gun-toting molls. To be honest, I still do.

Where there weren't bookshelves, the walls were done in wallpaper—a pleasant shade of yellow with tiny blue poppies. There was a massive oak desk at the far end and a smaller one with a typewriter against the wall to the right. The room was illuminated by standing lamps stationed in the corners, as well as a pair of lamps with frosted green shades on each desk.

Above the big desk was an oil painting as wide as I was tall of a gnarled tree standing in the middle of an empty, yellow field. I thought it was an ominous kind of picture to have looming over your shoulder.

Arranged in a loose semicircle was a collection of armchairs upholstered in the same light yellow as the wallpaper. The chairs looked practical rather than decorative, and their arrangement suggested regular gatherings of people whose attention was focused on whoever was planted in the seat of honor.

I sat in the largest of these chairs and waited. A small, ornate clock mounted on the wall ticked away the minutes.

Staring up at the painting I noticed a detail I hadn't before—a woman in a cornflower-blue dress sitting cross-legged in the shade of the tree. I was leaning forward for a closer look when the door opened and Ms. Pentecost strode in.

She was dressed as she had been three nights ago—three-piece suit that was definitely tailored for a woman, complete with a red silk four-in-hand tie. Illuminated by the room's warm lamplight, I could make out details I hadn't before. She was forty-five, maybe a little younger. She had thick cheekbones that rode high enough they threatened to intrude onto her eyes, a wide mouth, and a too-sharp chin. All of it set around a nose that wasn't quite a hook but had aspirations.

Her hair was the kind of dark chestnut most women get out of a bottle, but I was pretty sure hers was natural. A streak of iron gray traveled up from the center of her deeply lined brow and lost itself in the labyrinth of her braided bun. She carried her cane but barely leaned on it.

"I trust you've had the opportunity to wash," she said, planting herself in the leather swivel chair behind her desk.

"I have, thanks."

"Have you eaten?"

"Nothing since what they brought me for dinner yesterday," I told her. "Bologna and cheese. At least I think it was bologna. I didn't look too close."

She scrunched up her nose in disgust.

"Mrs. Campbell is fixing lunch now," she said. "Cornish hen. In this house we like our meat identifiable."

"Sounds good to me." An understatement. After three days of jail food and five years of circus chow, Cornish hen sounded more like a fantasy than a meal.

"Other than the de facto starvation, I hope your treatment by the police was not too egregious."

I'd never encountered the words "de facto" and "egregious" in casual conversation, but I managed to translate.

"There was a lot of shouting, finger-pointing, and calling me a dirty, rotten liar," I said. "But they kept their billy clubs tucked away."

She nodded. "Good. I apologize for the delay in your release. There were bureaucratic snags, or at least that's what my attorney was told."

"Yeah, I think they were hoping I'd crack and tell them you planned the whole thing. Whatever 'the whole thing' was."

Her hand came up like she was swatting away a fly. "The police sometimes have fancies. They have not learned the lesson that correlation does not equal causation."

My inner translator failed. "What's that again?"

"Just because they find me embroiled in the unraveling of a crime, it does not mean that I'm responsible for the crime. Quite the contrary. Though in this case, they have at least half a point, as my arrival did directly lead to Mr. McCloskey's death."

I considered that logic for a couple beats. "A guy like that, someone who bashes a man's brains in for his watch and wallet, he's gonna end up in jail or in the ground eventually. No fault of yours."

A slow, satisfied nod. "A very pragmatic philosophy. Perhaps a little too grimly optimistic."

"Okay, yeah. Right," I said, making like I knew what she meant. "So . . . what's the pitch?"

"The pitch?"

"Dee-Dee said you had an offer. That I should give it a long think before brushing you off."

"What do you know about me and my work?" she asked.

You've got to take something into account. The previous five years of my life had been spent crisscrossing a big swath of the country, cooped up in trailers and truck beds, and pursuing a rather unique education. That education definitely did not include the regular consumption of New York's news-papers.

If you're thinking: How could this girl not know who Lil-lian Pentecost is? The most famous woman detective in the city and possibly the country. The woman who tracked down the murderer of Earl Rockefeller. Who discovered the identity of the Brooklyn Butcher. Who Eleanor Roosevelt herself turned to when someone tried to put the squeeze on.

All I can say is this: I can pick a lock blindfolded, walk a wire twenty feet in the air without a net, and wrestle a man twice my size into submission. How about you?

To her I said, "All I know about your game is what I picked up from the police. You're some kind of private dick."

"A private investigator, yes."

"And people pay you to solve things the police have miffed."

"I generally take cases the police have been unable to solve or, for whatever reason, are unwilling to invest time and effort in."

"Like this guy Markel?"

"That was unusual. Markel was an acquaintance, so there was a personal element."

She glanced away at that. Not quite a tell, but close. I noted for the first time that there was something off with one of her eyes—the left one. It wasn't quite the same shade of gray-blue as the right. It looked just a little flat—like it was reflecting the light differently. I'd find out later that it was made of glass. She'd had several made over the years and none had managed to get the color quite right.

"So what's this got to do with me?" I asked.

"As you might have noticed, I have certain physical limitations."

"Yeah, I picked that up. Sclerosis, right?"

"Multiple sclerosis. That's very perceptive."

"I had a cousin. She was a lot worse off than you, though."
That was an understatement. Last I saw her, Laura had been
spending more time in her bed than on her feet.

Ms. P nodded grimly. "Yes, I'm told by my physicians that
my symptoms are progressing slower than most." She shot a
baleful look at the cane propped against her desk. "However,
they *are* progressing."

A glimmer of what could have been rage flickered in her
good eye. She took a deep breath and a long exhale and the
glimmer was extinguished.

"My profession is a stressful one, and can be physically and
mentally taxing. Unfortunately, these things exacerbate my
condition. This means I find myself frequently too exhausted to
answer letters, arrange interviews, and otherwise deal with the
more mundane aspects of my job. Mrs. Campbell is an excellent cook and housekeeper, but her skills otherwise are limited.
And, to be frank, her imagination has long-ingrained limits."

"So you want to hire me to be, what?" I asked. "A secretary?
Because I can't type and I don't own any pencil skirts."

"More an assistant than secretary," she said. "While you
would handle the day-to-day business of running the office, you
would not be confined to it. As you discovered the other night,
a certain amount of legwork is required, though rarely does it
result in bloodshed. As for the office-management portion of
the job, I feel confident you can learn to type. From what Mr.
Halloway told me, you have a sharp mind and are proficient at
picking up new skills quickly.

"And as for the dress code," she continued, "I see no reason
you cannot wear what you wish within the confines of propri-
ety. I prefer suits, myself. I've found the abundance of pockets
to be quite useful. In exchange, you'd be provided room and

board, as well as expenses for any training I'd require of you. You would also be given a salary, paid every two weeks."

She quoted a number that nearly sent my poker face packing. Just one of those checks would be more cash than I'd ever had in hand in my life. Still, in order to cash that check, I'd have to cut ties with everything I'd known since I left home. My friends. My family. My world. To come work for a woman I barely knew.

"Why me?" I asked. "If this is because of what I did the other night, you could slip me a few bucks now and call it even. There's got to be better people you could get. People who actually know how to do the things you want done."

She took a full ten seconds to respond. She doesn't like to be scattershot with her words, and has a tendency to make people wait while she sits stone-faced, mulling over an answer.

"You might be correct," she finally said. "But I've learned to trust my instincts. Seeing firsthand your powers of observation and of action, and hearing about your particular set of skills and your capacity to learn, I think you might be exactly who I'm looking for."

Basically, yeah, there were better people for the job, but I could catch up. The deal sounded good, but not quite too good to be true. Still, there was the thing with the watch. I just couldn't let it go.

"I appreciate the offer," I said. "But I've got to ask . . . Are you a spy or something? There aren't many lines I won't hopscotch over, but signing on with a Nazi is definitely one of them."

She arched an inquisitive eyebrow. "Why do you ask?"

"The thing with the trick watch. Didn't seem like the kind of piece you'd hide blow in. And gems are out. You'd want to hide those in something people wouldn't want to steal. I fig-ured it was some kind of message."

Her look confirmed that was exactly what it was.

"Don't worry," I said. "I didn't tip that to the cops. I figured what they didn't know couldn't hurt me. But I don't want that coming back to bite me, you know?"

Another long silence.

"I am not a spy, Nazi or otherwise. Nor was Mr. Markel," she said. "Though there was a message contained in the watch, it was of a personal nature."

"Oh."

She shook her head. "Not that kind of personal."

I wasn't sure I believed that but let it go.

"Did it have anything to do with what McCloskey said at the end?" I asked.

"What do you mean?"

"He said something I didn't catch. You got all excited. Asked him, 'Who told you that?'"

She gave me a look I couldn't decipher. Like she'd just real-ized she wasn't quite sure what breed of dog she'd brought home from the pound. She took a deep breath and twisted her fingers together, a rare nervous habit.

"If you were to take this position, I would bring you into my confidence in nearly all of my investigations. To do other-wise would be impractical. But you would have to be resigned to the fact that I won't share everything with you. There are certain cases—ones I have been engaged in for several years, and which involve an element of danger—that I am unwilling to expose you to. Do you understand?"

"Sure," I said. "Every performer I ever worked with held something back. Usually their best gag."

"Gag?"

"Gag. Trick. Gimmick."

She nodded approvingly at the analogy.

"I understand it's an offer that requires a certain leap of faith," she said. "I cannot promise that you will be happy. Happiness is, I've found, an elusive thing. But I think I can promise you will find the work interesting."

"Do I have to answer right now?"

"Of course not. Please take the day." She came out from around her desk and retrieved a package from a side table. "While I was leaving the circus grounds I was stopped by a Mr. Kalishenko. He asked that I give you this."

She handed me the package. It was heavy and small, wrapped in brown paper and twine and with a sealed envelope taped to one side.

"I'll be in the kitchen seeing about lunch."

When she was gone, I opened the envelope. I'd never seen Kalishenko's handwriting, but it was exactly as I'd imagined—cramped and elegant but somehow slurred. No Russian accent, but I couldn't help but read it in one.

> *My dear Will,*
>
> *You told me once that you consider the circus your chosen family. I think you know, having left my family behind in the steppes, that I feel much the same way. But for the young, families should not be things you cling to. They should be something that helps propel you to new heights. The trick, you see, is knowing when to let go.*
>
> *Your friend forever,*
>
> *Valentin Kalishenko, Dancer of Blades, Master of Fire,*
> *Last and Final Heir of Rasputin*

PS: I heard that the commissariat would not return your blade. I hope you will find these a suitable replacement. I also hope you will never have to use them in such a manner again. However, hopes are fragile and the world is hard. You should walk into it prepared.

I unwrapped the package and found not one but a whole set of throwing knives. Unlike the one I'd left in McCloskey's back, each of these had a wooden handle, worn smooth with oil and long use. These were some of Kalishenko's originals—taken with him from Russia when he fled the fallout of the revolution. They were the best going-away present I could have imagined.

Then it hit me. He assumed I really was going away. In his mind, I'd already said yes.

For the first time in years, I started to cry. Just for a moment. Then it passed and I wiped my tears away. I put the letter and the knives on the smaller desk.

My desk now, I figured.

The first time I left home, I ran as fast as I could. This time, I needed a little shove. But there's no sense arguing with an heir to Rasputin.

I walked into the kitchen to see what was cooking.

CHAPTER 3

Three years passed.

Enough happened during that time to fill a dozen books. And if you're wondering why I'm not starting there—with the first case Ms. P and I ever worked together—it's because I don't know how this is going to go.

It's possible I'll type "The End" and never want to hit another key again.

So if I'm only going to tell one story, it might as well be the Collins murder. In a lot of ways that was a threshold moment for both of us. It set a lot of dominoes falling and left me with more than a few scars, physical and otherwise.

But first, I realize up to this point I've been a little cagey about my biography. That won't do. Not if I want you to understand everything that follows. Here are the essentials.

Born in a small town. I won't give the name so you don't have to pretend to have heard of it. Only child; mother died when I was six; father a third-generation railroad man and fourth-generation boozehound. You probably won't be surprised to learn I ran away from home the day after my fifteenth birthday.

I footed it two towns over, where the Hart and Halloway Traveling Circus and Sideshow was wrapping up a weeklong run. I hitched a ride and made friends with a group of the spec girls—the showgirls who appear in the larger big-top numbers and in the strip-show tent after dark. By the time the circus reached the next town, they'd practically adopted me. I don't know if they thought of me as a little sister or the daughter they'd never had. Either way, they got me a job at the bottom rung of the crew. Actually, I had to crane my neck to see the bottom rung. I spent the first few months scraping out animal cages, emptying latrines—anything they wanted to foist on the new kid.

When I proved I could shovel manure without fumbling, I got recruited doing general setup and takedown, providing backup for the games, greasing the crowd for the midway performers.

I'd been there maybe half a year when the Lovely Lulu got laid up with the nine-month flu and both Mysterio and Kalishenko were down one shared assistant.

Between Kalishenko's personality and Mysterio's wandering hands, none of the spec girls wanted the job, so I got drafted. I was squeezed into an outfit that was mostly bare thigh, rhinestones, and a spangly bustier the girls helped pad out with fabric scraps. I spent each day being handed off from magician to knife thrower and back again.

I was definitely no Lovely Lulu, and no amount of padding made me look like anything other than what I was: a fifteen-year-old tomboy in borrowed sparkles. That didn't stop a lot of our male audience from making propositions you'd be shocked to hear coming from the lips of good churchgoing folk.

Or if you're a woman, maybe you wouldn't be shocked at all.

Mysterio lived up to his reputation but kept his hands to himself after I purposefully flubbed one of his tricks, embarrassing him in front of a sold-out crowd.

Kalishenko was a different story.

His nickname among the crew was the Mad Russian. Partly because he professed to be a descendant of Rasputin, partly due to his tendency to hiss and snap and toss the occasional knife at whoever rubbed him the wrong way.

My job was mainly to stand still and let him outline my body with thrown blades, hold balloons in my teeth that he would pop—that sort of thing.

"Just stand, smile, bend over every few minutes to show the crowd your ass, and don't talk," he slurred. "No reason for little girls to talk."

After a couple weeks of this, he had the idea to add a bit where I got mad at him, grabbed one of the knives from the wooden target, and threw it back. It was supposed to go wide left. Instead, the first time we did it live I cut it so close to his face I practically trimmed his sideburns.

After the show he asked, "Did you do that on purpose?"

"It's ninety degrees and these bloomers are riding up like gangbusters. So, yes, I did it on purpose."

He gave a big, bearded smile—something I'd never seen him do when a crowd wasn't watching.

"Fantastic!" he exclaimed. "We keep it. But we make you better, okay?"

We made me better.

Other performers saw me working with Kalishenko and figured if I could make the Mad Russian happy, maybe I was worth investing a minute in. Over the next five years, I apprenticed with everyone who'd have me. I learned how to juggle fire and walk over hot coals, the basics of costuming and makeup from the spec girls and the clown crew, bareback horse riding, sharpshooting, cold reading from Madame Fortuna, how to handle the big cats, and more about the residents of the reptile house than I was ever really comfortable with. I spent so much time in the House of Oddities, I could tell at a glance if a new exhibit was a fake and make a pretty good guess how the fakery was done.

There weren't many skills I could learn from the born freaks in the sideshow. You're either blessed with a tail or you're not. But I felt more comfortable hanging around with the sideshow crew than with just about anyone else at the circus. I burned away a lot of late nights listening to stories about the good old days from the Alligator Boy or the Tattooed Woman.

I spent some time with the aerialists, but the high wire didn't come natural to me. I can make it across a tightrope, but only at the cost of a bucket of sweat and a year off my life.

The lock-picking skills were developed during a short, ill-advised romance with a contortionist. He was only with the show for a summer, but during that time he taught me how to tackle any lock ever made; how to wriggle out of a straitjacket, both rigged and legit; and a few other things you don't put on a résumé.

I even apprenticed with Mysterio, who turned out to be a halfway decent instructor once he learned that making passes at me gained him nothing but grief. I had such fast fingers he began using me as an audience plant. In front of a packed tent, I'd execute the smoothest deck-switch you ever saw. Or didn't see.

In short, I became the circus's jack-of-all-trades—able to assist just about any of the talent and filling in when necessary. Never stopped having to pad the bustier, though.

That's where I was when my life intersected with Lillian Pentecost. The day after I accepted her offer, I began the next leg of my odd education.

She said in her pitch that she'd foot the bill for any training, and she was as good as her word. Over the next three years, I took classes in stenography, bookkeeping, law, target shooting, auto mechanics, and driving, among a host of other things. She even pulled some strings to mock me up a birth certificate, making me legally Willowjean Parker. With that bit of forgery in hand I was able to get a driver's license, a private investigator's license, and a permit to carry a pistol.

"I do not expect you will have much cause to use it," Ms. P said when I picked up the latter. "But there are places you will be asked to go where it would be imprudent to be without a weapon."

In reality, I spent more time in lecture halls than pool halls. A week didn't go by where she didn't announce a trip to see this or that expert give a lecture about invertebrates or astronomy or abnormal psychology.

"When am I going to need to know the difference between mold and a mushroom?" I asked before one such excursion. I was sore that this particular lecture was replacing a much-anticipated night at the Rivoli for the latest Hitchcock.

"I don't know," she said. "But it's better to have the knowledge at hand and not need it than the reverse."

I couldn't argue. Though no case to date has hinged on either of us knowing the life cycle of fungus.

Anyhow, that was life—at least between cases.

When we were hot on a job, there was no time for lectures or movies and barely time for meals. One of my unwritten jobs—and there were many—was to make sure Ms. Pentecost got at least one square a day. A lot of times that meant steering her into the nearest diner and refusing to budge until she shoved a roast beef sandwich into her mouth.

This was an extension of one of my other unwritten jobs, which was to keep an eye on Ms. P's health and make sure she didn't push it so hard it did her harm. Her disease didn't get too much worse in those first few years. There were good days and bad days. On the good days, you wouldn't know she was sick at all and could mistake the cane for a fashion statement. On bad days, she would limp and stumble, and that hitch would creep into her voice. She was also tired more and in pain, though she tried not to show it.

Then there were the really bad days. The kind that lasted a week or more. Luckily, she didn't have them too often.

All in all, it was a good life.

The Collins murder fell into our lap on a Tuesday morning in mid-November 1945. Much of that summer had been spent tracking down a firebug who was lighting up tenements in Harlem. Ms. Pentecost wrapped that up just in time for us to join the rest of the city in celebrating Japan's surrender. After we shook off the hangover and swept up the confetti, we were immediately thrown into a homicide dressed up as a suicide—a bit of chicanery the police were unaware of until Ms. P gracefully pointed it out.

Just so you know, the climax of those cases consisted of short phone calls to the authorities. No getting all the suspects in a room and laying out the facts before pointing a finger. As much as I might like that kind of mystery novel, most of the time our cases ended with a quiet whisper in the right ear. No dramatic unmasking.

On that Tuesday morning, we were only a few days into our first break in a long time. I had a quick breakfast of eggs and biscuits at the kitchen table courtesy of Mrs. Campbell. She lives in a renovated carriage house attached to the back of the brownstone, so no matter how early I get up she's already in the kitchen stirring and scrambling.

If you're looking for her bio, there's not much I can tell you.

She's widowed; she's been with Ms. P forever; she's originally from a place she calls the "Border Counties"; and while she can cook, clean, and generally keep a house, she can't drive worth a damn. She rarely talks about herself, and by that time I had learned not to ask.

I opened and sorted the mail, then skimmed through my copies of that morning's major New York papers, marking what articles to clip for our files. I moved on from that and began jotting down a list of phone calls I needed to make. Most were responses to requests for interviews, quotes, and pictures. Anything to keep Ms. Pentecost's name out there and the phone ringing. I was finishing the list when the phone did exactly that.

"Pentecost Investigations. Will Parker speaking."

A fussy patrician voice asked me if Ms. Pentecost would be available to meet with Rebecca and Randolph Collins that afternoon. At that moment, the great dame detective was still asleep. Since she's practically nocturnal, it's rare that you see her illuminated by morning sunlight. Luckily, she had long ago given me leave to use my best judgment when it came to scheduling consultations, and my best judgment was that we wanted in on the Collins case.

Neither the murder nor the arson case had come with a big paycheck attached. But I was sure the Collins family could fork over whatever fee we demanded. The papers over the last couple weeks had hinted at an air of weirdness attached to the thing that I knew would pique my employer's interest. And if that didn't do the trick, I had an ace up my sleeve.

I told the voice that Ms. Pentecost would be happy to meet with the Collins siblings at three o'clock. Time enough for me to drag her out of bed, get Mrs. Campbell to fix her some biscuits and gravy, and give her a summary of the last two weeks of headlines.

The Collins murder was big news in a city numb to lurid crime. And it wasn't the first time the family had made forty-point headlines. They had first hit the front page nearly twenty years previous when Alistair Collins, owner and CEO of Collins Steelworks and Manufacturing, married his secretary, Abigail Pratt. Abigail was thirty years his junior, decidedly working-class, and four months pregnant at the time. Shotgun weddings were a rarity in that tax bracket—at least such public ones—and the press had a field day.

Over the next two decades, Al Collins's name popped up pretty regularly in the business section, usually in the context of how deftly he was running the company. He hit the A section a couple of times in the thirties when he hired some leg-breakers to bust up a strike. That resulted in a number of cracked skulls and at least one death. Or at least one the cops knew about. Nothing too uncommon in those days, but it prompted one journalist to wax poetic by saying, "Collins is known to have a heart as hard and cold as the steel being shaped in his factory."

Five years ago, he got promoted to the front page when Collins Steelworks won a big government contract and Alistair announced the company would be refitting its factories to build military machine parts instead of office supplies, guns having become somewhat more lucrative than staplers.

Then the headlines turned grim for the Collins clan.

A year ago that September, Alistair sat down at the desk in his home study, put a revolver in his mouth, and took the express train to the end of the line. Interviews with associates revealed that the manufacturing magnate had been recently depressed, but no one knew about what.

A few of the papers made not-so-subtle suggestions that Abigail had given her husband a hand in pulling the trigger. In response, representatives for the family pointed out that Alistair had recently done away with a prenuptial agreement severely limiting his wife's access to the family checking account. That, combined with the fact that Alistair's will put most of the family fortune in a trust to be given to their children, put the kibosh on any motive Abigail might have had to hasten his death. No less than the district attorney himself came out and said the death was definitely a suicide.

All of this had recently been given a light dusting-off in the papers on account of what had happened Halloween night two weeks prior. According to the reports, Abigail Collins had been throwing her annual Halloween shindig—a masquerade party where the upper executives of Collins Steelworks got to play dress-up, groove stiffly to a swing quartet, and down an ungodly amount of champagne.

From the November 2 edition of the *Times:*

> Among the masked frivolity, guests lost track of Mrs. Collins. Sometime around midnight, smoke was discovered pouring from under the door of the late Alistair Collins's private study. The door was found to be locked from the inside. When it was battered down, it was discovered that a blaze started in the room's fireplace had spread. More horribly, Mrs. Collins was found sitting at her late husband's desk, bludgeoned to death.
>
> Police are baffled as to how the killer escaped the room after having committed this awful deed. According to one unnamed officer, "That door can only be locked from the inside. The only window is barred shut. And there are no hidden passages. We checked. It's a real puzzler."
>
> Lieutenant Nathan Lazenby said he could not comment

on the details of an ongoing investigation, but that the
police were following a number of promising leads and
expected to lay their hands on a culprit soon.

"Soon" had turned into two weeks. Apparently, it was
indeed a "real puzzler."

Nowhere in the papers was there a rundown of that evening's events. No timeline, no off-the-record interviews with
guests. Nothing.

The absence of those kinds of details made me curious. Either someone had spread some wealth around to keep
things quiet, or the police were hot on the trail of somebody
and working hard to keep the lid closed so their prey didn't get
spooked. Considering it had been two weeks without the hint
of an impending arrest, I was betting on the former.

When the clock struck one, I grabbed a mug of strong coffee from the kitchen and climbed to the second floor to knock
on Ms. Pentecost's bedroom door. There was no response.
Undeterred, I let myself in.

"Good morning," I said cheerfully, flinging open the heavy
curtains and bathing the room in gray November light. "Well,
not so much good morning as good afternoon, but the senti-
ment's the same. What time did you get to sleep?"

A four-poster bed dominated the center of the room. From
beneath its thick, white duvet, I caught a murmured reply.

"Six o'clock."

I set the coffee and copies of that day's papers on the night-
stand by the bed, careful not to jostle the glass eye staring up at
me from its nest in a folded white handkerchief.

"Is the sun up at six o'clock in the morning in November?"
I asked. "I'm an early riser, but not quite that early. Unless
appointments demand it or I've had a particularly late night and

I've yet to see a bed. Though if something's exciting enough to keep me out that late I'm usually not looking at my watch."

She threw back the duvet and glared—a glare made more menacing by the fact that half of it came from an empty socket. But the effect was undercut by her hair, which tends to frizz up when let out of its braids and lean toward full bog witch after a night in bed.

"Are you tormenting me for a purpose?" she hissed.

I put on a bright smile and shook my head. "Merely delivering coffee and word of potential clients who will be arriving at three o'clock. I thought you'd want time to shower and eat and wrestle your hair into submission."

"We have no appointments today."

"We didn't," I said. "Now we do."

I walked out.

This might seem like odd behavior for someone whose job title has "assistant" in it and who can be fired at will. But I've found that sometimes the best way of assisting Ms. Pentecost is to make sure that she's awake and fed and vertical enough in order to do the work she's devoted her life to.

Also, if I had said our potential clients were the Collins siblings, she might immediately have nixed it, or at least asked me to reschedule before burrowing back under her duvet.

Ms. P and I share a certain prejudice when it comes to the upper crust. Mine is the usual small-town, working-class chip on the shoulder. Hers stems from the fact that the wealthy are usually the least in need of her help. However, part of my assisting includes directing her to the occasional clientele who can write a five-figure check without breaking into a cold sweat.

We had expenses after all, not least of which was my salary.

An hour later, showered, fed, dressed in a navy blue tweed, and hair tortured into her customary bundle of braids, she

walked into the office. She'd left her cane upstairs, which sug-
gested that the day was a good day, or she was being stubborn.
She sat at her desk and I gave her the rundown, including the
Collinses' timeline of headline-producing scandal and woe.

When I finished, she took a full two seconds before asking,
"Is there any reason to consider taking this case other than the
clients' bank account?"

"Their bank account is nothing to sneeze at," I told her. "At
least according to the latest stock prices in the *Journal*. But if
filthy lucre doesn't interest you, there's also the fact that it's an
honest-to-God locked-room mystery. A locked-room mystery!
How often do you get one of those?"

"I don't have the same fascination with pulp conceits as you."

"How about that it's the brutal murder of a woman and the
police have come up dry, and you have a civic duty to do your
best to see the killer brought to justice?"

"There are many murders I could turn my attention to,"
she countered. "Most affecting families who are unable to
leverage their wealth to hire a private consultant."

I arranged my limbs in a posture of defeat. "You got me," I
said. "I guess I'll just have to call and cancel."

I reached for the phone but froze, as if suddenly remembering something. "Oh, there is this." I pulled a newspaper clipping from my vest pocket and casually tossed it across her desk.
Cautiously, she picked it up and scanned it.

It was from a day-three follow-up on the murder. I'd circled
a name buried on the jump page. When she came to it, Ms.
Pentecost perked up. Or at least one eyebrow raised a quarter
of an inch, which is as perky as she gets.

"Why haven't I seen this before?"

"You've been braids-deep in the Palmetto case, so you're
still catching up on the clippings," I said. "Also, this is an

Enquirer story. We don't usually pick up that rag. Lucky I even saw it."

"Are we sure it's accurate? They could be making it up. You said that no other paper included a guest list."

"It's possible," I admitted. "I don't have a person at the *Enquirer*. But I could probably ferret somebody out within a day or two and slip them a twenty. No, scratch that. They'd be a new contact so it'd have to be a C-note. Then we could cross our fingers that their information's legit, because it's the *Enquirer*, after all. They'd frame their mother on the front page if it would sell a paper. Or . . ."

"Or we could ask the Collinses when they arrive just who was at their party," Ms. P finished with a dollop of sarcasm.

"That's certainly something to consider," I said.

She tapped a finger against the side of her not-quite-hook nose and stared off into space. After a few seconds' hard thinking she said, "Go up to the archives and retrieve any clippings on the Collins family, including the father's suicide."

"You think there's a connection?"

"I don't think anything yet. I don't even know if I'll take the case. But it's better to have the information at hand than to be found wanting."

I asked her if she'd like the files on the other character—the person whose name I'd circled—but she told me no. She was already familiar with it.

I hurried up two flights to the high-ceilinged room that takes up the entirety of our third floor. The space is filled with rows of tall shelves and resembles certain areas of the Forty-second Street library. A giant Egyptian carpet creates an island in the middle of it all. A comfortable armchair and a tall Tiffany lamp hold a place of honor in its center. The sea of shelves surrounding the island is filled with file boxes, hundreds of them.

Each firmly sealed to protect their contents from the light streaming through the skylights that checkerboard the ceiling.

The boxes contain years' worth of meticulously organized clippings on crimes, notable events, and citizens of interest, as well as case notes, curiosities, evidence, and assorted strange objects that Ms. Pentecost has picked up over the course of her career.

I found the correct box, and sure enough there were clippings on Alistair Collins's suicide. One of my tasks is to cut out any articles on unsolved deaths or general weirdness and file them away for possible future use. I've tried to convince her that this is wasted energy, since each newspaper has its own morgue, to which I can gain easy access. But she likes having everything close at hand.

I brought the files down and she read through them while I clipped new articles from that morning's papers. The choices that day included the drug overdose of Charlie Silverhorn, a semifamous jazz musician, and the latest in a string of burglaries plaguing the Central Park–adjacent crowd.

At three on the dot, the bell rang. I opened the door to Rebecca and Randolph Collins, whom I recognized from their pictures in the papers, and Harrison Wallace, who introduced himself as acting CEO of Collins Steelworks and executor of the Collins estate. He was the fussy patrician I'd spoken to over the phone.

Relieving the three of their hats and coats, I directed them to the chairs facing Ms. Pentecost. Then I planted myself at my own desk, where I could get a good look at our visitors.

Wallace was a lawyer right out of central casting. Somewhere between middle age and retirement, he was tall and stoop shouldered, with a high forehead and half-moon glasses centered in a profile that could have been handsome if you made a dozen or so adjustments. His skin hung too loose in some places and adhered too tightly to his skull in others. His gray two-button was fashionable enough but suffered from the same poor fit as his face. He carried a leather briefcase and set it down next to his chair, giving me a look like he was afraid I might pull a snatch-and-run. Perched between the siblings, he looked like a pigeon who'd fallen in with doves.

I describe Wallace first to get him out of the way, because the Collins twins were two of the most beautiful humans I've ever laid eyes on, and my days in the circus had introduced me to some lookers.

I knew from the papers that they were a hair under twenty-one. What I didn't know was which was prettier: Randolph with his knife-edge cheekbones and Cupid's bow mouth perched atop a six-foot-tall swimmer's body? Or Rebecca with her gentle Gene Tierney overbite and not-so-gentle Rita Hayworth physique squeezed down into a size-two frame?

They both sported blue eyes and white-blond hair, his slicked back, hers in ringlets that dangled to just below her ears. He was in a light gray suit whose casually rumpled cut likely cost at least three bills for a tailor to get just so. She wore a dark blue dress with white polka dots that left her arms bare. Not something I'd usually care for, but she made a case for it.

I looked up to find her watching me watching her. Something in her look brought the blood to my cheeks. I found myself wishing I'd taken more than two minutes on my hair.

The pigeon chirped first.

"Thank you for seeing us on such short notice, Miss Pentecost," Wallace said.

My boss held up a hand. "Ms. Pentecost, please. I am unmarried and, I believe, have long outgrown 'Miss.'"

Wallace was ruffled, but not overly so. "Of course. Ms. Pentecost. I suppose it's no mystery why we've asked to consult with you."

"I despise making assumptions," my boss declared. "If forced, I'd assume it's concerning the recent death of Abigail Collins and the police's inability to locate a culprit."

Wallace snorted. "That's a very polite way of saying that the police are idiots. Which they are."

"I've found New York City homicide detectives to be quite dogged."

"If by 'dogged' you mean chasing their tails, I agree," he sniped. "They assured us this would be handled swiftly. Two weeks later, not only do they have no culprit, they have no leads, no suspects, and have taken to badgering the Collinses' friends and associates."

"It's not all that bad, Uncle Harry." This was from Randolph, who arranged his Cupid's bow into a soothing smile. "They're just doing their job."

"Uncle," by the way, was a purely ceremonial title. In the papers Wallace was described as a senior partner at Collins Steelworks and longtime family friend. No blood relation.

"It *is* bad," Wallace corrected him. "The longer this goes on, the worse it is for the company."

"Could you elaborate, Mr. Wallace?" Ms. Pentecost asked.

"With the death of Mrs. Collins unresolved, the majority control of Collins Steelworks remains in legal limbo. If you've read the Business section of the *Times,* you probably know all about it. With the war over, the company's military contracts are up for renegotiation. If we lose them, we'll be forced to return to a prewar footing manufacturing office supplies. Millions of dollars are at stake, and everything is up in the air because the police can't do their job."

"I just wish they'd let us finally bury her." This was from Rebecca, whose voice was a full octave deeper than I'd expected. Something you'd hear out of the throat of a jazz singer, not a socialite. "They still have her . . . body."

Wallace patted her knee. "Of course, dear. I shouldn't have started off by focusing on business. That was thoughtless of me. You see, Ms. Pentecost, the police are not just playing with the finances of a multimillion-dollar company, but with the emotions of my godchildren. They deserve closure."

"What makes you think I will find success where the police cannot?" Ms. P asked. "And why turn to me specifically? There are larger organizations."

"You come highly recommended by several members of our board. By their wives, really," Wallace explained.

This wasn't a surprise. Ms. P made a specialty of investigating crimes against women. Though it *was* a surprise that Wallace dropped this comment without the usual condescending tone you get from most men his age.

"They praised you for your ingenuity but, more important, for your discretion," he continued. "Those larger firms? We've used several in the past for other jobs. Suspected industrial espionage and that sort of thing. But they're such large organizations, with so many men hired freelance. Too many chances for certain elements of the case to slip out."

"And that worries you?"

The three shared a look I couldn't decipher.

"There are certain details around Abigail's death that are . . . embarrassing," Wallace said. "If you agree to take the case, you'll hear all about them."

"I'm afraid I'll need to hear about them first," Ms. P said, casting her eyes over the group. "I never take a case blind."

Wallace puffed up his feathers. "I'm afraid that's unacceptable. We need assurance that what's said here will never be made public."

I decided to dip my toe in.

"You've got the assurance of Ms. Pentecost's reputation," I told him. "If you don't trust that, you should probably go with one of the big firms. They'll take a case no questions asked."

Wallace squinted at me, like he was trying to figure out just what species of bird I was—pigeon, dove, or other.

"This is ridiculous," Randolph blurted. "The girl's right. We should go to Sterling and Swan. Father trusted them implicitly. Remember that . . . incident . . . with the labor organizer?"

Wallace shook his head. "No," he said. "Too many staff; too many variables."

I could tell Ms. Pentecost was getting impatient.

"Mr. Wallace," she said with more than a little steel in her voice. "I've handled any number of sensitive cases, many of which my reputation is *not* built on, since no one but myself and my clients has ever heard of them. Whatever you have to tell me, I can assure you, unless it includes evidence of a crime or the intent to commit one, I will safeguard it."

"Just tell her," Rebecca demanded, borrowing a little metal from my boss.

Still, Wallace hesitated.

"It's going to get out eventually—you know that." Rebecca turned to Ms. Pentecost, leaning in toward the big desk. "People already think they know who killed her."

"You believe you know who killed your mother?"

"I didn't say that. I just said people think they know."

"Becca, please. Don't be silly," Randolph scolded.

"It's what everyone's whispering. They think it was our father."

"I was under the impression your father committed suicide over a year ago," Ms. P said. "Did your mother remarry?"

Rebecca shook her head. "Oh no. That's who I mean. People think she was murdered by the ghost of our father."

CHAPTER 4

If Wallace and Randolph were women, I'd probably use the word "tizzy" here. Actually, I'll still use the word. They went into a tizzy.

"You've got to stop saying that," Randolph flittered.

"There is nothing to suggest this is anything other than the work of a . . . a madman," Wallace fluttered, the loose skin around his cheeks shaking. "Anyone saying otherwise is being stupid, cruel, and foolish. It's superstitious gossip and I won't have it. Not among company people."

"I'm not saying it," Rebecca countered. "Other people are."

"Please." Ms. Pentecost held up a quieting hand. "Perhaps if you would start from the beginning. But first, would any of you like a drink? Some brandy, Miss Collins?"

"Gin, if you have it."

We did have it and I fixed her a healthy three fingers with a little water. Wallace had scotch and milk, which I didn't agree with, but to each his own. When I asked Randolph what he'd like, he shot a look at his sister. "No thank you. I like to keep my wits."

I immediately disliked him. Not for the sobriety—I don't drink, myself—but for the judging.

"Suit yourself," I said, pouring Ms. Pentecost her usual glass of honey wine. Mrs. Campbell has the stuff imported from Scotland at an expense that is, if not ungodly, at least embarrassing.

Once drinks were distributed and we were all settled again, they began telling the story, trading off when needed and prompted occasionally by questions from Ms. Pentecost. It was clear they'd gone through the tale more than once, probably in front of a rotating cast of men with badges.

The story began on Halloween night. The holiday had fallen on a Wednesday, so most of the city had celebrated the weekend before. On Saturday and Sunday the streets had been awash in costumed revelers stumbling from party to bar and back again. By midweek most of the celebrating was finished unless you were saddled with kids.

"Mother wanted it held on Halloween night. Even if it was a work night. She said the veil was thinner," Randolph said.

"The veil?" Ms. Pentecost prompted.

"Between the living and the dead." Randolph's voice practically dripped sarcasm. Wallace looked at the floor, embarrassed.

Only Rebecca kept a straight face. "Every year there was some form of special entertainment," she said. "This year—"

"We're getting there, Becca!" Randolph snapped. Their looks might have echoed, but I didn't think they'd be singing harmony any time soon.

Wallace picked up the narrative.

"Al began the tradition shortly after they were married. It was partly to give Abigail a chance to socialize, to have fun with planning a to-do. Mostly it was to entertain company executives. This year, there were about a hundred guests—down from previous years. That was due to Al . . . passing away last year," Wallace said. "Nearly all in attendance were company men and their wives."

The festivities kicked off around nine o'clock. There was

a string quartet in the ballroom, waiters passing out an end-less stream of hors d'oeuvres, and three bars—two inside and one on the veranda—assuring nobody had to wait in line to get sloshed.

As in previous years, everyone arrived in costume. No rented gorilla suits here. A lot of gowns and capes, black ties, and elaborate masks, most only covering the top half of the face to allow for eating, drinking, talking, smoking, and so forth.

I was surprised to learn that Wallace had gone full-on Uncle Sam with a red, white, and blue tuxedo; spangly top hat; and fake beard.

"My wife talked me into it," he said, blushing. "To celebrate the victory overseas. She said people would get a big kick."

"They did, Uncle Harry," Rebecca said, giving him a buck-up smile.

Wallace returned the smile, but his was a tad sickly.

"A little after midnight, Abigail had everyone gather in the study on the second floor. This was Al's study that he used as an office," he explained. "When we walked in we found black velvet draped everywhere. Covering the bookshelves and most of the furniture. Al's desk was done up in gaudy silks with this absurd crystal ball in the middle. And she had that woman there, sitting right in Alistair's chair. It was ridiculous."

"It was awful," Rebecca added. "Hideous."

"What woman was this?" Ms. P asked.

"It was a séance, you see," Wallace continued. "She'd invited her spiritual advisor—Abigail's phrase, not mine. This woman was going to tell fortunes and read tarot cards and speak with the dead."

Ms. Pentecost leaned forward ever so slightly. "What was this spiritual advisor's name?"

"Belestrade." The word twisted in Wallace's mouth so he practically spit it out. "Ariel Belestrade."

There it was. The name from the newspaper clipping that I'd circled in red. The hook I'd used to get Ms. Pentecost in on this case.

Belestrade was one of those citizens of interest whose name I'd been trained to pick out whenever it appeared in print. As a spiritual advisor to a handful of the city's elite, she made the papers occasionally, though usually in the society pages, and only in passing.

In our third-floor archives there were two boxes dedicated solely to her. Why was Ms. Pentecost so interested in the movements of a woman who was basically Madame Fortuna working a better zip code? I had no idea. When it came to her strange fascinations, I'd learned not to ask. She'd tell me when she thought I needed to know.

Have I mentioned how the woman infuriates me?

Across the desk, I saw the signs of Ms. Pentecost's excitement—the tensing of the fingers, the eyebrows raising a fraction of an inch, that gleam in her winter-sky eye.

"Belestrade," Wallace muttered. "Probably not even her real name. With these types, it never is."

"These types?" Ms. Pentecost prodded.

"Frauds. Charlatans," Wallace sneered.

"Becca thinks she's the real deal," Randolph said, scowling.

"I never said that," his sister said. "Never. I only said that . . . she's good."

Ms. Pentecost raised another steadying hand. "What exactly did Ms. Belestrade do at the party?"

The three settled down and went on to describe something that would have been right at home in Sideshow Alley. There was some fortune-telling for the wives, in one case letting a not-yet-announced pregnancy out of the bag. Then came the tarot readings. By then some of the men were getting into the act. Belestrade outed one older gent as planning his retirement, something that came as a bit of a surprise to his bosses.

For the climax, the electric lights were turned off. The only light came from the fireplace. It was a cold night and the furnace had trouble reaching that room. The spiritualist asked for a volunteer. When no one leaped forward, Belestrade beckoned to Rebecca.

"Come, girl. I sense there's someone who wants to speak with you," she declared.

"She had me sit across from her," Rebecca told us. "Then she asked me to take her hands, which I did, and she set them down on the . . . on the crystal ball."

The medium closed her eyes and instructed Rebecca to do the same. After a long minute of awkward silence, Belestrade's head rolled back and she began speaking in a low, sonorous voice.

"'There's a spirit here . . . Close to you . . . Someone who . . . who passed over in this very room. Someone who is still here.' That's when her voice changed again. It became . . . deeper. Rougher . . ."

"It set the entire room off," Randolph said.

"Why?" Ms. P asked.

"Because it was our father's voice," Rebecca said, her own voice quivering. "His voice exactly."

"And what did it say?"

Rebecca closed her eyes, remembering.

"'Who's there? Who is it? It's dark here. I can't see. I . . . I smell lavender. . . . White Orchid. Is that you, Becca? Is it from the bottle you stole?'"

A shiver ran through her.

"Was that significant?" Ms. Pentecost asked.

"Yes," she said. "When I was little, a friend dared me to steal a bottle of White Orchid from the counter at a department store. I felt bad and told my father about it later. He promised not to tell anyone else but made me pay the store back. I . . . I still wear that scent."

My boss gave her a moment, then asked, "What happened next?"

"I think I . . . I think I said something. I don't . . . I don't remember what."

"You said, 'Daddy? Is that you?'" Randolph said. His eyes were on his lap, embarrassed for her. Wallace's eyes, on the other hand, were fully stoked with anger.

Rebecca continued.

"Then he . . . she . . . said something like 'I'm so lonely. I just want to move on. I want to be at rest. Please, let me be at rest.' And I heard our mother behind me ask, 'What do you mean, Allie? How can we help you be at rest?' and the . . . the medium said, 'Don't betray me. Don't betray me, my love.'"

Rebecca shook her head, like she was shaking off the reins the memory had on her.

"I couldn't take it anymore," she said. "I tore my hands away, then ran to my bedroom and locked the door."

"What happened next?" Ms. P asked.

"Becca running away broke whatever . . . spell . . . the woman was under, or at least she pretended it did," Randolph explained. "Then our mother ordered everyone out. She said she wanted to be alone in the room with . . ."

"With her husband. With Al," Wallace finished. "She asked everyone to go back to the party, including Belestrade."

Understandably, the mood of the party turned sour after that. People began to beg off. Randolph joined a few friends on the veranda for a smoke, while Wallace quickly made the rounds before too many people fled.

"I wanted to have a chat with some of the more influential members of the board," Wallace explained. "I didn't want any tongues wagging. Not with the company's future on such a precipice."

Wallace must have put the fear of God into them because no one had yet leaked the séance to the papers, and "Speaking to Dead Leaves Socialite Slain" would sell a hell of a lot of morning editions.

"Do you have any idea what 'Don't betray me' might refer to?" Ms. P asked.

Wallace shook his head. "None at all."

Ms. Pentecost downed the last of her wine and I moved to pour her another. "And you, Miss Collins? Did you return to the party?"

"I didn't. I stayed in my room."

"The entire time?"

"Yes," she said. "Then I heard . . . Well, I heard yelling. When I came out, they had broken down the study door."

"The papers said there was a fire. That someone smelled smoke?" Ms. P asked.

"I did," Wallace said. "At first I thought maybe someone had left the veranda door open, but it didn't smell like cigarettes. Then I went upstairs and saw the smoke coming out from beneath the office doors."

"What did you do then?"

"I tried the door, but it was locked. I started yelling."

"He was so loud, we heard him outside," Randolph said.

"Who is 'we'?" Ms. Pentecost asked.

"Me and John Meredith—he's the senior floor manager at the Jersey City plant. We ran inside and up the stairs. I found Uncle Harry here trying to batter down the door. Meredith put his shoulder into it and charged. Nearly took the thing off its hinges. Smoke was billowing out, but John just rushed in. He's that kind of man."

"Impetuous?" Ms. P asked.

"A man of action," Randolph said. "A little fire didn't scare him."

It was clear that neither Wallace nor Rebecca shared his hero worship, but both kept mum.

"Once the smoke cleared a little, the rest of us followed. There was a fire going in the fireplace and it had caught on some of the black velvet. I tore it down and stamped it out. I didn't . . . I didn't even notice her at first. Not until I saw Becca and where she was staring."

"I heard the shouting," Rebecca explained. "I opened my door and there was all this smoke in the hall. I ran into the study. People were rushing about, and she was just sitting there. Slumped over the desk."

I retrieved the gin from the liquor cart and refilled Rebecca's glass. She didn't even notice.

"At first I thought Abigail must be unconscious," Wallace said. "Because of the smoke, you know? I pulled up her up by the shoulders and . . ."

He needed a little prompting and Ms. Pentecost gave it. "And you realized she wasn't merely unconscious."

"Her head was . . . there was blood. And her eyes . . ."

He didn't finish the thought, and no one picked it up for him. No one needed to. Ms. P and I had seen more than a few bodies, including ones who'd been bludgeoned to death. Our imaginations were up to snuff.

"It was the crystal ball," Randolph said, his voice cracking. "We found it in the fireplace. It was cracked and . . . bloody."

Wallace took a swig of scotch and milk and grimaced, from either the taste or the memory. "We telephoned the police," he said. "They arrived within minutes and . . . And everything else you have almost certainly read in the papers."

Ms. Pentecost shook her head. "You overstate what can be found in those articles, or understate your own efforts at keeping out the more lurid details."

"Can you blame me?" Wallace asked. "It's terrible enough without turning the whole thing—including my godchildren—into a public spectacle."

Another shake of the head. "My comment wasn't to cast blame, but to point out that there is much I don't know, but which I will certainly need to know before I can proceed. For example, I will require a full list of guests as well as servants and hired staff, as well as a detailed timeline of when each person arrived and departed, with particular attention paid to who was still present when the body of Mrs. Collins was discovered. I will also require a complete description of Mrs. Collins's life, both her day-to-day existence and her history."

"Of course," Wallace said. "I hadn't even thought of the hired staff. The waiters and musicians and so forth. It was probably one of them. A thief or madman."

Ms. P shrugged. "Perhaps. Though I suspect the police have done a thorough background check on the hired help. That's usually the first place their imaginations turn. After the family, of course."

That caused our guests to squirm a little but they didn't

object. Apparently two weeks had been enough time for them to realize that they were possible subjects for the frame the police were building.

"Abigail kept a calendar that should document her general movements. Who she met for lunch. What appointments she had. That sort of thing," Wallace said. "As for her history, I can tell you about her life after she came to work for the company, since she was my secretary."

"Your secretary?" Ms. P asked, eyebrows raised. "I thought she was Mr. Collins's."

"Technically, Al and I shared her," Wallace said. "But my side of things required the most clerical support, so she worked out of my office. Unfortunately, she never discussed her youth or her personal life before she came to work for the company, so I can't be of much assistance there."

Ms. Pentecost looked to Rebecca and Randolph, who synchronized a head shake.

"She never spoke about her childhood," Rebecca said. "At least not to me."

"Or me," Randolph added. "Just that she was orphaned and grew up poor somewhere in upstate New York."

Ms. P frowned. She didn't like having holes in a victim's biography. Experience had shown her that that's where killers liked to hide.

She turned to me.

"Before we discuss my fee—Will, are there any questions I'm neglecting?"

"You were probably just saving it for later, but was Belestrade still there when the . . . when Abigail was discovered?" I asked.

"I believe she left after the séance broke up," Wallace said. "But I can't be sure."

"Also, did she bring anyone with her? An assistant or partner?" I was thinking of the times I'd worked with Madame Fortuna. It always helps having someone working the crowd.

Wallace shook his head. "I don't believe so. She had a driver, I remember. But he never came inside."

Rebecca placed a hand on his arm. "Uncle Harry. You're forgetting that college professor."

"Of course. She was so quiet, I forgot she was there. She arrived with Belestrade."

"I spoke to her a little," Randolph added. "She didn't leave much of an impression."

"What professor are we talking about?" I asked.

"A Dr. Waterhouse. Not a medical doctor. A university sort," Wallace said. "I can't remember her first name."

"Olivia?" Ms. Pentecost asked. "Dr. Olivia Waterhouse?"

"You know her?"

"I know her work. Are you sure she accompanied Ms. Belestrade to the party?"

"I'm sure she wasn't there with anyone else," Wallace said. "She didn't know it was a costume party. She had to borrow a mask from one of the waitstaff."

"She said something about appreciating the theatricality and wanting to view it close up," Randolph said. "To be honest, I wasn't paying much attention. Just being polite."

"She will have to be interviewed," Ms. P said. "Many people will. But first I would like to visit the house and see the room for myself."

"You'll take the case?" Wallace asked.

She nodded. Wallace seemed relieved. Rebecca and Randolph were neutral.

"And you'll be discreet? I don't want any of the more sordid details to get out."

"I will be as discreet as I'm legally able, Mr. Wallace. However, it's inevitable that the sordid details, as you call them, will make their way to the press. Such things always do."

Wallace's shoulders slumped. "Hopefully by the time they do the company will be on firmer footing. Now, about your fee."

Ms. Pentecost quoted a number that made all three blink.

"Do you charge that much to everyone?" Randolph demanded.

"Of course not, Mr. Collins. Nor are you obligated to pay it. I charge what is reasonable for the case and the client. Speaking of which, who am I working for? The Collins family or Collins Steelworks?"

"Neither," Wallace declared. "The company cannot be on record as hiring you."

He reached into the case sitting at his feet and pulled out three bank-wrapped bundles of bills. He set them gingerly on Ms. Pentecost's desk.

"This is my personal money, Ms. Pentecost. If you must attach a name to your efforts, use mine. I'm acting as godfather and family friend, not in my role as acting CEO of Collins Steelworks."

The only giveaway that he was handing over what was probably a year's salary in currency was the layer of cold sweat covering his forehead.

"That is a significant investment for an individual, Mr. Wallace."

"I have been a friend of the Collins family for most of my adult life," he said, straightening out his spine. "Al was my best friend. Abigail is the mother of my godchildren."

Ms. Pentecost gave a single, satisfied nod, then stood, wobbling only slightly.

"Will, please gather the necessary information and make

an appointment to visit the Collins residence as early tomorrow as is convenient."

Having handed me my orders, she shook hands with our new clients, wished them good day, and walked out of the office.

As instructed, I gathered phone numbers and schedules and made an appointment for us to visit the Collins house at ten the next morning. Then I retrieved hats and coats and saw them all out. Rebecca lingered at the doorway.

"She's a strange woman."

"I guess," I said. "I find I'm not always the best person to diagnose strangeness in others."

She gifted me with a small, polite smile.

"Is she as good as people say she is?" she asked.

"Better," I said with a straight face. "But I thought you believed a ghost did it."

"I said other people think a ghost did it."

I decided to take a shot. "If you had to pin it on someone, who'd get stuck?"

She opened her mouth to pass me an answer but then looked back at the sidewalk, where her brother and godfather were waiting. She closed her mouth, shook her head, and turned away without a goodbye.

CHAPTER 5

After seeing out the Collins crew, I put the cash away in the safe—a custom job hidden under some trick floorboards beneath my desk. Then I made my way up two flights, where I found my employer sitting cross-legged in the middle of the Egyptian rug, back propped against the armchair. A pair of file boxes were on the floor next to her and clippings were scattered about. Ariel Belestrade's name was underlined in each.

"Popular woman," I noted. "Don't suppose you want to tell me why you're so interested in a glorified sideshow act?"

"I'm interested in many people. Did you note anything about our clients and their story?"

When it comes to changing a subject, my boss enjoys the hard left turns. But if she didn't want to spill, nothing I could say would force her to tip.

"I found a lot worth jotting," I said. "Do you want it chronologically or in order of importance?"

She twirled an impatient finger.

"No love lost between the twins," I said. "I'd like to know what's behind that. Is it the usual sibling rivalry or something more recent? Rebecca's definitely holding something back. Not sure if it was from us or from the other two."

"Agreed," she said, sorting through the clippings.

"Then there's Wallace. He plays the affronted godfather

pretty well. 'Oh, the charlatan! Surely it was a madman amongst the hired help!'" I struck a clutching-my-pearls pose. Ms. Pentecost gave me a look that long-suffering maiden aunts could rent by the hour.

"But he's cagey," I continued. "I don't care what kind of talking-to he gave the guests. To keep this quiet he'd have to be slipping some bills to reporters. Maybe even editors. At least four figures a person for this kind of hush job. That takes a lot of know-how and finesse. Makes me suspect he's not a virgin with this kind of cover-up."

I wondered whether Wallace was cagey enough to have committed the murder himself, then try to muddy the waters by hiring Ms. Pentecost. It wouldn't have been the first time the person signing our checks was the one who got fitted for bracelets in the end.

"Also, did you notice the barely controlled grief at Mrs. Collins's passing?"

"I noticed there was very little."

"Yeah," I said. "What do you think that says about Abigail Collins?"

"I think it says we don't have enough information," my boss declared, eyes skimming over a story about a museum fundraiser where Ariel Belestrade had played a starring role. "You remember Professor Waterhouse, of course."

"Of course."

She had been one of our lecture-night outings a year or so back. An anthropologist who made her nut as a university professor. She had been holding forth on why superstitions persist in modern culture. Dry subject, but she'd been entertaining enough to keep me awake. I vaguely recalled reading a page 3 piece in the *Times* about a scuffle she'd gotten into with the Father Divine crowd up around Harlem. Scuffles are the least you can expect when you try to take people's god away from them. Even if their god is a grifter.

"A séance is a pretty strange place for her to turn up," I said. "Would be nice to know what she was doing tagging along with Belestrade."

"Yes."

About thirty seconds of silence passed without a word and I considered tiptoeing out. Sometimes Ms. P's brain conjures the words "you are dismissed" but she's too distracted to push them out her lips.

I was about to tip the first toe when she asked, "Is Hiram working tonight?"

"Don't know," I said. "He should be. It's not Shabbat and the holidays don't kick off for a couple weeks. Besides, it's not like Hiram keeps tight with tradition."

"Will he be awake now?"

I checked my watch—four-thirty P.M. Stuck on the night shift, Hiram was a late riser even by Ms. P's standards, but I figured he should at least be up and at breakfast. I told her as much.

"Call him," she ordered. "If he's on shift tonight, tell him we'd like to pay a visit around one A.M."

"Just so you know, we have an appointment at the Collins manse for ten tomorrow morning. So you might want to curtail your usual late night."

The look she gave me would definitely not have come from a maiden aunt. Although the only aunt I had ran a roadhouse outside Chicago and had done three years for manslaughter, so what did I know.

She gave a great sigh and told me to ask Hiram if eleven P.M. would work.

"Anything I can do in the meantime?"

She shook her head. "Choosing a direction now would be a waste of your energy. We need to ascertain what ground the police have gone over, what they have discovered, and exactly what kind of crime we're dealing with. Call Hiram."

She dove back into the boxes.

I went downstairs to call a man about a corpse.

Homicides made up a pretty small chunk of the cases that we tackled. Still, I've seen more bodies—in situ and on slabs—than ninety-nine out of a hundred New Yorkers. It's not something you get used to.

It's not the gruesome ones that get me. Bullet holes, stab wounds, the broken-china insides of car wrecks and jumpers—I can handle all that.

It's the ones that look like they're sleeping that I have a hard time with.

Eventually, I notice the stillness. The absence of things I take for granted: the slow in-and-out of regular breathing, the thrum of blood pulsing under the skin. It hits me that they're not just playing a champion game of possum. It sinks in just how thin the line is between me and them. One thimble of poison in my coffee and that's that.

That's when the cold finger runs up my spine.

Abigail Collins was somewhere in between. From the neck down she looked pretty good, if you discounted the chalk-white pallor from being in the morgue's freezer for two weeks and the telltale Y incision of the autopsy. It was clear that in life she'd been a good-looking woman, a youngish forty who shared her children's fair features.

Above the neck was another story. The tip of her tongue stuck out of the corner of her mouth, giving the socialite the look of a petulant child. Her left eye was filled with blood and the pupil was cocked at a grotesque angle. The other eye had gone the blue-white of corpses.

"Show me the wound?" Ms. Pentecost asked the man standing beside her.

My boss never demanded anything from Hiram. Everything was a request. She knew how much he was putting on the line letting us into the morgue after hours. A little over five feet tall, with a close-cropped black beard and deep-set eyes, Hiram carried himself with the solemnity of a rabbi.

Working as an assistant to the medical examiner for nearly a decade, he'd seen a healthy cross-section of mankind's creative ways of doing away with one another. If it weren't for his being Jewish, he'd have been his boss's boss by now. Maybe even a coroner if he'd had the patience for politics. On the flip side, his vocation put him at odds with his community, making him a pariah twice over. But nobody in that room, dead or alive, was mistaking the world for fair.

He gently turned Mrs. Collins's head. High on the left side, where pale forehead met golden-blond hair, was a crater set off by a jagged cut a good three inches long. Ms. Pentecost ran a gentle, white-gloved finger across the cut.

"I am told it was from the base of a crystal ball," Hiram said, his voice low and reverent. "A single blow struck with considerable force."

"Would the assailant have needed to be particularly strong?"

Hiram shook his head. "Not particularly, no."

Since the victim had been found sitting, the angle of the wound meant nothing, other than that she probably saw it coming. Which meant our murderer was a man or woman of unknown strength and indeterminate height.

Excellent! We could rule out infants and the comatose.

Ms. Pentecost worked her way down the length of the body, examining every inch. She stopped at Mrs. Collins's left wrist, leaning in so close her nose almost brushed the cold flesh.

"You observed these bruises?"

Hiram nodded once.

"They're very faint," she noted.

"They likely occurred very shortly before her death."

"Made by the killer?" she asked.

"I could not say," he told her. "That is your charge, Lillian. Determining the possibilities. Mine is caretaking the dead."

I can count the number of people who call her Lillian on my fingers and still have digits to spare. She'd helped his family out of a jam a few years back. I don't know the details. It was before my time. Whatever it was, he calls her Lillian and sneaks us into the morgue when needed, and she tries not to wear out his hospitality.

Still, before we left, I slipped a couple bills from our clients' bundle into the pocket of his white lab coat. He didn't put up a fight. He had a family and was a practical man. He gave a quick nod of thanks, then saw us out the back door and into an alley behind the building where the morgue is housed.

I'd parked the Cadillac several blocks away. Even though it was after midnight and there weren't many cops around, it wouldn't do for someone to see the great lady detective sneaking in and out of the morgue. On the way back to Brooklyn, I thought I spotted a tail. But after a few loop-de-loops around some choice blocks in Midtown, the headlights disappeared. So either I was imagining things or they were very good.

Once home, the boss disappeared up to the third floor and I retired to my room. It was the same bed that had been there when I'd arrived. I'd furnished the rest out of my own pocket: a couple of low bookshelves I was slowly filling up with detective novels, a not-too-battered end table, a tall lamp, and a wing-backed armchair I'd rescued from an empty lot. The walls were decorated with framed movie posters and signed lobby cards from Broadway shows. I sneak in the occasional musical or cabaret when I can. It reminds me a little of the circus. The room had a small fireplace, but it wasn't quite cold enough to get it going.

I slipped into a pair of green silk pajamas that had been a gift from Ms. P the Christmas before and lay in bed for a long time digesting the day. Locked rooms and vengeful spirits and dead women tucked away in the cold. I listened to a familiar patter from the floor above me: the rhythm of a pair of slip-pered footfalls interspersed with the hard rap of a cane.

When I finally managed to fall asleep, I dreamed of the cir-cus, of clowns beating on drums and the sound of knives carv-ing a path to their target.

CHAPTER 6

The Collins place wasn't exactly the Vanderbilt mansion, but it was within spitting distance. A four-story granite edifice lodged in the heart of an Upper East Side block, it had the gray, flat face of an upscale asylum. We were greeted at the door by Sanford—a whippet-thin man in traditional butler's attire. He had a carefully waxed white moustache and the practiced remove of the longtime servant.

Having read more than my share of detective novels, I'm always hoping for a "the butler did it" moment. Taking in Sanford's cultivated detachment, I doubted he could have ginned up the passion to raise his voice, much less a blunt instrument.

Inside we found Randolph waiting with barely concealed impatience. Wallace, we were told, had been called into a board meeting, so the ten-cent tour had fallen to the young Mr. Collins.

"Rebecca had a late night," he said with disdain. "She's still asleep."

"Lucky girl," Ms. P muttered.

She was allowed to be resentful. She'd been dragged out of bed a good four hours too early for her. But she'd filled up with enough coffee to get Rip Van Winkle doing the jitterbug, so I hoped at least three out of four cylinders were firing.

Randolph was wearing dark gray trousers and a heavy-duty work shirt. When I commented on it, he said, "I'm going to be on the floor of the plant later today. It's no place for a suit and tie." It came off as posturing and reminded me of a little boy playing dress-up.

While the outside of the house leaned toward grim, the inside was pleasant enough. The first floor was a sprawl of sitting rooms, a dining room, kitchen, and what Randolph referred to as "a modest ballroom."

The second floor contained the siblings' bedrooms, as well as Alistair's office and bedroom. The third floor held the master bedroom suite, which Abigail had used, along with a suite of vacant servants' quarters. Neither Sanford, the cook, nor the part-time maid lived on the premises. The fourth floor had a conservatory and nursery and was mostly unused.

I made a mental note of the separate sleeping arrangements for Abigail and Alistair. Maybe it was something. Or maybe one of them snored.

We kept the walking portion of the tour to the first two floors. Ms. P wasn't having a bad day but there were a couple stumbles going up the stairs.

Randolph led us into the study, which he told us had been left as it was since the night of the murder. I was surprised to discover that this extended to the black velvet draped on the walls and over the room's single, barred window. It turned the room into a dark, claustrophobic womb with old Alistair's desk, at least twice the size of Ms. P's, hovering in the center. The candles, the bloodstained silks, and, of course, the murder weapon had all been collected by the police.

There was a lingering smell of scorched fabric and paper. It was strongest around the fireplace to the left of the desk.

Ms. Pentecost strode over and sat heavily in the desk chair.

Randolph stayed in the doorway, trying to look nonchalant and failing.

"The police insisted we keep the scene intact, whatever that means," Randolph said. "To be honest, once the estate is settled, we'll probably gut this entire room. Tear it out and turn it into . . . anything else."

Who could blame them? Both their parents dead by violence while sitting in the chair my employer was currently occupying. I'd want to do some extreme renovating myself.

"The locks on these drawers appear to have been forced," Ms. P noted.

"The police," Randolph said with more than a hint of contempt. "If they'd asked, we could have provided the key, but why ask when you can just destroy an antique?"

I wouldn't have called anything "destroyed" but I didn't argue.

"They were locked the night of the party?"

"Yes," he said. "They were always locked. Though everything of real value was removed after our father's death."

While my boss rummaged the desk, I checked behind every velvet drape. All hung pretty close to the wall or a bookcase. No room for somebody to hide without their feet sticking out the bottom. There was one space near the door—a gap between the bookcase and the wall. I squeezed in and found it a very tight fit. A person could hide there if they were small and didn't put too much of a premium on breathing.

"Did you find anything?" Rebecca stood behind her brother in the doorway. She was dressed in white silk pajamas, barefoot, blond ringlets twisted by sleep.

"Thank you for joining us," Randolph muttered.

"Sorry. I haven't been sleeping well."

"Maybe if you didn't stay out until all hours," he said, a little more forcefully than required.

But Rebecca wasn't listening. She was staring at the desk, at the chair she had sat in during the séance.

"I used to love this room. Now it's ruined," she said. "That séance alone would have been enough to keep me from ever coming in here again."

"Do you believe the séance to have been legitimate, Miss Collins?" Ms. P asked. "Now that you have had time to consider?"

Rebecca took a moment before responding.

"I suppose not," she finally admitted. "But if the woman is a charlatan, then I have to accept that she tricked me. Thinking my father was reaching out from beyond the grave—that would have been less painful."

"Uncle Harry's spent good money making sure talk like that doesn't spread," Randolph said.

"Would your father's spirit have any reason to harm your mother?" Ms. Pentecost asked.

"Don't be silly," Randolph snorted. "What kind of question is that?"

"A necessary one," Ms. Pentecost said. "Assuming the culprit is not your late father, then it could be someone who wishes us to think it was him. In the latter case, the real killer would seem to know of a reason such a thing might be believed."

Randolph muttered something not fit to print.

"To rephrase," Ms. P continued, "were the relations between your mother and father cordial when he was alive?"

"Yes," he blurted. "They were fine. They were happy."

Rebecca said nothing.

"Was there any suspicion that your father's death was anything but a suicide?"

This poked a hornet's nest behind Randolph's eyes.

"There was not! No matter what the press tried to dredge up, it was very clear that . . ." He sputtered into obscenity. Rebecca put a hand on his arm. The gesture got him back on track. "Look—it was Uncle Harry's idea to hire you. I told him to go with someone we've worked with before, a company we can trust. But now you're on board to help clean this up and digging up more mud won't do it. It's obvious this Belestrade woman had a hand in it. Why don't you go talk to her?"

I didn't disagree, but I still had the urge to tell him where he could shove his suggestions. Ms. P just cocked her head like she was inspecting a painting by a deeply mediocre artist.

Rebecca opened her mouth to add something, but Sanford chose that moment to pop his blank-faced head into the study.

"Mr. Wallace has returned. He's waiting for you in the sitting room."

My employer brushed some stray ash off her jacket and turned to me. "Willowjean—would you mind finishing the inspection of this room? I have questions I'd like to pose to Mr. Wallace."

"No problem, boss." To the Collins twins, I asked, "Do you mind if I take down the drapery? It'll make going through things easier."

"Do whatever you want with it," Rebecca said. "I won't ever come in here again."

Ms. P followed Randolph out of the office and headed downstairs. Rebecca veered off to the right.

"I'm going to shower and dress," she threw over her shoulder. "I'll be down in a bit."

Randolph, still simmering, grunted in response.

I counted to twenty, walked out of the office, veered right, and stopped in front of the door to Rebecca's bedroom. Ms. P and I have developed a few codes over the years. When she addressed me as "Willowjean," that was her giving me a cue to poke around and see what I could find out.

I knocked. A voice called from the other side.

"Yes?"

I opened the door. Rebecca had taken off her pajama top and I was greeted by a view of her bare back. I had a split second to wonder whether the rest of her was as smooth and flawless. Startled, she slipped the top back on and quickly did up the minimum of buttons.

"Sorry," I said. "I thought you might want to exchange a few words without your brother or uncle listening in."

"I really don't think I should," she said.

"How about I ask a direct question? If you feel like answering, you answer. If you don't, no hard feelings."

She brushed an errant blond ringlet out of her eyes. "I'm not in the habit of inviting strangers into my bedroom to grill me."

"I'm not exactly a stranger."

"Strange enough," she said with half a grin.

"Then I guess we need to be properly introduced. I'm Will Parker."

I held out a hand for her to shake. After flipping a coin in her head, she did. Her fingers were long and smooth, but with a certain amount of iron in the grip.

"Pleased to make your acquaintance, Miss Parker."

"Just Will."

"Then you'll have to call me Becca," she said.

"Now we're not strangers," I said.

She let loose with a real smile then—one that stretched all the way up to her eyes. "Fair enough. Ask your question."

"Was it true what your brother said? That your mother and father were happy?"

Her smile died by degrees. She sat back on the bed and turned her baby blues to the floor.

"I wouldn't say happy. Maybe content. Or satisfied. Not all relationships are built on passion."

"Did your mother tell you that?" I asked.

"That's two questions, Will."

"Lend me a little credit."

She curled her toes into the lush carpet.

"My father said it. He said that lives might be built on a foundation of ideals, but that the rest of the construction is made of compromises."

"That's a hard way of looking at life," I said.

"My father could be a hard man. He was not . . . sentimental."

That tracked. Anyone who had kept a company alive and thriving during the years after the Crash had to have a little cutthroat in him. More than a little if the papers' accounts of Steel-Hearted Al Collins were to be believed. Though that didn't quite match up with a man who'd eat his own gun.

"Do you think he really committed suicide?"

That snapped her head up. Fire sparked in her eyes. It wasn't the sputtering anger her brother had shown. It was something else.

"Yes, I do," she said. No hesitation. No doubt.

"It didn't surprise you?" I asked. "The way the papers told it, it came out of nowhere."

I don't know what flickered in and out of her head while she was coming up with a response, but I would have given a sawbuck to catch the matinee.

"Yes, I was surprised," she finally said. "He was a . . . He didn't seem the type."

"But you don't think anyone killed him."

"No. No, I don't," she said with resolve, or at least a decent counterfeit. "Now, I'm afraid I need to shower and dress. And you've run out of credit." She stood and gently but firmly led me to the door.

Just as I crossed the threshold she asked, "Can I ask you a question, Miss Parker?"

"It's only fair."

"Do you dance?"

"I, um . . . I . . . Yes?" I sputtered. "I mean, yes. I dance."

"Good."

She closed the door in my face.

CHAPTER 7

I stood on the other side of the bedroom door for a solid half minute trying to regain my balance. I don't know what I was thrown by more—the dancing question or the fact that I was positive there was a lie hidden somewhere in what she'd told me. I just couldn't put my finger on where.

I went back into the office and, after pulling the drapes off the walls, spent the next hour and a half giving the room a thorough searching. This included shaking out every book in the bookshelves, using my penknife to unscrew electrical sockets to search for hidden stashes and test for loose floorboards, and going over the desk inch by inch.

Not a thing. Or, I should say, a thousand things, probably none of them relevant.

I found a couple hundred scraps of paper, mostly receipts from bookstores, tucked into pages. I found canceled checks and a few innocuous company documents. I found two dozen errant paper clips, more than a few dust bunnies, and a cigarette tucked into the back of a drawer that Mr. Collins must have been saving for a rainy day.

No revelations in the lot. I was disappointed but hardly surprised. It's a rare case that hangs on a keystone clue.

I confirmed that the bars on the room's single window were legit, and that the window had long ago been painted

shut. With cat burglary crossed off, I spent the next fifteen minutes on the door trying to lock it from the outside using picks.
No dice. It could only be locked from the inside.

The only thing I found that was really interesting—though
I'd hardly call it a clue—was a framed family photo on one
of the bookshelves. In it, Al Collins was sitting on the main
staircase of the house. He looked as dark and cold as he did in
the papers—wide forehead, receding widow's peak, carefully
groomed moustache set above a razor slash of a mouth.

He held a smiling toddler on his lap I presumed to be
Rebecca, though he didn't seem all that pleased to have her
there. Next to him sat Abigail trying to comfort a shrieking
Randolph. A man sat on the step above them—younger than
Alistair, but not by much, and very handsome in an asymmetri-
cal kind of way.

After a few moments of study I realized that I was looking at a young Harrison Wallace. The years hadn't been kind,
but back in his prime he hadn't been far from a heartthrob. He
was leaning down between the couple in what I assumed was
an attempt to help calm baby Randolph. The gesture had him
pressed very close to Abigail. Of all the people in the photo—
toddlers and adults alike—he had the biggest smile.

Harry and Abigail. That was a thought.

Was Abigail sharing more than just her secretarial skills
with the two men? Neither twin resembled their father much.
They didn't look like Uncle Harry, either. Still, it was something to think about.

Downstairs I found Randolph, Rebecca—I made a note to
start referring to her as Becca—Wallace, and my boss arranged
in a sitting room. Randolph was mid-rant.

"I'm not saying that, as businesspeople, we shouldn't have
ethics, but—for crying out loud, it was war. It would have been

unethical not to have done our part to arm our soldiers," he declared. It didn't take much to see the cranky toddler hovering just underneath Randolph's pretty face.

"And your mother disapproved?" Ms. P asked.

"She said we had the blood of everyone killed with our bombs on our hands."

"Which was never something she cared about before," Wallace said, jumping in. "Not until she got involved with that spiritualist. And we're talking millions. More when you think about the company's stock prices."

As Wallace worked himself into a lather, Ms. P shot me a look. I shot her one back. I was still on poking-around duty.

I walked through the modest ballroom and into the kitchen. There I found a squat woman in her fifties sporting an apron and attending to three steaming pots and what smelled like half a cow sizzling in the oven.

I gave a polite cough and she turned to see who was intruding on her kingdom.

"Can I help you?" she asked with a hint of Irish in her voice.

"Willowjean Parker. I'm Lillian Pentecost's assistant." I pull out the full first name for court officials and women of a certain age. It keeps the confusion to a minimum.

"I'm Dora. I'm the cook. In case that wasn't obvious."

"Do you have anything cold to drink? A soda, maybe?"

"I think there are a couple in the icebox. I'll check."

"Don't bother yourself," I told her. "I can open an icebox door as well as anybody. You keep doing what you're doing. Don't want the gravy to get lumps."

"No, I certainly don't," she said, going back to stirring. "Mind you, a few lumps wouldn't be noticed. Young Mr. Collins inhales his food, Miss Collins eats like a bird, and Mr.

Harry never stays for meals anymore. But I spent the better part of twenty years making gravy for the late Mr. Collins and he liked things just so."

Thank God for chatty house staff.

I stuck my head in the icebox and pulled out a bottle of something labeled "lemon fizz." I cracked it open and took a sip. It was disgusting, but a drink in hand gives you a purpose and it makes it harder to kick you out. I sat down at the little table in the corner of the kitchen where I assumed Sanford and Dora took their meals.

"I'll take good gravy any way I can get it," I said. "But I understand wanting something just so. He was like that? The late Mr. Collins?"

"Oh, yes. You don't get to be where he was, an important man, head of a company, by neglecting the details." She never took her eyes off the dishes on the stove except to turn to a counter and grab a pinch of this or a dash of that. Mrs. Campbell would have approved.

"You should meet my boss," I told her. "She can hear me make a typo at a hundred paces."

"Read about her in the papers," Dora said. "Those Central Park killings. Neat trick figuring that one."

"Yeah, that was a tense couple of weeks."

"Seems like a smart woman. Good at ferreting things out."

Her tone walked a line. I couldn't tell whether she thought Ms. Pentecost's ferreting was good or bad. I waited for her to pick up the thread, but she'd gotten absorbed in tending to a pot of greens.

"You've been with the family twenty years, you said?"

"Little more than twenty." She measured out a pinch of salt in her fingers. "Jeremy and I came on a few years before he and Miss Abigail married."

I assumed Jeremy was Sanford's Christian name. From the way she said it, I took it they were a matched pair. I couldn't quite picture the two in wedded bliss, but I try not to judge the strangeness of bedfellows.

"It must be a nice place to work if you stayed this long."

"We were lucky to find ourselves here. Especially back in those days. Hard times, they were," she said. "Then the children arrived—the twins. I'd worked as a nursemaid, so I spent a lot of time with the two of them."

She cracked open the oven and peered at the sizzling roast. She must have liked what she saw, since she closed it again with no additions or subtractions.

"When I said Mr. Collins was particular, I didn't mean it in a bad way," she said, wiping sweat off her brow with a dish towel. "He was always very generous. Bonuses on Christmas and our birthdays. Any time he was getting rid of furniture or clothes or anything like that, he let Jeremy and I have first pick. Jeremy has quite a few suit jackets that used to belong to Mr. Collins."

Whenever someone bends over backward to tell me so-and-so was a saint, I always wonder what sins they're trying to sweep away.

"How about Mrs. Collins?" I asked. "Was she particular?"

A bit of silent stirring from Dora.

"She was particular, too, I guess, God rest her soul. But her particulars kept changing, if you know what I mean."

"Mercurial kind of woman?"

She let out a little bark that I took for a laugh. "Mercurial. That's a good word. Always trying new things, new hobbies, new fashions. Horseback riding, archery, knitting for about a week, that kind of Mexican dancing with the big dresses. And her diet kept changing along with the rest. Seemed like she loved a dish one week and pulled faces at it the next." She gave her head a brisk shake. "I shouldn't say things like that. She wasn't a bad employer. Just a little hard to please."

I let out a lemony burp. "Excuse me. Did, um . . . Did she and Mr. Collins get along?"

"They were married," she said, patly.

"There's married and then there's married," I said. "My parents, for instance. Lovebirds their whole life. They'll be holding hands and splitting chocolate malts until the day they die. But I have an aunt and uncle—this is on my father's side. Pick an afternoon and listen at their door and you'd swear you were eavesdropping on a Bowery barroom."

None of that was true, but I've never been one to shy away from sacrificing honesty for a good story.

Dora turned to me, lips pressed in a hard line.

"I know what you're asking. I'm not a stupid woman."

"I'd never mistake you for one," I said. "Anyone who keeps a bowl of bacon fat on hand and knows how to use it can't be a dummy."

"All right," she said. "I guess you and Ms. Pentecost are doing the Lord's work. I've got a friend who works at a boardinghouse in the Bronx. Met your boss a couple times, she has. Nothing but good things to say."

I knew what boardinghouse she meant. It kept a handful of rooms open for women who found themselves suddenly in need. Ms. P occasionally stopped by to provide free consultations. Half the time the problem was booze or a husband too free with his fists, or both. Usually Ms. P's assistance boiled down to helping the women find a way to get out and get out quick.

Dora turned the burners down and started giving things a final stir.

"I never saw the two of them fight. Arguments, sure. All couples argue. Usually about money. Though I tried not to listen in."

"Of course."

"Anyway, I wouldn't say they were the most affectionate couple—not in that hand-holding way. A lot of couples aren't."

She was doing some contortionist tricks to make out that Al and Abigail were doing fine, but I was reading between the lines well enough: cold, distant, and fighting over money. She grabbed a pair of mitts, opened the oven, and reached in.

"Did his death surprise you?" I asked.

She stayed half in, half out of the oven so long I thought I might have to rescue her before she started to broil.

"Certainly, it did," she said, hauling out the steaming roast. She turned away from me and set it on a counter and started slicing into it. "But that kind of thing. Can't always see it coming, can you?"

I think she wiped away a tear, but she had her back to me so it could have been sweat. I could feel her wriggling off the hook, so I didn't tug any harder on that particular line.

"What did Mr. Collins think about his wife seeing a spiritual advisor?"

The gnomish woman whirled around, meat fork in one hand, oven mitt in the other.

"Advisor!" she spat. "That woman was nothing but trouble." With each syllable, she jabbed the air in front of her with the fork.

"Why was she trouble?"

"Say what you will about Miss Abigail being mercurial. But at least she had sense. Then she tries out this woman. Everyone figured it was another of her whims. She'd be done with it in a week or a month or however long. She just kept going. Then she started bringing her here."

"Ariel Belestrade? What for?"

"Something about reading the rooms. Divining the energy of the space—that's what she said. I remember very clear because she came in here while I was in the middle of fixing a chocolate soufflé, which takes a bit of care. She said there was bad energy in this room. Unkind energy. Looked at me like it was my doing."

She threw her hands in the air so hard, the oven mitt flew off, bounced off the ceiling, and nearly fell in the pot of greens.

"See? Even thinking of it gets my back up. And of course, the soufflé didn't turn out. Had to fix it into pudding."

"Terrible thing to do to a soufflé," I said, shaking my head gravely. "What did everyone else think of her?"

"About like I did, far as I could tell. Mr. Collins ignored her. Mr. Randolph threw faces at her behind her back. Miss Becca avoided the woman altogether."

As she spoke, she took pots off the stove and started ladling things into dishes.

"What about Mr. Wallace?" I asked. "He's around a lot, isn't he?"

"Oh, yes," she said with a genuine smile. "Mr. Harry's practically family. Old, old friend of Mr. Collins. And, of course, he's the children's godfather."

"What did he think of Belestrade?"

"Not much. Especially after what she said to him. You can't blame him, really."

"Of course not," I said, sipping my lemon awfulness and trying to look casual. "What were her exact words again?"

"That he was a terrible source of energy for the whole household. That he was spiritually poisonous. Mr. Harry! One of the sweetest men. A second father to the children. If that man is poisonous, I must be Typhoid Mary."

"Did she give a reason why?" I asked.

"Not to me. I gather it was because he and Mr. Collins were always talking business. Money, she said, muddied the well of the soul." If she dripped any more sarcasm I'd have to get a mop. "Anyone who says things like that hasn't had to worry about money a day in their life."

"What did Mrs. Collins think about that?" I asked. "Did she come to Harry's defense?"

She might have had an answer for me, but Sanford took that moment to walk in. He saw me sitting at the table and for a split second his mask of reserve fell away and beneath it was . . . what? Panic? Anger?

"Can I help you, miss?" he asked, slipping the mask back on.

"No thank you. I found what I was looking for," I said, saluting with my lemon fizz.

"I was telling her about that Belestrade woman," Dora told him. "How she got her hooks in."

A little tension went out of Sanford's shoulders and I wondered what he had been worried we were talking about.

"Do you think she had something to do with what happened to Mrs. Collins?" I asked.

Dora was about to answer but her husband jumped in. "We really couldn't say. We were assisting in the kitchen the whole time. And certainly when . . . when the incident occurred."

His wife fell in line and nodded.

"That's true," she said. "Went over it all with the police."

"I believe they are finishing in the sitting room," Sanford told me. Unminced, that translated to time to skedaddle. I thanked the cook for the soda and the chat and left.

Back in the sitting room, things were indeed wrapping up.

"I don't know why it's necessary," Wallace was saying. "These are busy people."

"Which is why it's best to interview as many at once without requiring them to travel to my office." The between-the-lines message here was that either Wallace acquiesced or the Collins Steelworks muckety-mucks would be forced to schlep out to Brooklyn.

"Fine," he said. "I'll tell everyone to make themselves available."

We said our goodbyes and Ms. Pentecost promised to keep them updated on any progress. Driving back to our house in that dreaded borough, she let me know I'd be making a trip to the Collins plant in Jersey City later that week. There I'd find a number of executives and managerial types, along with assorted others, who'd been at the party. Sure, we could have gotten them to come to us, but she wanted me to get a feel for the atmosphere of the place.

"It seems that there was something of a crisis point developing within the company prior to Mrs. Collins's death," Ms. Pentecost explained from her leathery nest in the backseat of the sedan. "The board overwhelmingly favored renewing the military contracts. However, over the last year, Mrs. Collins had expressed a change of heart. She spoke about moving the company back to a domestic footing. It seems she'd acquired ethical concerns about prospering from the war."

"Did she catch these ethical concerns from Belestrade?"

"That is the prevailing opinion," Ms. P said. "With forty percent of shares remaining under family control, it's possible that she could have found favor among the minority of other shareholders who held similar concerns."

I swerved to avoid an errant pedestrian and presented him

with a single-digit salute, our bumper passing within inches of his knees.

"So, who votes those forty percent now?"

"Once the estate is settled, the shares will be split evenly between the children but will be held under care by a trustee until next year, when they turn twenty-one. Would you like to wager who the trustee is?"

"No bet," I said. "It's Wallace."

I caught Ms. P's nod in the rearview.

"Where's Uncle Harry stand?"

"He would not commit either way."

I gave that some thought. It was a sure bet that guns were always going to remain more lucrative than staplers. A lot of money might have swung on that decision. If Mrs. Collins had been pushing for staplers, that was a grade-A motive. Then I thought about the picture in the office. Add into the money thing a history of illicit love?

I jumped off that train of thought and filled Ms. P in on my conversations with Becca and the cook and the thoughts inspired by the family photo. I left out the glimpse of bare back and the question about dancing.

"So what do you think?" I asked. "Could Uncle Harry be Daddy Harry? Or at least Lover Harry?"

"There was certainly the suggestion of strong emotions whenever he discussed Abigail, but he hides it well." She twisted in the backseat, trying to find a more comfortable position. That meant she was aching, which meant she was tired, which meant I'd have to prod her to take a nap before dinner or tomorrow might turn into a bad day.

"Of course, it could be exactly what it looks like," I conceded. "A working girl seduces the big boss, gets a pair of buns in the oven, and wins the Irish lottery. Hard to make that call without knowing a little more about what kind of woman we're dealing with."

"Unfortunately, both Mr. Wallace and his godchildren were unable, or unwilling, to provide many details about Abigail's life prior to her marriage," Ms. Pentecost said. "She arrived in New York City in 1924, obtained a position as secretary to Mr. Collins and Mr. Wallace that fall, and became pregnant within the year. To their knowledge, she kept no documents or mementos of her life prior to coming here."

"What are the chances the dominoes that tipped her murder started falling that far back?" I asked.

No answer from the backseat. It was a rhetorical question, and besides, she knew I was aware of how she felt about missing chapters in victims' lives.

"I foresee a considerable amount of research in my future," I said.

"Not a difficult prediction."

"Speaking of seeing the future, what about Belestrade?" I asked.

"What about her?"

"She was there that night. She orchestrated that whole show in the office. There are a lot of strong feelings bouncing around. Whether she had something to do with the murder or not, she definitely had her fingers in the Collins family."

No response from the backseat. I glanced in the mirror and saw that she had her eyes shut. I couldn't tell if she was thinking hard or pretending to.

"What I'm saying is this woman is possibly good as a suspect, and definitely good as a source of information, and since I'm not heading to Jersey until Friday, maybe we should pay her a visit tomorrow."

More silence from the backseat. I was about to prod her again when she let out a slow, "No. I don't think so. Not yet."

"What are we waiting for? Honestly, boss. If I had the reins we'd be heading to her place right now."

"I know. But you don't have the reins, so we will wait before confronting Ms. Belestrade." It's not often she puts her foot down, so I stuffed a sock in any follow-ups.

"Okay. Fair enough. What do we do with the next two days?"

"I believe a visit to Professor Waterhouse is in order," she said as the sedan descended into Brooklyn. "She was observing Ms. Belestrade. I'd like to know what exactly she saw."

"I'll call up the university and see if she's available. That'll eat up an hour or two. What else?" Yes, this was aggressively coy. I wanted to get on Belestrade and I wanted to get on her right then. My employer ignored it.

"I think you'll save time during your visit to the plant if we know just where the police are in the tracking down of alibis and so forth," she said. "Reach out to your contacts in the department. Save any homicide detectives for last. I don't want to risk tipping our hand."

I pulled the Caddy in front of the town house, edging the front bumper to within a few inches of a familiar unmarked sedan.

"I think we're about to be saved a dime," I said, throwing the car into park.

The cops were here.

CHAPTER 8

Lieutenant Lazenby was polite enough to wait in his car while we went inside and got a couple drinks poured—water for me, bourbon for Ms. P to take the edge off the ache. Not exactly doctor's orders, but I had learned to choose my battles.

Three sips in, he rang the bell.

"Are you in with the family or the company?"

Squeezed into the largest of our guest chairs, Lazenby looked very much like the man I'd first met across an interview table. He'd added an inch or two to his waistline and a lot of silver to his beard but was still very much the NYPD's sharpest blade when it came to cutting to the heart of their toughest cases. He also cut an impressive figure in a dark gray wool pinstripe, the color of which matched his eyes. Its quality probably made a few people wonder if he was on the take. He's not. I happen to know he has a cousin who's a tailor to the Madison Avenue crowd.

He repeated his question. "The family or the company?"

Ms. P leaned back in her chair and sipped her bourbon.

"So . . . *you're* pursuing the company," she mused, a twinkle dancing in her good eye. It was a statement, not a question.

Lazenby scowled and shifted his bulk. "We're pursuing a number of leads."

"But you prefer the company. You think the murder is business, not personal."

"I think for a lot of people, business *is* personal," the policeman noted. "But, again, what makes you think—"

"It's simple." Cutting him off midsentence infuriates him. But he knows she knows it infuriates him, so it doesn't bother him as much when she does it, or at least he tries not to let it show. Follow? "You didn't ask if I was investigating Abigail Collins's death. You took that as a given. How you discovered as much, I'll chalk up to your skill as an investigator."

Lazenby snorted, though the compliment was sincere. I flashed back to the tail I'd spotted when we were leaving the morgue.

She continued. "Our paths have crossed during domestic cases before. Frequently to our mutual benefit."

Another snort.

"Which suggests that your concern is that I am employed by Collins Steelworks, and thus that my involvement will interfere with an ongoing avenue of investigation."

"You still didn't answer the question," he squeezed out through clenched teeth.

"No, I didn't," she said with a hint of an echo of a smile. "I am not compelled to release my client's name. Unless you've come armed with a warrant."

Lazenby started to object, but she cut him off again.

"However . . . In the interest of professional courtesy, I will answer. I am *not* employed by Collins Steelworks."

The big man relaxed a hair in his seat.

"Which does not mean I will not search for a motive originating within the company," she added. "Will shall be interviewing executives at the Jersey City plant this Friday—

focusing primarily on those who were at the party Halloween night."

He tensed again.

"Yeah, it'll probably be an all-day affair," I added. "Might spread into Monday or Tuesday. Lot of people to talk to."

I smoothed out some nonexistent wrinkles in my trousers. "Of course, if I had the nuts and bolts of who was where during the last inning of that party, I'd be in and out a lot quicker. Fewer opportunities for me to accidentally stick my nose into whatever you've got cooking."

"*Accidentally.*" Something unpleasant was brewing behind his eyes. "Like either of you ever do anything accidentally." After a few seconds of thundering, his face settled. "Let me see what we have. In the interest of professional courtesy." This time he was the one who smoothed some nonexistent wrinkles. "So . . . why don't you think this came from the company end?"

It wasn't a throwaway. He really wanted to know. More than once, Ms. Pentecost had come sideways at a case and uncovered a culprit in a spot the police had never checked. It was natural that he was feeling snakebit.

"I did not say that. Merely that my involvement in the case comes at the behest of the family."

"Yeah, you said. But you're playing this too cute. If you thought the murder came out of company business, it'd be you heading to Jersey City and not your sidekick here."

I prepared something indignant to fling at him, but Ms. P beat me to it.

"Ms. Parker is my assistant, not my sidekick, and an investigator licensed by the state of New York. Her talents should not be underestimated."

He waved it off. "Sidekick, assistant, conspirator—whatever you want to call it. I've seen you operate enough to know where you're looking. Why do you think this came out of the family and not the company? Our numbers men tell us that if Abigail Collins got her wish and the company went back to office supplies, it'd mean a nine-figure swing over the next decade. That's a big, fat motive. What do you know that I don't?"

"As far as this case is concerned, you assuredly know far more than I. You've been working on it for two weeks. I've been involved a single day. As it stands, I don't have nearly enough to make an informed conclusion and so am working on instinct."

"And your instinct says it's not the company."

She gave a noncommittal shrug. Even the great lady detective can play coy when she wants to.

"Have it your way. Just stay out of mine."

He heaved his bulk out of the chair and headed for the door. I ran ahead, grabbing his coat from the rack in the hall and slipping him a couple questions of my own.

"I'm assuming you came up empty on prints on the murder weapon? Since it got tossed in the fireplace?"

The look he shot me was a nicely blended cocktail of annoyance and suspicion.

"We played some of our cards faceup," I said, handing him his coat. "Play fair."

"That you think this is a game is part of the problem," he said. "We found prints. Not that it does us any good. They were all ones we expected: this spiritualist, her assistant, the daughter—the other guests she roped into playing her game. And some smudges our print guy says came from somebody wearing gloves."

"Interesting," I said. "The killer came prepared."

He shrugged into his overcoat and opened the door. He was about to leave when I tossed him another one.

"Dig up anything interesting on Belestrade?"

He turned and glared. "Such as?"

"Her real name, for instance?"

"Sorry to disappoint you," he said, "but as far as we can tell Belestrade *is* her real name. Either that, or someone's gone to a lot of trouble to fudge her paperwork.

"Not *everyone* walks around with a counterfeit moniker," he added with a hangman's grin.

So he knew Parker wasn't what I was born with. I forget sometimes just how good a detective he had to be to keep his job as top homicide cop in the city.

"Try and keep your nose clean on this one," he said. "Your knives, too."

The jab stung and I felt every inch of my five foot nothing.

A lot of the time, Lazenby and his men treat me like a little girl playing at being a detective. More mascot than serious player. Three years of working cases, Ms. P vouching for me, but he never let me forget that the first time we met I was on the other side of the table.

Not that I let him know I was thinking any of that. Instead, I threw on a pout.

"Lieutenant, you wound me. I haven't stabbed anyone in ages."

But he was already three steps down the stoop and gave no sign he'd heard me.

Back in the office, Ms. Pentecost was standing at our little bar, pouring herself another bourbon. I shot her a disapproving look, which she deftly ignored.

"Not the company, huh?"

She didn't respond.

"So, why not?" I asked. "Somebody pass you a note?"

She sat back down behind her desk, cradling her full glass of Kentucky gold.

"I did not say that I believed the murder was not related to Mrs. Collins's relationship to the business."

I got half a syllable of a protest out before she raised a hand.

"I merely told the good lieutenant that I was employed by the family, that I did not currently have enough information to make any informed conclusions, and that I was working on instinct. Everything else was inference on his part. And yours."

I invested half a minute in thinking about that before responding. "So he leaves thinking that you're going to be picking apart the Collins clan and that my trip to Jersey is just the standard nailing down of alibis. Which makes it a little less likely I'll have one of Lazenby's boys standing over my shoulder when I'm there."

Her answer was a long, slow sip of her drink. I know you've only just met her, but my boss—in case you haven't inferred as much—is a genius.

"What are the chances the lieutenant will relinquish any of his notes on the party guests?" she asked.

"Ten to one against," I said. "Five to one if he's really concerned about us tripping over something they've got going. Who knows if they really have a hook into anything. He might be flipping a coin and it came company-side up."

She shook her head. "No, I think they are investigating in earnest. He said 'our numbers men.' That means he's called in assistance from the fraud squad."

"You think that's what we've got here? Somebody had their fingers in the till and Mrs. Collins caught 'em?"

"I think in a company as large and turbulent as Collins Steelworks, a thorough investigation will find many fingers in many tills. Whether or not those fingers found their way around the murder weapon, I do not know."

This time I only had to invest half a minute of thought to follow that line to its end.

"If it's something like that—straight-out embezzlement—Lazenby's going to get there before us."

"Almost certainly," she agreed. "We cannot match the NYPD's manpower, nor do we have the luxury of seeking warrants."

"And Sid's good, but I'm not sure he's up for a job this big."

Sid was our numbers man and a former member of a certain fraternal organization. His job had been to move the club's dough around in such a way that it became invisible from the feds. He did a little till-dipping of his own, got caught, and was moved to the top of the club's agenda. Ms. Pentecost managed to get Sid out from under by solving the decade-old murder of the club boss's uncle. Instead of payment, she asked for Sid to be spared. So he owes her his life and he was paying her back on the installment plan by providing assistance when we had financials that needed combing.

"You're right," Ms. Pentecost said. "However, that does not mean you shouldn't keep your eyes and ears open on Friday. Perhaps inquire about warrants and just what questions the police have asked and see who reacts and how."

"Got it," I said. "Ask questions. Get answers. Pay attention. I might even remember to bring a pencil and paper so I can write things down."

My sarcasm went unremarked.

"Now, if our schedule is free, I'd like to grab lunch out and take a tour of some newspaper offices. See if there's anything that wasn't fit to print but which might be fit for us. I'm not worried about tipping off our involvement in the case. If the cops know we're in the mix, it's a sure bet the journos are only about half a step behind."

"I agree," she said. "But first, call the university and inquire about Professor Waterhouse's schedule for tomorrow."

I did and I found that she had a full day—two classes in the morning, two in the afternoon, with barely enough time to inhale a sandwich in between. We decided to hit her up after her last lecture. No warning her ahead of time. Who knew where she fit into this thing.

With that settled, I grabbed my coat and hat and left to put my underestimated talents to use.

CHAPTER 9

When I began the chore of writing all this down, I found I had to keep making the same big decision over and over again. What do I keep and what do I toss? There's a lot that cropped up during this case that has no bearing on anything or anyone, or at least nothing worth committing ink to paper—the mundane stuff that accumulates during any big investigation. Those are easy tosses.

Then there are the things that aren't so much relevant to the investigation as they are relevant to me or to my boss. Private things that would not otherwise see the light of day but that you might find illuminating. Those are harder. I'm taking those on a case-by-case basis.

Then there are the moments where I did not acquit myself as well as I would have liked. In plain language: the screwups. I'm human. Humans screw up. Back then I was still learning and flubbed things on a semiregular but hopefully diminishing basis. What follows is an instance where I tripped over my feet in a big way. I could probably find a way to cut it, but I respect you as a reader and I hope you'll view it in a generous light.

I did just what I told Ms. P I would do and swung by some newsrooms. A lot of the journos saw me as part source, part cub reporter, which came in pretty handy. A certain portion of those also saw me as a young, single woman who sometimes bought them drinks, so they got ideas. I wasn't above mixing pleasure with business, as long as they knew it was a casual thing and not to get attached. It's not that I was averse to going steady, it's just that I had rules: no cops, no clients, no reporters. Nothing that could get in the way of the work.

This time out, I limited myself to asking some roundabout questions and making a few oblique promises that I'd feed information when I had it. I confirmed that, yes, Ms. Pentecost was on the case but left it vague as to who was signing the checks. And to the perennial "Who does she think did it?" I gave the all-purpose "No comment."

A few of the things I managed to squeeze out in return were, in no particular order:

Alistair Collins had underbid a lot of competing companies to get those military contracts, accumulating some powerful enemies in the process.

Money was definitely changing hands to tamp down the headlines.

And Becca Collins had had a reputation as a straitlaced schoolgirl until her father died. Now she was a borderline wild child. Though "wild" by the standards of her tax bracket might constitute using the salad fork on the entrée.

I said adieu to the inkmongers and made my way to the New York Public Library at Fifth Avenue and Forty-second, rubbing the foot of one of the lions for luck on the way in. My objective was Hollis Graham, who ran the library's periodical archives. Before settling into that role, he'd been a world-class reporter. Hollis had tracked the ebb and flow of the city's elite for the better part of three decades—first on the social-scene beat, then crime, then City Hall, before he was pushed out by a scandal of his own. During his heyday, not only could he tell you where the bodies were buried, but he knew who did the digging and what brand of shovel they used.

I was informed by an assistant that he was on a rare vacation and wouldn't be back until the following week. I left a message for him to call me when he returned. Then I walked a block to grab a late lunch at a corner diner.

After doing away with an egg salad on rye and a slice of lemon meringue, I walked the forty blocks south to my destination. It was a clear, crisp day in New York, and I figured we wouldn't get too many more like it before winter settled in.

On my way, I swung by a newsstand to buy a used twelve-cent mystery for a nickel, a bag of popcorn, and a cherry soda. Then I followed the street signs to a little neighborhood near Greenwich Village. I made my way down a block of identical brownstones broken only by a church on one side and a tiny park on the other.

I headed toward the park, careful to keep my face turned away from number 215. Out of the corner of my eye, I managed to make out the words etched into the glass of the door.

ARIEL BELESTRADE

SEEKERS INQUIRE WITHIN

The park was just big enough for a tree, a scrap of grass, and a bench on either side. I took the one empty bench. The other was weighted down by a pair of old women in black sack dresses and colorful babushkas. They each had a tiny bag of birdseed and were chatting quietly away in Russian while the pigeons danced and pecked at their feet.

I cracked open my soda and my book and munched popcorn while half paying attention to the hard-boiled hero and half to the front of number 215, which I had a decent enough view of through the bare, low-hanging branches of the lone tree. There was a light in the window, and at one point I thought I saw the shadow of someone moving inside. The spiritualist was in.

I rationalized that I wasn't really disobeying Ms. P's instructions. She said we weren't ready to question Belestrade. I had no intention of questioning her. I just wanted a look at this maybe murderer. The papers didn't have a good snapshot, and I wanted to get a glimpse of the woman who had my boss so on edge. She was suspect number one, after all. It was ridiculous to put her on the back burner.

That's what I told myself, anyway.

Really, I was still sore from Lazenby's jab. I wanted to prove something. To him, to Ms. P, to myself. Maybe to Becca, too.

I passed the time imagining scenarios straight out of *Black Mask*. In them, I'd hear a scream from inside Belestrade's place. I'd kick down the door to find the crone with a knife to Becca's throat.

"Move and she dies," the witch would hiss.

Faster than the eye could follow, I'd draw my .38 from my shoulder holster, putting a bullet right between her eyes. Becca would collapse into my arms. Things progressed from there.

Eventually the sun began to set and the babushkas abandoned their post. I took up the slack, tossing popcorn to the pigeons, but eventually I ran out and the birds abandoned me as well. Between five and six, foot traffic on the little street picked up with men and women returning home from work. Then the rush died down, and the street was dark and quiet.

Night fell and the streetlights flickered on. The wind picked up and I began regretting I hadn't brought a pair of gloves or grabbed my knit hat instead of my cap.

I kept up the ruse of reading but that cover was becoming less plausible now that I was turning pages by streetlight. The

hard-boiled detective was debating whether to follow his bru-
nette bombshell of a client into her bedroom and I was debating going home when the door of number 215 swung open and
a woman stepped out.

The first thing I noticed was her height. She pushed six
feet, and it wasn't a willowy seventy-two inches either. She was
broad shouldered and solid. She had on an ankle-length white
fur draped over a formfitting black dress and matching heels.
She sported a black bob that framed a soft, open face and large,
dark eyes.

No burning gaze. No viper's grin. Not that I could see,
anyway.

I'd managed to get a description from one of my newspaper
contacts. He'd told me she resembled a sized-up Myrna Loy, but
with the sultry edges buffed away.

He nailed it.

Belestrade hit the sidewalk, took a right, and started hoof-
ing it away from me. I decided on the fly that a look wasn't
enough. I gave her a respectable head start and followed.

As I walked, I conducted a mental inventory of the contents
of my wallet. I expected her to grab a cab as soon as she hit a
main drag, requiring me to find a cab of my own and play a
game of "follow that car." I had enough cash to take a loop
around the island, but I was hoping it would be a short trip.
Even if a cabby is up for playing a game of rabbit, they almost
always botch the job.

Belestrade surprised me. Instead of hailing a cab, she went
to the nearest subway entrance and headed down. I followed.
She hopped on an uptown train and I did the same, staying one
car back from her. With her height and that fur, it was a cinch
keeping her in view.

A handful of stops later, she got off and headed west. After a couple blocks, she walked into a bookstore. This one didn't have a lot of dime novels, but Ms. Pentecost sent me there monthly for her supply of European magazines.

I gave Belestrade half a minute, then went inside. There was no sign of her. I spent a breathless few minutes going up and down the aisles before I heard the bell above the door give a ring and looked out the store window to spot her heading back the way we came.

I darted out in time to see her descend into the subway again. I managed to catch up just as she boarded an uptown train. This time I ended up in the same car as her, but it was full and she didn't spare me a glance. We only went a couple more stops before she got off near Times Square. While it wasn't tourist season, that area is never vacant. I struggled to keep her in sight while not drawing attention. Tailing is one of the few places where my size can be an advantage, letting me slip between people without jostling too many elbows.

A few blocks down, she made a sharp turn into a theater. Now her outfit made sense, I thought.

I'd seen the show the week before. It was a new comedy that veered toward bawdy when it would have been better served keeping its skirts down. Luckily, the skirts in question belonged to one of my favorite actresses, so I'd led the applause.

I figured I'd better go in and make sure she was seeing the show and not meeting someone. Or bludgeoning somebody to death in the ladies' room. I was following a cluster of theater-goers to the entrance when suddenly the door opened and Belestrade glided out.

She passed so close we brushed shoulders. After my heart dropped under two hundred beats a minute, I followed. Back into the subway we went.

For the next two hours I followed her on an aimless journey around the island. This included stops at a diner on Fifth Avenue that makes a killer Reuben; two other bookstores—one that has a great collection of mysteries and another that pads its bottom line with some back-room forgery work; a cop bar that's a good place for station house gossip; and an after-hours club that doesn't like to advertise. I didn't follow her into the last two, since they knew me in both places and I didn't want to chance someone yelling "Hey, Will Parker! How's your boss, the famous lady detective?"

During our travels, I had time to consider what Belestrade was up to. At first I thought she was trying to lose a tail, or at least seeing if she had one. But if she was savvy enough to do that, she was savvy enough to have clocked me in the first half hour, in which case why keep bouncing from place to place?

Then I thought maybe she was checking sources. If she was a con artist, she'd need to finger likely marks. I could see all of those places being good spots to meet contacts and suss out information.

I was mulling over that possibility when I followed her down into the subway again. This time we took the IRT to Brooklyn and got off at the stop I was most familiar with. I followed her a couple of blocks, made a right, a left, a right again. When I realized where she was heading, the short hairs on my arms stood at attention.

I peeked around the final corner and saw her standing on the sidewalk looking up at a front door, the keys to which I had in my pocket. I slipped my hand into my coat and felt the comforting grip of my .38 stashed nice and tight in my shoulder holster.

No, I wasn't trigger-happy as a habit. But this was a woman Ms. P seemed unusually wary of, and my boss isn't someone

who scares easy. And it wouldn't have been the first time someone had taken a run at my employer.

After a couple minutes of looking up at our door, she turned
on her heel and began to walk back in my direction. I ran to the
other end of the block, ducked around a corner, and crouched
behind a rowhouse stoop. A few breathless moments later, I
heard the tapping of my quarry's heels go past.

I picked up the tail again and followed her back to the subway, getting off at Greenwich Village. A traffic jam of bodies
on the steps put me farther behind her than I liked. I lost sight
of her a couple times, and by the time I turned the corner onto
her block, the door to number 215 was closed and the lights
were burning.

I glanced at the windows as I walked past, hoping for a peek
inside. All I got was the back side of the curtains. As I continued
sidling down the block, I wondered. What had all that been
about? Had she spent the night meeting contacts, then planned
a visit to Ms. Pentecost but chickened out? Or was it something
more sinister?

As I passed the tiny park, a voice called to me.

"Do you have a light?"

I turned and there she was. All six feet of black dress and
white fur lounging on the bench I'd sat on not two hours earlier. She had an unlit cigarette dangling from her long fingers.

"I seem to have left my lighter in the house," she said.

Trying to keep my breaths coming in even increments, I
pulled a lighter out of my pocket. I don't indulge, but I keep a
lighter on hand for such occasions.

I walked up and lit her smoke. She inhaled and the ember
glowed like an eye in the dark. She crossed her legs and pulled
the fur tight around her.

"It's a cold night," she said in a voice like spiced honey—rich with a little bite to it. "November is a tricky month. That slow turn from autumn to winter. You think you've made yourself comfortable and then a gust comes along and cuts you to the bone."

She looked up and smiled.

There it was. Just a little bit of the viper around her lips. And more than a little fire lighting up those big, dark eyes. I thought of about twenty things to say in reply, but none of them made it to my tongue. She reached down and pulled off her heels.

"These will cut you, too. One of the many things men don't have to worry about. I applaud your choice. A nice pair of oxfords. But I so enjoy the click-clack of heels against the concrete. Like you're tapping out a secret code only the initiated can decipher. You understand, don't you, Miss Parker?"

That fight-or-flight instinct I'd learned about in one of Ms. P's lecture-hall field trips should have been kicking in about then. But her voice—rich and thick and rhythmic—was like an elixir. Gentle and calming.

She stood up and brushed by me for the second time that night. Heels dangling from one hand, she padded barefoot across the street, trailing a line of cigarette smoke behind her. As she walked up her front step and opened the door, her free hand caressed the message etched into her glass.

SEEKERS INQUIRE WITHIN

She disappeared inside. I waited for the door to click shut, but it didn't. It stayed open a couple of inches. A beam of yellow light fell out and spread across the street like an invitation.

I thought about it. I had questions, and the answers were on the other side of that door. I took a step, then another. I was standing at the bottom of the steps when somewhere down the block I heard the squeal of brakes and a horn screaming in protest.

The music of the city snapped me out of my trance. I decided I'd proved myself enough for one night and hurried back to Sixth Avenue and the storefronts and still-bustling sidewalks.

I flagged down a cab. On the way back to Brooklyn, I thought about the questions I'd left in front of that door. When did she know I was on her tail? How did she know my name? How'd she find out we were on the case? Did somebody tip her off? What would have happened if I'd gone through that door?

As I pondered, the cab passed the after-hours club, where the night would just be starting. As we drove by, a quartet of women disappeared inside, their heels tapping out a secret code.

You understand, don't you, Miss Parker?

In a flash, I *did* understand. The whole night rushed back and slammed into me like a wave at Rockaway Beach. I muttered a few choice expletives. The cabdriver gave me a nervous glance.

The theater, the bookshops, the bars. Some I knew well enough that you could call them haunts, others I visited only occasionally. But I did visit them. Some would take work to link me to, the after-hours club especially. But she'd done it.

The night was a map of my life in New York City. That last gesture and the open door? That was the message: *I know you. You want to know me, all you have to do is knock.*

The whole night had been one long tent show. And I had been the mark.

CHAPTER **10**

The dead play a key role in every civilized culture, from the tribes of the Amazon to the deserts of Arabia, to right here in New York City. We venerate them. We speak to them. We ask them for guidance. They are present in every action of our waking lives, whether we are conscious of it or not. In many ways, we are ruled by the dead."

I stifled a yawn.

Not because the woman holding forth on the university lecture-hall stage was boring. I'd spent too many hours lying awake replaying every move Belestrade had made, every word she'd said.

I should have caught on to her game earlier. I'd let her lead me around like a show pony. Putting me through my paces.

What's worse, she knew things about me I preferred not to advertise. I'd only been to that particular after-hours club a handful of times, and not in half a year. But if it hit the grapevine that I spent time in places like that—and who I spent time with—I wasn't sure how far the news would spread.

Ms. P and I had made enemies. Some of them wore badges. And there were plenty of laws on the books they could leverage if they wanted to get back at us.

I hadn't told my boss about my evening adventure. How could I? I'd gone out to show I had what it took to be called a detective and ended up putting on a much different kind of display.

I was ashamed.

But she knew something was bothering me. She'd asked three times at lunch if I wanted more of Mrs. Campbell's seafood stew. For her, that was practically fawning.

Now we were settled in the back row watching Dr. Olivia Waterhouse kick off her last class of the afternoon. A petite, almost child-size woman, Waterhouse looked more like one of her undergraduates than a respected fortysomething professor. She had an unruly mass of curly brown hair that looked like it chronically resisted a brush and wire-rim cheaters over a pair of dark eyes. She was sporting a brown wool skirt and jacket that had seen better days, and were probably bought off the rack in the junior's section.

"I know what you're thinking," she told the half-filled lecture hall. "You're thinking, 'I am a rational citizen of the twentieth century. I am not beholden to a fallacy. The idea that the dead speak, that we are controlled by our long-dead ancestors, is something we left behind in the Old World. It has no place in the New. We are free to pursue our destiny. There are no chains of superstition on me.' I'm here to tell you you're wrong."

Her voice was high and light, but there was a power and passion behind it. Dr. Waterhouse was someone you probably wouldn't spare a second glance if you passed her on the street. But standing onstage, holding forth from her favorite academic soapbox, her eyes lit up and she drew from a hidden well of charisma.

Her hundred or so students were certainly paying attention, which is saying a lot for a late afternoon class of undergraduates.

"Think on this," Waterhouse continued. "How many churches are there in this city? How many cemeteries? How many crypts? How many statues carved in the semblance of long-dead men? Each of these exists because we believe the dead are more than just dust and bones. Most modern religions—Christianity especially—have created complex hierarchies of the dead that put the ancient Egyptians to shame. We are taught that the dead are still around us. Hovering. Whether above or, in the case of our more freethinking ancestors, below."

She squeezed a polite chuckle out of that.

"Let me employ a little exercise. How many of you, as a child, stole something? Something small, like a piece of candy from a shop?"

I didn't know where that left turn was heading, but I raised my paw along with a scattering of others. She made a show of counting the sparse number of hands.

"Now," she continued. "How many of you, as a child, thought about stealing something—really considered it—and decided not to."

About five times as many hands went up. Waterhouse smiled and nodded.

"For those of you who chose not to steal, what swayed you to choose not to?" she asked. "Was it a surge of civic pride that suddenly made you loath to transgress our society's laws?"

I started to see where she was leading us. The first time Ms. P and I had seen Dr. Waterhouse speak, I'd been struck by how good a performer she was. Most academics aren't. It's like they don't realize they're on a stage and it's their job to grab their audience and not let go. But Waterhouse knew when to breathe, when to gesture, when to raise her voice, and when to lower it to make the crowd lean in and listen.

"Or was it guilt that kept you on the straight and narrow?" she offered. "Was it because, even as a child, it was impressed into you that there were people somewhere high above you looking down, watching, judging? Much harder to steal a Mars bar if you think it might damn you. Or if you think Great-Aunt Grace is looking over your shoulder."

There was a wave of laughter as her little joke let some of the tension out of the room.

"I led you on this tangent to make the point that we modern women and men of the twentieth century are not so far removed from the ancient cultures that we are studying. We are as beholden to our superstitions as they were to theirs," she said with true earnestness. "I'm not saying this to provoke you. Just to remind you that we are not so far out of the cave as we'd like to think. Now, please, open your books to chapter fifteen."

She moved into a more traditional lecture, spending the next hour on the Sumerians, whose gods, as far as I could tell, were a lot more interesting than any saint you'll find hanging out in St. Pat's.

When she finished, we weaved our way through the departing students, introduced ourselves, and begged a few minutes of her time.

"Of course," she said. "This is my last class, and as usual, I have no social plans. Please, come to my office."

As we followed her through a warren of narrow hallways, she asked, "What did you think of the lecture?"

"Surprising," my boss said. "Less for its content than for what you judiciously left out."

"And what was that?"

"It seems that the argument you were leading to was that religion has been used through the centuries as a goad to enforce the law," Ms. P explained. "That the ones hovering above are not just the dead but whoever happens to be in power, whoever is holding on to that goad."

"It did seem like that, didn't it?" Dr. Waterhouse said, stopping in front of an office door.

"I wish my students were as swift to make that leap as you," she added, fumbling a key out of her pocket. "Sadly, most of them are in the class to fill some requirement or other. The few that do make the leap—well, I've frequently found that life's already taught them about power and abuse."

She opened the door and we entered an office that was about twice the size of a bathroom stall. Dr. Waterhouse squeezed behind a postage stamp of a desk, while we sat in a pair of rickety wooden chairs.

Except for a scattering of papers and books, the room was practically bare. The only personal touch I could spot was a glass case mounted to the wall above her desk. It held a row of stone arrowheads, like the kind I used to stumble upon in the tilled-out fields where I grew up. It caught my boss's eye as well.

"The Illinois?" she asked, nodding at the case.

Dr. Waterhouse looked surprised.

"The color of the stone," Ms. P said, answering the unasked question. "And the barbed tips."

The professor smiled.

"I must say, you're exactly as perceptive as advertised," she said, flipping over a folded copy of the *Times* that was sitting on her desk.

On page 3, there was a follow-up to the Collins murder under the headline FAMOUS LADY DETECTIVE BROUGHT IN ON COLLINS KILLING. It included a photo of Ms. P that had to be at least five years old. I made a mental note to schedule a photo shoot whether the famous lady detective wanted it or not.

"You were at the party the night Abigail Collins was killed?" Ms. P asked. It was a softball, but we had to start somewhere.

"I was. Though I'm not sure what help I can be." The professor removed her spectacles, squinted, then put them back on. "The police have spoken to me, of course. They didn't seem to find my testimony very interesting. I've been racking my brains trying to remember more details from that evening."

"Let's start at the beginning," Ms. Pentecost suggested. "How did you come to accompany Ms. Belestrade?"

"Well, I hadn't expected to," Dr. Waterhouse said. "She had invited me a while back, but I'd declined. I don't really like those kind of events. They're like faculty mixers, you know? I always feel so awkward and out of place, and then I get going on the unspoken caste system in modern American culture and how in some ways it's more regressive than older civilizations, especially in regards to how women are treated, and . . . Well, people don't seem to want to engage in that kind of dialogue at a party, and I try and change the subject and that just seems to make it worse. Then I was talking with my editor and he suggested I needed what he called a concrete set piece in the last chapter and I thought that this might provide it."

I glanced over at my boss and was comforted to find her as lost as I was. She waited for Dr. Waterhouse to take a breath, then raised a hand.

"Perhaps we should start with more basic details," she suggested. "How do you know Ms. Belestrade?"

Being a pale redhead, I'm a master blusher. But the doc gave me a run for my money.

"I'm sorry. If I don't have a lecture plan, I tend to ramble," she said. "I'm working on a book, you see? Actually, it's with my editor now, so most of the work is done. In it, I interview a number of clairvoyants, psychics, spiritualists, and so forth. Men and women who claim to have supernatural powers or profess to have contact with the dead. That sort."

"This was in order to debunk them?" Ms. P asked.

"I don't use the word 'debunk.' Certainly not in the interviews," Waterhouse said. "I'm less interested in how they do what they do than how they fit into the overall scheme of our culture. Our willingness to believe the unbelievable if it provides comfort. Because most of these spiritualists target the poor and working-class, that comfort usually comes in the form of hope. That things will get better. That, as they say, their ship will come in."

"Ms. Belestrade's clientele are hardly working-class," my boss pointed out.

"True! Ariel—Ms. Belestrade, I mean—is something of a holdover from the last century. The drawing-room séances, the theatricality—those things have mostly gone out of fashion. The revolutions in science and technology started it, but it's the Depression that really did them in, you see?"

We couldn't see and told her so.

"For the rich and powerful, spiritualists' comfort was wrapped in the message that everything would stay the same. That all was well and would stay well. Even beyond death." Waterhouse was on the edge of her chair, revving back into lecture mode. "The Crash proved that message to be a lie. And the years that followed drove that proof home. Things would not be well forever. Not even for the rich and powerful."

She finally took a breath and Ms. P took the opportunity to toss in a question.

"How does Ms. Belestrade thrive where others do not?"

Thrown off her rhythm, Waterhouse took a moment to think.

"A different message, I suppose," she finally said. "In her practice, it's less about communing with the spirit world and more about maximizing her client's success in this one. There's also her considerable talent to consider."

"Her talent?"

The professor leaned back in her chair. Which, because of her office's jail-cell dimensions, meant angling catty-corner to the room.

"I met her at some party I was dragged to years ago. We started chatting. She'd heard of my research and invited me to visit her at her home. I interviewed her on a number of occasions and sat in on several of her meetings with clients. She very quickly became a focus for my book. At the time, she was not as in demand as she is now, but I was sure she would be."

"Because of her talent?" my boss prompted.

"Ariel has a very . . . powerful personality," Waterhouse said.

Glasses off, squint, glasses back on. If I didn't know better, I'd have said the good professor had a bit of a crush on the clairvoyant. And I didn't know better.

"Are you familiar with cold readings?" she asked.

My boss turned to me.

"I've had a little experience with those kinds of operators," I said. "They ask sort of broad questions or say the kinds of things that might hit home with anyone. Like 'I sense you've lost someone.' If that's a yes, the easy follow-up is 'I sense they were dear to you' because if you're thinking in terms of 'lost,' then of course they were dear. Then they narrow things down from there. To the mark, it seems like the fortune-teller knows things they shouldn't know. But really, the mark is playing their cards faceup."

"Yes, yes, exactly!" A little of the lecture-hall glow came back into the prof's eyes. "A person going to this kind of— 'operator' is the word you used. I like that. I wish I'd used it in my book. Anyway, a person walking in to see a medium or a fortune-teller is almost always emotionally vulnerable in one way or another. Even those that don't believe, deep down they *want* to believe."

I added, "And if the medium or whoever hits the bullseye right off the bat, it puts the mark in the frame of mind that they know things other people don't. So even if they miss the target farther down the line, the mark will give them the benefit of the doubt."

Waterhouse nodded thoughtfully. I got the sense she was seeing me for the first time.

My boss grabbed the reins of the interview and pulled. "What makes Ms. Belestrade different from the rest of these so-called operators?"

"Not only is Ariel able to glean information from every word or gesture her clients make, but she has such a magnetic presence," the professor explained. "She's able to relax the subject in such a way that they divulge more information than they want to. Her voice, the way she holds herself, the cadence of her words. All of it combines to set the person at ease and make them susceptible."

"You make it sound like hypnotism." Ms. Pentecost's tone let slip exactly what she thought of that practice.

Waterhouse shook her head. "No, no. Hypnotism on unwilling subjects without a soporific is a myth. She's more subtle than that."

I thought of that honey-spice voice slipping into my ear.

"Also, there were occasions when we were speaking during which she revealed things about me that I absolutely did not divulge, unwittingly or otherwise. Things very few people know about me. She said they had been revealed to her by the spirits."

"Did you believe her?" Ms. P asked.

Waterhouse cracked an embarrassed smile. "I have to

admit that I almost did. I guess I was just like everyone else—someone who wanted to believe."

"But in the end you didn't."

"In the end, I recognized her assistant," she said. "He used to be a student here. Neal something. Watkins. Neal Watkins. A focus on history and anthropology, but he dropped out before graduating. Lack of funds, I believe. I asked around and his professors remember him as an excellent researcher. I surmised that he'd been tasked with digging up obscure details about me."

"So you did find her out in the end?"

"Not that I could prove it. At least not enough that I could put it in my book. I don't believe in making unsubstantiated charges. And . . ."

"And?" my boss prodded.

"Some of the things she knew about me . . . They weren't the sort of things that could be discovered through casual research. I don't know how she did it. Even with assistance."

The way she said it, it was clear that whatever those things were, they weren't open for inquiry. Ms. P must have gotten the same cue, because she changed course.

"From descriptions of the Halloween party, she did much the same thing with Rebecca Collins. What was your impression of her performance?"

"It's interesting you call it a performance," she said. "Because that's what she is. A performer. Usually a very good one. But that night . . ." She leaned back again and half closed her eyes. "At the beginning it was the usual fare. The card readings, the little tricks. Then there was the . . . incident . . . with the Collins girl and channeling her father. No subtlety. No grace."

"You've been present before when she purportedly channels the dead?" Ms. P asked.

"On two other occasions—neither was like that."

"Were you still at the party when the body was discovered?"

She shook her head and rocked her chair forward again. "No. I left immediately after the séance."

"Have you had the opportunity to speak with Ms. Belestrade regarding her performance that evening?"

"No, I haven't. I've left messages for her, but she hasn't returned my calls." The words came out draped in regret. I decided Dr. Waterhouse's interest in the clairvoyant was definitely a little extracurricular.

Ms. P shot her a few more questions about the party and the people and what she heard and saw there, but there were no further revelations. We thanked her for her time and were retracing our steps through the warrens when we heard her hurrying to catch up.

"Would it be possible to interview you at some point, Ms. Pentecost?" she asked after she caught her breath. "I'd be fascinated to see the same techniques my collection of charlatans use put to the cause of justice. It would make a wonderful chapter in future editions of my book."

For a second, I thought Ms. P was going to take her up on it. Then she shook her head. "No, I think not, Dr. Waterhouse. Like your collection of charlatans, I like to keep my tricks a secret."

Ms. P didn't say a word the entire way back to Brooklyn. Neither did I. I recognized her deep-thinking face and I don't like to disturb her when she's working her way through a line of thought.

Instead, I did some deep thinking of my own. About Ariel Belestrade and Abigail Collins and what might have gone off the rails on Halloween night. Pulling up in front of the brownstone, I noticed a car parked across the street. I noticed it because a maroon Pierce-Arrow—the 1935 V12 model, I believe—was as out of place on our avenue as an opal in a Cracker Jack box.

A man was behind the wheel—young and slender with a carefully cascading mane of black hair. As we went up the steps, I eyed him eyeing us.

I'd barely gotten the key in the lock when Mrs. Campbell opened the door, her usually steely warden's face clouded with worry.

"You're back," she said with a snarl that was half relief and half annoyance. "I told her you weren't in, but she wouldn't take no for an answer. Said she'd wait as long as she needed to. That it was a matter of life and death. Then she strolled right into the office and made herself at home."

Ms. Pentecost asked if the woman had identified herself, but this time I was a step ahead of her. It wasn't genius, though. Behind Mrs. Campbell, hanging from the coatrack in the hall, was a familiar long, white fur.

CHAPTER 11

I'm sorry for imposing myself on your housekeeper, but I had a feeling—a very powerful feeling—that we needed to meet. And it needed to be today."

The clairvoyant lounged in our most comfortable guest chair—all long legs and black bob, dressed in white slacks and a violet blouse that stood in stark contrast to Ms. Pentecost's earth tones. Her choice in nosebleed heels remained constant— these in a purple that matched her blouse.

"Why did it need to be today?" Ms. P asked, seeming to take Ariel Belestrade's sudden appearance in stride. I knew the nonchalance was a put-on. There was a tension just beneath the surface. It showed around her eyes and in the way she flexed her fingers against the arms of her chair. She was staring at a tiger cage, wondering if she could trust the bars.

"I don't know why, but I know it's important," Belestrade said. There was less spice and more honey in her voice today. Not that Ms. P had an appetite for either. "She's been calling out," the medium said, adding just the right amount of strain around the edges. "She needs help. I feel you're the only one who can provide it."

"Who needs my help?"

"Abigail," Belestrade said, as if the answer couldn't have been more obvious. "A person who dies by violence can linger for so long before moving on. They're trapped by pain and fear. The rage grounds them to this world. Like a terrible millstone around their neck."

I could see a dozen arguments flit across my employer's face—all the ways she could take apart the spiritualist's superstitions. I'd seen her reduce somebody to tears because they refuted evolution.

Instead, she surprised me. "Did Abigail Collins pass on any more information?" she asked in a tone of perfect seriousness. "The identity of her killer, perhaps."

Belestrade shook her head sadly, her eyes wide and filled with sincerity, or at least a good replica. "I'm afraid not. Spirits who die by violence aren't as clear as others. The rage disrupts things."

My boss didn't take her shot, so I decided to.

"I get the same problem trying to tune into the Dodgers game on a windy night," I quipped, giving her my third-snidest smile. She responded with a woe-is-you head shake.

"I don't expect you to believe me."

"Then what do you expect?" Ms. P asked.

"That we could confer. I know you're curious about me. I see no reason we couldn't simply meet instead of sending Miss Parker to surveil me."

Ms. P raised an eyebrow my way. Her way of saying we'd talk about this later. My stomach twisted at the thought of describing how Belestrade had played me.

For the clairvoyant, all of this may as well have been sketched out in neon.

"Ah," she said, turning toward me. "So you weren't sent by your employer. Perhaps our meeting was happenstance."

There was that viper smile again. I wondered just how poisonous this woman was.

I didn't find out because my boss rescued me.

"I give Miss Parker leave to use her own initiative in gathering information on suspects," she told the medium.

"I'm a suspect? How exciting." She said it with a perverse hint of glee. "Ridiculous, of course. I had no reason to wish Abigail harm. But it is thrilling in a very morbid way."

"You live a rather morbid life—in the strictest definition," Ms. P offered.

"My work is far more about the living than the dead," Belestrade explained. "Providing comfort and guidance."

Ms. P shifted a bit in her chair, arranging her limbs into what I think of as her interrogator pose. "Now that you've delivered your message from the late Mrs. Collins, would you be so kind as to answer a few questions?"

The clairvoyant thought about it—or pretended to think since she must have known the request was coming. "I'm a very private person, Ms. Pentecost."

"Yet you do not shy away from attention, if your press clippings can be believed."

A hit. A palpable hit.

"You've looked up my clippings? Did you have to seek them out? Or are they in your extensive files? The ones you keep upstairs."

Apparently I wasn't the only resident of our house she'd done research on. If my boss was fazed, she didn't show it.

The medium waved a hand, as if brushing her own question away. "No bother. The times I've been mentioned in the press have always been as a supporting role in the lives of others. Never my own personal story. Which I feel is what you're seeking."

She put on another thoughtful face and I was reminded of poker games during my circus days. Specifically of my buddy

Pauly, the clown. Even through three layers of greasepaint, he couldn't hide when he was holding a big hand.

"I'll make you a deal," the clairvoyant said. "I'll give you an hour right here, right now, to answer any questions that you pose. In exchange, the two of you must visit me at my parlor and give me an hour of your time."

A big bet.

"For what purpose?" Ms. P demanded.

"To read your past and tell your future," our guest said matter-of-factly. "And to provide what guidance I can."

A long silence followed. I could practically hear the gears turning behind my boss's eyes. Inside I was yelling, "Fold! Fold, damn it!"

We couldn't trust any answer she gave. Besides, we'd eventually dig it all up ourselves given time and legwork. I didn't want Ms. P walking into that spider's parlor. Not that I'd ever call my boss a fly, but better safe than swallowed.

"Agreed," Ms. Pentecost said.

I tried not to let my disappointment show, but considering the perceptive skills of the two women I was in the room with, it was probably a lost cause.

The smile from Belestrade belonged to someone who'd just made their flush and were waiting to rake it in.

"Ask away."

CHAPTER 12

One of the first classes Ms. P had me take was short-hand. Twenty-year-old me, still insisting on overalls and flannel shirts, plunked down into the middle of two dozen prim and proper Midtown secretaries in training. Not my favorite three hours a week, but in the long run some of the most useful.

During that hour with Ariel Belestrade, I barely looked up from my notepad. True to her word, the clairvoyant answered everything thrown at her. No hemming, no hawing, no pauses as she internally edited. If she was fudging anything, I couldn't tell.

If what Dr. Waterhouse said was true, she was a master of deception, so I took nothing for granted.

Here's a transcript of the highlights.

LP: Where were you born, Ms. Belestrade?

AB: Please, call me Ariel. And I was born in New Orleans, but I grew up in many places. Louisiana, Florida, Tennessee, Texas, California, for a short time London and Paris, and then most of my teenage years in Savannah, Georgia.

LP: What accounts for such an upbringing?

AB: My mother traveled.

LP: For work or pleasure?

AB: That . . . is a thorny question. You see, she was a professional mistress. Men would hire her to be their companion for a week or a month. Sometimes longer. Sometimes for a single special event. Or a vacation. Once a man hired her for a six-month tour of Europe. Thus my time in London and Paris.

Do you find that shocking?

LP: I find little shocking when it comes to how women are forced to make their way in the world. You accompanied her everywhere?

AB: Not always. When I did, a nursemaid or some other companion would travel with us. Or she would leave me with a friend she trusted in the city. During our trip to Europe, my grandmother accompanied us. At the client's expense, of course.

LP: Your mother must have been very beautiful.

AB: That's just it, Ms. Pentecost. She wasn't. Or, I should say, she was attractive and fit but hardly stunning. Still, she was personable. Men found her to be a pleasure to be around.

LP: You mentioned your grandmother. Did she approve of your mother's profession?

AB: Certainly not. But she learned early on that nothing she said could change my mother's course. However, her disapproval was not rooted in sexual mores, but in her fear for me and my education and training.

LP: Your training?

AB: It was during our trip abroad that my gift was first noticed. My grandmother would catch me playing by myself. Having conversations with people who weren't there. My mother had seen me do this, but I was a child—eight or nine—and imaginary friends are not uncommon.

But my grandmother took notice. When she asked me who I was talking to, I said Charlotte. When she asked who Charlotte was, I told her that she was a little girl like me who had been very sick. Then she woke one morning and no one could hear her or see her, not her mother or father or brother. And she was very afraid.

LP: *Charlotte was a ghost?*

AB: I don't like that word. "Ghost." The connotation it has with ghost stories. That their purpose is to frighten us. We don't need to be afraid of the dead. That's what my grandmother taught me.

She convinced my mother to let me come live with her in Savannah. The gift ran throughout that side of the family. Not in my grandmother, but in her sister and her mother. She knew how to help me and train me to use my abilities.

WILL HERE: I'm going to skip over her time in Savannah learning how to speak to spooks. A lot of sitting cross-legged on crypts waiting for spirits to appear. A whole sidetrack on the interpretation of tarot cards and which deck is better: the eighteenth-century French version or the more modern Rider-Waite-Smith deck.

Interesting if you're into that kind of thing. It's just that I prefer my fiction properly labeled. Besides, I want to get to the present-day murder mystery.

I will say this. Belestrade told the story of her upbringing with a sense of dramatic timing that can only come from long practice. My guess is that these hard-coaxed private revelations had been hard-coaxed by any number of her clients.

Back to it.

LP: *How did you meet Abigail Collins?*

AB: A museum gala about two years ago. She was introduced to me by another client. I can't remember who. We had an immediate connection. She made an appointment to come see me the following week.

LP: This immediate connection—can you describe it?

AB: It's different with each client. For me, it means that there's a clarity about a person. I can clearly see and feel the poisonous elements in their lives. For them, it means they see in me something they need in their life. Some are lost; some are struggling against something; with some there's just an ease in speaking with me that they have nowhere else.

LP: It sounds like the relationship between a patient and psychiatrist.

AB: I suppose it is. Though, unlike a psychiatrist, I recognize that the inner world cannot always provide the answers. There is a world beyond this one.

LP: Which type of client was Mrs. Collins? Lost, struggling, or was she just looking for someone to talk to?

AB: She was a seeker. She wanted something more from this life.

LP: Can you expand on that?

AB: No.

LP: No?

AB: The details of what I discuss with my clients, of the spiritual journeys we go on, are sacrosanct. I'm bound to keep them private.

LP: Ms. Belestrade, a spiritual advisor is not a legal advisor. The law does not recognize confidentiality with your profession. Even if it did, that confidentiality would be eased with Mrs. Collins's death.

AB: But it hasn't! Abigail might have departed her body, but she has not left this plane of existence. She still holds her passions and her secrets close, and I must respect that. And, please, call me Ariel.

LP: Ariel . . . You must see that somewhere within what Mrs. Collins discussed with you, her passions and secrets, there might be a key to understanding her murder. If, as you say, she reached out from beyond the grave to direct you toward me, perhaps confidentiality can be ignored.

AB: I understand. And I sympathize. At the same time, I do not want to splay out her most intimate details for strangers.

I will say this. Abigail's marriage was . . . difficult. She remained with her husband for the sake of her children and she paid a price for this, in her mind, heart, and soul.

LP: By "difficult," do you mean she was physically abused?

AB: I'm afraid I can't say any more.

LP: And how did you go about helping her?

AB: I showed her that there is light in the darkness. That she was not trapped. That there were paths back into a life where she could be happy.

LP: This was shortly before the death of her husband?

AB: Are you insinuating something?

LP: Merely establishing a timeline.

AB: Let me be clear. Abigail had no hand in her husband's death. I have no reason to believe it was anything other than suicide, and she expressed the same to me many times.

LP: Did she have an opinion as to why her husband took his own life?

AB: Again, we're stepping into intimate details of her life and emotions that I'm not comfortable discussing.

LP: What of her recent change of heart regarding her company's contribution to the war effort? Are you comfortable speaking about that?

AB: As it's something that Abigail expressed publicly, I am. Her conscience could no longer allow her to take part in man's brutality to man.

LP: Was this change of heart due to your influence?

AB: Absolutely. When you understand that the veil between the living and the dead is so thin, and that the pain of life lingers far beyond that final breath, it's much harder to dismiss the violent taking of a life. Even one taken in a so-called noble cause.

LP: Speaking of the veil between the living and the dead, let's move on to the events of Halloween night. Whose idea was it to feature you as the party's entertainment?

AB: It was entirely Abigail's. I rarely do public readings like that. So many people; so much negative energy. My talents work best when I can focus on the intricacies of a single person, a single heart. Things like this have a tendency to turn into spectacle.

LP: Why did you agree?

AB: A feeling. A very strong feeling that I needed to be there. That a message needed to be passed on.

LP: Were you paid for your performance?

AB: I was provided a generous stipend.

LP: Was Abigail similarly generous throughout your relationship?

AB: Don't be so coy. It's beneath you. Just ask if I charged her for my services.

LP: Did you?

AB: Yes. And I don't come cheap. I would think you'd sympathize. Being a woman whose talents are rare and in high demand.

LP: Please describe the events of the night of the party from your perspective.

AB: I arrived a little after eleven. Abigail wanted everything to be a surprise, so she didn't want me mingling with guests. I came in through the back and was quickly ushered upstairs to the study, which had been set up according to my specifications.

I spent the next half hour there meditating and centering myself. Then Abigail brought her guests in. I began with simple readings, which are less about predicting the past or future and more about showing the person what paths are available to them. That seemed to go rather well, but overall the group was rowdy, a little drunk, and not very open.

Then we began the séance.

I felt a strong need to speak with Rebecca Collins and I asked her to sit for me.

I assume you've spoken with others about what happened. I'm afraid I can't tell you much about what was communicated. When I'm connected to the other side, I have very little memory of it afterward.

LP: *According to witnesses, you spoke in a voice not unlike that of the late Mr. Collins. You said, "Please, let me be at rest. Don't betray me, my love."*

AB: Then that's what I said.

LP: *Do you have a sense of why the spirit of Alistair Collins would say this?*

AB: I'm sorry, I don't. At the best of times, I can facilitate a conversation. In most cases—like this one—I'm merely a conduit.

LP: *That sounds very frustrating. To be used that way. Against your will.*

AB: It's a privilege, Ms. Pentecost. Few can do what I can. It's my duty to follow this calling. As I'm sure you feel it is your duty to follow yours.

LP: *Once you . . . emerged from your trance, what did you do next?*

AB: When I came back to awareness, Abigail was telling everyone to leave. I was hurried out along with everyone else. I left the party soon after.

LP: *After you left, where did you go?*

AB: Home. Neal, my assistant, drove me.

LP: *Where was he during the party?*

AB: Waiting in the car. And before you ask, yes, he was there the entire time, and no, he didn't see anything of note. I would have invited him to the party as well, but I was already imposing on Abigail's generosity with one guest.

LP: You're referring to Dr. Waterhouse. Why did you invite her to come and observe?

AB: I rarely go out of my way to provoke skeptics, but Olivia is so adamant in her disbelief and so passionate about discovering my so-called tricks. I can't help but have a go at her.

LP: We've spoken with Dr. Waterhouse and she mentioned that you have extraordinary abilities when it comes to reading people. Would you agree?

AB: People are not books. I don't open them up and flip through their pages. Rather, I open *myself* up. I become supremely sensitive to the world and the souls around me.

LP: During your time in the Collins house, did you . . . feel . . . anything notable from the other guests?

AB: Most people there were more interested in being seen than finding pleasure in one another's company. Many felt disengaged. They were either waiting for a chance to talk business or putting in the time before they could leave. Sad, really. To waste your life like that.

LP: Do you believe that Abigail Collins was murdered by the spirit of her husband?

AB: I have experienced countless spirits piercing the veil.

I have seen them manifest corporeally. I have felt them enter my body and use me to speak with their loved ones. I have seen them enter the bodies of others and move within them. I have walked into houses beset by poltergeists—spirits so lost and forgotten they are little more than mindless rage given form. But I've never seen a spirit murder a living human being. In my experience, as I'm sure in yours, we mortals know enough of murder. We don't need to rely on the dead.

CHAPTER 13

Now that I've made myself available to you, when would it be convenient for you to make yourself available to me?" Belestrade asked at the end of the interview. "You can visit me at my studio at any day or hour."

The unflappable lady detective squirmed but eventually settled on the following Wednesday in the late afternoon. I think she was hoping we'd have the case wrapped up by then and could welch.

I walked Belestrade to the door.

"I hope you'll join us next Wednesday, Miss Parker," she said, pitching her voice in a way that sent shivers down my spine. "The invitation is open to you both."

My eager smile fooled no one. "Wouldn't miss it."

Back in the office, I sat down in the chair that Belestrade had just vacated, took a steadying breath, and spilled the events of the night before, leaving out nothing.

I capped it with an apology. "I'm sorry I didn't tell you. I got caught and I was embarrassed."

"You're sorry you didn't tell me, but not sorry that you went in the first place— Let me finish! That you disobeyed a direct order and approached the woman when I expressly told you not to. You're not sorry about that?"

My cheeks grew hot. I thought about quibbling over "direct order" and "approached," but I bit it back.

"I'm sorry," I said. My voice was weak and wavering. I hated it. Yeah, I was ashamed. My boss had trusted me and I'd flubbed it. At the same time . . .

"Yes?" Ms. P said. "You have something else to say?"

"Yeah," I said, gathering my guts. "I regret getting caught. I regret getting played. But I don't regret trying to scope the woman out. She's a suspect in a murder case. She's head-and-shoulders the oddest bird in the flock. And she's got you nervous like no one I've ever seen."

My boss opened her mouth to deny it but I didn't give her a chance.

"She knew things about me she shouldn't have known," I said. "Places I go that I'm real careful about. So unless you believe she's got a direct line to the dead, she had an eye on us before the Collins case ever came along. I know there are some cases you work alone, and I'm usually okay with that. But this time I need to know. I think you owe it to me to tell me what's going on."

For about three breaths' worth of stony silence, I was weighing the odds on whether I was about to be fired. It was so quiet, I could practically hear the coin flipping through the air. Then it landed and she gave a nod.

"You're right, Will. I do owe it to you." She sounded tired and care-heavy. She stood up and walked to the bookcase on the far side of the room to retrieve a book. She teetered three times—twice on the way there and once on the way back. I hadn't realized until then how much the interview had taken out of her.

"What do you know about Jonathan Markel?" she asked.

"The man whose murder introduced us? As I recall, you've never said word one about him."

"As you've proven, you are not afraid to seek out answers on your own initiative."

I gave her the point and thought back to the hours I'd spent poring over old newspapers.

"Jonathan Markel—thirty-five, never married, oldest son of a wealthy clan," I began. "Not Collins wealthy, but high-six-digits comfortable. Social butterfly. Content to spend his days gallivanting about town and burning off the top layer of his inheritance. Early afternoons at his club, early evenings at the theater or opera, late nights at the seedier establishments his proper peers wouldn't be caught dead in. A new date on his arm every night. As one particular journo said to me over a beer, he was a man without a passion except for all his passions."

"Excellently put," Ms. P said, nodding her approval. "Though almost laughably inaccurate.

"It's not your skills as an investigator that are at fault," she added. "It's Jonathan's skills as a dissembler. While his family had been wealthy, the Crash had not been kind to them. His inheritance was more modest than he led most to believe. He supplemented it by acting as a broker of sorts."

"What kind of sorts?" I asked.

"Information, mostly. Jonathan deftly walked many worlds. He was equally at home in the upper rooms of power as he was conversing with gangsters in a downtown club. He had an uncanny ability to ferret out even the most secreted bit of information. Whether it was for use in industrial espionage or blackmail or for less criminal reasons—he would take all clients if the price was right. People paid dearly for his services."

"Were you one of them?"

"I was," she said. "On more than one occasion. Though I did not pay as dearly as Jonathan did."

She cracked the book open, flipped to a page in the middle, and removed a small slip of paper. She held it delicately between two fingers.

"In the years before we met, when I was not quite so well-known and my health allowed me a modicum more stamina, I frequently took it upon myself to look into crimes I had not been hired to investigate. Many times I was able to pass on suggestions to the police or to the newspapers."

I nodded. "You were drumming up business."

"That was part of it."

She didn't have to mention the other part. Ms. Pentecost with free time on her hands is a dangerous thing. She has a tendency to take unsolved crimes personally.

"There were some cases that resisted my talents," she continued. "Over time, I started to see a pattern in some of them. There was the bank president who fell from the Brooklyn Bridge. The garment tycoon who was burned alive in his penthouse apartment. The zoning commissioner who disappeared from his bedroom with his wife asleep beside him and was never seen again. Others like it. I can show you the files. All involve wealthy or influential people who were involved in activity that was, if not criminal, then at least suspect. Their deaths or disappearances had far-ranging ripples, and all contained certain inexplicable elements."

That explained some of my standing orders when it came to scouring the newspapers. I'd always thought she had a thing for weird crime. Now I saw she was looking for more threads in the pattern.

"Other than their . . . resemblance, I could find no . . . other commonalities," she told me. "At the same time, the cases that I was managing to solve were . . . bringing more clients to my door. I had less and less time to pursue my hobby. So I went to Jonathan. I . . . told him I was looking for a person . . . or persons linked to several if not all of these crimes. For any connection. I paid . . . a retainer I could not quite at the time afford and he went to work. That was . . . five months before his death."

I was starting to see where this was going, and I didn't think I was going to like it. I also didn't like how tired she sounded.

"You don't have to tell me all this now," I said. "Take a break. Get a nap in before dinner and we can go into this later."

"We will do it now," she snarled.

I knew she wasn't angry with me. She was angry at the disease. I walked to the drinks cart and poured her a water. She accepted it with a nod and took a big swallow. She came up coughing. I handed her my handkerchief.

"I'm sorry, Will."

"It's okay," I said. "You take your time."

Another swallow, slower this time. Then she continued.

"The evening before his death, Jonathan contacted me and let me know he'd found something. Or someone," Ms. P said. "I asked him to . . . tell me. He refused. He said what he had for me was . . . worth more than I was paying him. He asked to meet the . . . following afternoon. In a public place . . . A park. He sounded . . . worried. I said yes. I was . . . to bring the rest of . . . his fee. That night . . . he was murdered."

That's what I'd seen coming. And I was right; I didn't like it. A man with information about a string of crimes gets offed less than twenty-four hours before he's supposed to hand it over?

"What are you saying?" I asked. "That McCloskey didn't do it?"

"Oh, I'm quite sure he did," Ms. P said. "Do you remember McCloskey's final words?"

I cast my memory back and went fishing.

"As I recall, his last words were something like 'In for a penny, et cetera.' What came before that, I didn't catch. I was too occupied getting ready to put a knife in his back. I do remember that whatever it was got your hackles up."

"What he said, what interested me so, was 'She said it wouldn't come back on me.'"

I let that bit of information sink in.

"I'm guessing the 'she' he was referring to wasn't his dear, departed mother."

"Mr. McCloskey did not seem the type to think often of his mother."

"Okay, I'll bite," I said. "Who was he talking about?"

"That's what I asked Mr. McCloskey," she reminded me. "Unfortunately, he was soon far beyond answering."

I wound up a sardonic apology for saving her life, but before I could throw it she slid the slip of paper across the table.

"This is what I took from Jonathan's watch. A hiding place few, if any, knew about," she said. "This is the message he was going to pass on to me."

On the paper, written in tight, spidery script, was "Ariel Belestrade."

She leaned back in her seat, as if the very act of telling me had drained her. I picked up the strip of paper and studied it, piecing together the questions in my head.

I dredged up what else I'd been able to learn on the sly about the incident that brought me and Ms. P into each other's orbits. I knew the police had no doubt that McCloskey killed

Jonathan Markel. As soon as they started picking apart his life, they uncovered a dozen other bash-and-grabs he was good for. Several of those had also left the victims dead.

"Any connection between Belestrade and McCloskey?" I asked.

She shook her head. "None that I can determine."

"Was Belestrade on your radar before that?"

"No," she said. "I'd never heard of the woman."

"What about these other cases?" I asked. "Does Belestrade turn up in any of them?"

"None."

"She have anything to gain?"

"Not that I've been able to discover," Ms. P said. "I can find no instance in any of the cases where she benefited, directly or indirectly."

She arched her back, trying to find a comfortable position. I could tell she was in pain—partly physical and partly the mental pain of butting against dead ends.

"How about revenge?" I suggested. "Maybe each of these people were clients of her mother that treated her wrong."

"Now that I have a better grasp of Ms. Belestrade's background, if indeed any of what she told us is true, I'll have to consider it. Though for something as seemingly complex as this, revenge as a motive seems far too . . . raw."

I thought about my own mother and how she'd been treated in life. The lengths I would go to, given the temperament and opportunity, to get a little payback.

Sometimes the rawest motives are the ones that last, I thought.

Out loud I asked, "Why come here? Is she playing with us?"

"Certainly," Ms. P said, leaning back and closing her eyes.

"She knew we would soon approach her. This way it's all on her terms."

I thought about it a little more. Not that I hoped to hit on an answer my boss hadn't already considered and discarded. One thing did occur to me, though.

"What are the chances Markel was wrong?" I asked.

"He built . . . his reputation on . . . accuracy," she said, eyes still shut.

"Okay, then maybe wrong on purpose."

"What are you suggesting?" she said, peeking open one lid.

"You said he was looking for more dough. That he was living a champagne life on a nickel-beer bank account. Maybe he was running short and decided to throw you a name."

Her eyes shot open again and a rogue's gallery of emotions ran across my employer's face.

"Jonathan would . . . not . . . have done that. He was . . . morally compromised . . . but he lived . . . by his reputation," she said. "I trusted . . . him as . . . I trust . . . you."

"Okay," I said. "If you trusted him, he was worth trusting."

I didn't drop the idea but stashed it on a mental shelf to pick up later. It's not that I don't think Ms. Pentecost is a good judge of character. She hired me, after all. I just had the sense, reinforced by her reaction, that maybe her relationship to this character went beyond the professional.

In the handful of years I'd been with her, Ms. Pentecost had never shown a romantic interest in anyone, man or woman. Of course the vast majority of the people she encounters are criminals, victims, or cops. It's not a life that lends itself to improving one's dating prospects.

That said, I wasn't fool enough to think that she was incapable of feeling that way. She'd given me advice from time to time, things they didn't put in the ladies' magazines, that suggested she definitely had a romantic history.

I wondered if Markel had been part of that history. Sure, he was "morally compromised." But he was also a handsome man-about-town with a curious, sharp mind who crossed class lines with ease. Does that sound like someone we know?

Ms. Pentecost closed her eyes again and her breathing slowed. Soon she was softly snoring. I slipped out on mice feet and into the kitchen to tell Mrs. Campbell to make a few revisions to dinner, then I went back in and gently shook Ms. P's shoulder.

The famous lady detective woke with a snort.

"Come on," I said. "You're going to bed."

"I'm fine," she said groggily. "Dinner will be ready shortly."

"Dinner is postponed. Mrs. Campbell's gonna turn the roast chicken into sandwiches. I'll bring you up a couple."

She didn't argue. That told me how tired she was. I helped her out of the chair and up the stairs. At the door to her bedroom I handed over her cane.

"Want me to help you into bed?"

"I'm not an invalid," she growled. Then she took a shaky breath. "I'm fine, Will. Thank you. If I'm asleep when you come up, leave dinner by the door."

"Yes, boss."

I left her to it and went downstairs to my desk. I listened for her footsteps as she moved across the bedroom, to the bathroom, and to her bed. I didn't stop listening until I heard the creak of the springs.

I sat there for a while thinking about Belestrade and Markel and the Collins clan. Basically shifting the puzzle pieces around on the table. Not only couldn't I get them to fit, I couldn't even get a sense of the big picture.

I also thought of what Ms. P had said.

I'm not an invalid.

Specifically I thought about the word I'd thought she was going to say next. Even though she didn't, it still hung there. Silent and awful.

Yet.

CHAPTER 14

The next day was Friday and I was scheduled for a full day of interviews at Collins Steelworks. We'd never heard back from Lazenby about what ground his men had covered, so I was starting from scratch.

I was up before dawn, almost but not quite beating Mrs. Campbell to the kitchen.

"You look smart," she said when she saw me. "Like somebody's secretary."

"That's the idea," I said, draping my wool blazer over the chair and pulling down my pencil skirt as I took my seat at the kitchen table. "I'm hoping this pile of executives I'm combing through will let their guard down if I look more like their secretary and less like . . ."

"Like someone who keeps a gun in her pocket?" the housekeeper suggested.

"Exactly."

I tucked a napkin into my collar before digging into the eggs and cheddar biscuits. I wanted to wait until at least lunch to get the first stain on my white blouse.

Right before I left, I asked Mrs. Campbell to check on the boss around lunchtime and see if she was sleeping, eating, or other.

Strictly necessary? No. But when we're working a case I get

a little touch of the den mother and Ms. P lets me get away with it until she doesn't.

I made it out of Brooklyn just as the sun was coming up and into Jersey City along with the rest of the nine-to-fivers. I followed the directions to a sprawling industrial area on the banks of the Hudson. To call the plant a factory is underselling it. It might have started as a single building, but over the years it had spread like a fungus of concrete and steel to take up some serious waterfront real estate.

At the center of the complex were the Collins executive offices, which were housed in a five-story brick square that an architect clearly didn't waste much creativity on. Harrison Wallace greeted me at the door. I couldn't tell if his sour face was for me or for someone else, or if that was just how his features were sorted.

"I've arranged time for you with everyone who was at the party," he said as he led me through the maze to a small conference room with a bank of windows overlooking the river. "They'll come to you one at a time. All except John Meredith— he's one of our floor managers. You'll have to speak to him on the plant floor."

Not exactly how I would have fixed it. Everyone would be walking in with their guard up. I'd have no chance to see them in their natural habitat.

But Wallace was the client and I needed to squeeze in close to forty interviews over the course of the day.

"Are the police still poking around?" I asked.

"My God, yes." He struck a martyr's pose. "Hours and hours. A pair of them spent all of Wednesday and Thursday going through our financials. I'm not sure they've even talked to everyone who was at the party. Like I said—incompetent."

He went to send in my first interview, and I was left to

ponder what scent Lazenby and his boys were chasing. Wallace was wrong on that score. Lazenby was a lot of things, but a time-waster wasn't one of them. If they were following the money, there was money to follow.

I'll spare you a blow-by-blow of the day. It was easily one of the longest, driest slogs I've ever been ordered to march. I spoke with forty-three executives—forty of them men. Most were married, divorced, or widowed, and seven out of ten had middle age in their rearview. My script, as it developed, came out something like this.

How long have you been with Collins Steelworks?

Was this your first time at the Collins residence? How did you like it?

Were you close to Abigail or Alistair Collins?

What did you do at the party? Who did you spend your time talking with?

Did you see or talk to Abigail Collins before midnight? What about?

Did you happen to see or talk to Rebecca or Randolph Collins?

Were you in the office for the séance? What did you think?

How was everyone else taking it? Did anyone seem particularly upset other than Abigail and Rebecca?

When did you leave the party?

Were you there when the body was found?

What's the best time to phone your wife? I promise not to bother her. Really, I promise.

There were variations, but that was more or less my day. While Ms. Pentecost might have been able to make gold out of that heap of straw, I wasn't seeing it.

The only tidbits that piqued my interest were the following, in no particular order.

Al Collins was almost universally admired and feared in equal measure, and he logged in more hours at the office than any two of his subordinates put together.

Abigail Collins was . . . less admired. Everyone made the appropriate sympathetic noises, but I got the impression that a lot of the management resented her poking her nose into the company after her husband's death. That she had grown a conscience and was considering pulling the company out of military contracts made more than a few of them grind their teeth.

The man who got outed at the party by Belestrade as planning a secret retirement admitted it hadn't been so secret. He'd told several friends and colleagues and had been cutting back on his hours. Even if nobody had squealed, deductions could have been made.

The husband whose wife's pregnancy Belestrade had divined? He'd let slip that his missus was a famous lover of champagne. Not a drunk, he stressed. A connoisseur. However you phrase it, her sticking to ginger ale at the party might not have gone unnoticed.

Speaking of drunk, I discovered that "indisposed" was white-collar code for throwing up in the bathroom. Used in a sentence: Conroy from accounting was indisposed in the second-floor bathroom from the end of the séance up until they started yelling "fire." In between, he didn't hear anyone enter the study. That wasn't saying much as he was "loudly" indisposed. He emerged when they started battering down the study door but said he never went in.

One of the executives' wives had recently taken up photography and had brought her brand-new Kodak to the party. She'd spent the evening burning through film. This perked me up, but the man, a middle manager in sales whose chin had been repossessed, assured me everything would turn out blurry, overexposed, or both. I made him promise to send me copies as soon as they were developed.

Were all of these things actually notable? Or were they just moderately less boring than the rest of the dross? I wasn't willing to wager. Not right then.

I took a break at twelve-thirty for lunch and spent it in the company's basement cafeteria, which was big and clean with some not-half-bad grub. It was used by both the suits and the factory staff, but there was an invisible but very firm demarcation line between the two.

I split the difference and planted myself at a table of secretaries. I played coy and waited for one of them to make the first move.

Eventually a tall number sporting tortoiseshell glasses and a jet-black ponytail leaned over and, in an almost conspiratorial whisper, said, "You work for Lillian Pentecost, don't you? What's that like?"

I started in on a few of my favorite anecdotes and pretty soon had the whole table hanging on my every word. A few scoffed and scowled and clutched their pearls at the idea of a woman getting her hands dirty with rapists and murderers. But I noticed that they leaned in just as hard as everyone else at the dramatic moments.

Another thing that shorthand class taught me is that the life of an executive secretary is one of quiet desperation and gossip is as good as gold. Soon, I had them talking, too. To be honest, that wasn't exactly a feat worthy of Hercules. The violent death of the company's matriarch does a lot to grease the conversation.

A few things that I picked up from the secretaries that I hadn't gotten from their bosses:

Harrison Wallace hadn't been the same since Al Collins's death. The words "moody," "depressed," and "irritable" were used, none of which were qualities he'd exhibited before. So he hadn't been born with the sour face.

One of the older secretaries noted that this change in mood predated his friend's suicide, and that the two may have been arguing. Wallace and Collins used to have connecting offices, but a few months before Collins's death Wallace relocated to new digs on the other side of the building.

"He said it was because the air-conditioning in his office never worked right," the gray-headed woman said. "But I don't think that's true."

When I asked why, she said it was because Wallace didn't seem to really want to change offices.

A couple of the women had been there long enough that they remembered when Abigail had been Harrison and Alistair's shared secretary.

"The pregnancy was a huge scandal," another of the gray-hairs said. "And when Mr. Collins came out and said they were his? It was unheard of!"

"Did anyone suspect the two were an item beforehand?"

"Not a peep," she said. "But it didn't surprise me. Abigail was . . . friendly."

"Anyone else she might have been making friends with?"

I was hoping she'd point the finger at Harrison Wallace, but she shook her head.

"Oh, I didn't pay *that* much attention," she assured me. "It was just known. She was a jazz girl. And that was before every girl was a jazz girl."

That got all the gray-hairs chuckling and nodding along. Shortly after that they all excused themselves and headed back to work.

So Abigail Collins was friendly. That was interesting.

Of course, a twenty-year-old rumor like that could have meant squat. A beautiful young woman who snares her wealthy boss, either accidentally or on purpose, is just the kind of person who'd be retroactively smeared.

Still, it made multiple contestants for fatherhood a stronger possibility.

One other thing I'd managed to squeeze out of the secretaries: The police were passing out a lot of subpoenas. They were being cagey about it—handing out paper for files, employee records, expense reports, and doing it across a lot of departments. Basically the DA's office was playing three-card monte with their investigation. It made me wonder where the queen was.

CHAPTER 15

I put in a few more hours in the conference room, then at three-thirty sharp Wallace reappeared to escort me to the main factory building. I was handed a hard hat and led out onto the factory floor.

It was a stark contrast to the quiet, antiseptic offices. Everything reeked of chemicals and scorched metal. The heat was tremendous and I immediately began sweating through my blazer. Wallace seemed untouched by the heat and even shivered once or twice, as if grazed by some arctic breeze only he could feel.

Machines were hammering, folding, riveting, and generally turning heaps of steel into more elegantly shaped heaps of steel. Most would be used to house explosives that could then be dropped, fired, launched, or otherwise used to blow someone or other to kingdom come. The war might have been over, but the war business was going strong.

A couple hundred people moved in and around the machinery, all sweating through more or less identical blue coveralls. I was pleased to see that at least half were women, but I knew that wouldn't be the case for much longer. The boys were on their way back from overseas, and companies had already publicly declared that their jobs would be waiting for them when they returned. Rosie the Riveter was heading back to the kitchen or to the unemployment line.

Wallace and I weaved through the factory, dodging elbows and forklifts, and basically trying to avoid an awful death. Not too different from the circus really. Just replace the smell of manure with the smell of solder.

I followed Wallace up some stairs to a catwalk overlooking the factory floor. There we found Randolph having a heated conversation with a character who could have passed for the circus strongman: six feet and change, completely bald, with shoulders and arms that tested the structural integrity of his coveralls.

I'd have pegged him for a smelter or a grinder or some job that required lifting heavy things and putting them down again, but the white shirt and tie peeking out from the top of his coveralls said management. Randolph and the strongman cut their chat short when they saw us.

"Ms. Parker—this is John Meredith, our senior floor manager!" Wallace shouted above the din. "Meredith, this is the, um . . . the individual I told you about. Please answer whatever questions she might have for you."

"Yes, sir, Mr. Wallace," he said. He had a voice like somebody had slipped gravel into his Grape-Nuts.

"You want me to sit in?" Randolph asked Meredith. It was an odd question from a part-owner to a floor manager. Wallace's scowl told me he'd caught the disregard for rank as well, but he kept mum.

"That's all right, Randy," Meredith said with more smirk than smile. "If I can run the floor, I think I can handle a little girl with some questions."

I let the "little girl" jab slide. I was in prim and proper disguise, after all.

"Come on, Randolph," Wallace said. "We should go over the quarterlies if you're going to sit in on the next board meeting. Ms. Parker, will you be needing me after you're done here?"

"I don't think so," I said. "If I do, I know how to find you."

He nodded, then followed Randolph down the stairs.

Meredith led me along the catwalk to a door. Beyond that was a small, dank hallway, and another door that opened to reveal an office. Or a broom closet with ambition. There was a metal chair and a wooden desk so scarred it was useless as a writing surface.

He shut the door behind us, but the factory noise seeped through. I took the one chair, while he hopped up on the desk. I waited a breath for it to collapse, but it defied the odds.

"Don't use this much," he said. "Don't have much use for it."

He was so close that I could smell him—shirt starch, talcum, and sweat. His face was only about four feet from mine. It wasn't a great face to see in close-up. His nose had been broken more than once, and he had the little cuts around his eyes that were the mark of a brawler.

"What do you want to know?" he graveled.

"Have you been with the company long?" I asked.

He laughed. "Since I was old enough to use a hammer without smashing my fingers. Started on the floor when I was fifteen hauling scrap. Then I moved to stacking boxes in the warehouse. Then riveter, assistant floor manager, crew manager, floor manager. Now I get to oversee the whole damn lot ten shifts a week."

He looked to be on either side of forty-five, which made him one of the longest-serving Collins employees I'd talked to.

"You must have known Abigail Collins back when she was Abigail Pratt."

"Not really," he said. "I mean, I knew her to say hello. She'd come onto the floor with her old man—I mean her boss. Taking notes and all that. He'd be over here all the time. Didn't trust us to do our jobs. That kind of guy. But I didn't know her much except to say hi."

"You seem to be friends with her son," I pointed out.

"I don't know about friends," he said, wiping away a sheen of sweat from his dome. "We're friendly. He's a good kid. Gave him his first tour of the factory floor back when he and his sister only came up to about my knee."

"Was he the one who invited you to the party?" I asked.

"I got invited to the party because I'm management," he said, leaning another inch toward me. "You know, I volunteered for the army but they wouldn't take me. Said my job here was vital to the war effort."

The massive chip on his shoulder wobbled a bit, but he righted it.

"All right," I said. "You were there because you belong there. Who'd you talk to?"

"Mostly Randy," he said. "Couple guys from shipping and distribution. I made small talk with the head of personnel—always good to make nice with the guy who signs off on your overtime, right?"

I smiled and nodded like, yes, we're both just two blue collars in white-collar masquerade.

"Did you talk to Mrs. Collins at all?"

He shifted his weight and the table creaked dangerously. "Little bit," he said. "Thanked her for having me. Being polite, you know?"

"Did she return it?"

"What?"

"The politeness," I said. "Was she polite to you?"

He was really sweating now. Then again, so was I. There were no vents in the office, and the room was starting to bake.

"Sure, she was polite. Why wouldn't she be?" he asked.

"I've been talking to other people around here, and she doesn't seem to be so well liked. Especially with people who knew her from before."

"That's no surprise. She had aspirations and she let people know it."

"How could you tell?" I asked.

"You can always tell a girl like that," he said. "Girl who thinks she's better than everyone around her."

If it was a jab at me, it wasn't subtle. I shrugged it off.

"What did you make of the séance?" I asked.

His lip curled into a sneer. "I thought it was nonsense. Kind of thing you waste money on when you've got it to waste. That's why I didn't go up."

"You didn't go into the office?"

"Nah," he said. "Got one of the bartenders to make me something stronger than champagne, then went out back for a cigar and a snort. Didn't know about the thing until Randy came out and told me."

"What did he say?"

"That this voodoo woman or whatever she calls herself had played some tricks and really upset Becca." He cracked his knuckles, one at a time in slow succession. "She didn't deserve that."

I had the feeling he took Becca's discomfiture personally.

"Are you as friendly with Miss Collins as you are with her brother?" I asked.

"Not so much, I guess," he said. "Never got to know her like I did Randy."

"You don't like her as much?"

"I like her plenty. She's just more . . . standoffish."

There was definitely something there. Bitterness, maybe? Like he'd tried to make nice with Becca and she'd shot him down. I wondered if Meredith had a crush on the boss's daughter.

"Anyway, if somebody should have been clubbed, it should have been that Belestrade woman," he said. "Toying with people like she did. Somebody should catch her in a dark alley and teach her a lesson."

With each word, he leaned in a little farther until his face was barely two feet from mine. I couldn't help staring at his battered nose. I wondered who'd had the guts to take a swing at him, and what they'd looked like after.

The metal chair began to feel a lot harder. I crossed my legs, and he glanced down to take in an eyeful. He wasn't quick about it either. When he looked back up, our eyes met, and he knew he'd been caught. He didn't even blink. Just gave a little what-are-ya-gonna-do smile.

It occurred to me how isolated we were. Two doors between us and the factory floor, and the din so loud any noise from the office would be lost.

"I, um . . . I understand you were the one that managed to get the door down," I said.

"Still got the bruise on my shoulder."

"What did you see?"

"Not a thing at first. It was all smoke," he said. "Then I saw the fire and smothered it with some of those black curtains. Then Becca yelled and I saw . . . I saw Mrs. Collins."

"Who followed you in?"

"Wallace, Randy. Conroy was there, but I don't think he came into the room. Becca was there. And what's-his-name—the butler. And that voodoo woman."

I looked up from my notebook.

"Belestrade was still there?"

"Yeah, I think in the hall with Conroy. Right behind him."

Conroy hadn't mentioned seeing the clairvoyant after the door had been busted down. But he'd also admitted to drinking two bottles of champagne and being nearsighted.

"You're sure it was her?" I asked. "Could it have been someone else?"

"Yeah, I'm sure," he said. "The woman's kinda memorable."

Belestrade had still been there when the body was found but gone by the time the police arrived. That little tidbit might have made the entire slog of a day worth it.

I gave a half grin and wound up my last pitch. "Do you want to nominate a murderer?"

He hopped off the desk and stared down at me like I was a rat that had made it through the traps.

"No, I don't," he said. "Is that all? I have a shift change to supervise."

"That's all," I said with whatever smile I had left. "Thank you for your time, Mr. Meredith."

He was already opening the door and walking out.

CHAPTER 16

I left the factory along with the shift change. It was a good sixty degrees colder outside than in, and I was drenched in sweat. I was shivering by the time I made it to the car. I cranked the heater to full, pulled out of the factory parking lot, and immediately ran into rush-hour high tide.

I used the delay to think about Meredith. Sure, he was big and ugly and an obvious brawler, but that didn't make him a murderer. Still, he was the first player in this game I'd run into so far who looked like he'd be comfortable beating someone to death.

I felt like I hadn't gotten my money's worth with that interview. The tight space and his attempt to run his eyes up my skirt had thrown me more than I'd thought. There were follow-up questions I'd missed.

I began to wonder if Meredith had deliberately been trying to throw me and not just catch a glimpse of thigh.

On the other hand, his motive for the murder was iffy. Resentment against Abigail for leaping up the social ladder? A thing for Becca, but her mother got in the way? Neither quite held together—not yet anyway.

On the *other* other hand, he'd poked the first hole in Belestrade's story, putting her in the house when the murder occurred. Decisions, decisions. Luckily, I didn't get paid to make them. My employer did.

When I got home, I found Ms. P still in bed but on the mend. It had been a bad day, but not a really bad one. She was propped on a mountain of pillows and working her way through the evening editions. Her hair was brushed out and hung loose to her shoulders, its streak of iron gray lost in the waves of brown.

"I am home from the wars," I declared, falling into the armchair in the corner. "You want the full report now or the highlights?"

"Highlights," she said, putting down the paper. "Then type up the interview notes so I can read them in full tomorrow evening."

"Brace yourself," I warned. "It's a short and not-very-thrilling ride."

I gave her the headlines, spending half the time on Meredith. As far as I could tell, Ms. P kept a resting heart rate throughout, even when I told her Belestrade had been seen after the murder room was cracked open.

"It opens up possibilities," I said. "She knocks. Mrs. Collins lets her in. She does the deed, locks the door, lights the fire, and waits. Door is busted down, but the room's full of smoke. She slips out into the hall and skedaddles before the police arrive."

The only response I got was a "hrrrrmm" from the bedridden detective.

"You don't like it?"

"On the contrary," she said, "it's an excellent theory. It deftly explains the door being locked from the inside."

I was so unused to compliments on my deductive skills that I didn't trust it. Still, I let it stand.

"I'm sorry you had to endure such a grueling day, but it

was necessary," Ms. P said, picking up the paper again. "Dinner will be somewhat delayed. Mrs. Campbell managed to procure scallops at the fish market this afternoon. She's soaking them in some kind of butter concoction."

That was my dismissal. I went to my room and showered away the reek of solder and sweat. I considered burning the skirt, but who knew when I'd need to play prim and proper again. I changed into a pair of dungarees and a men's undershirt, both left over from my circus days. We didn't stand on ceremony at dinner, and Ms. P would likely show up in pajamas.

Since I had a few minutes to spare, I decided to get to work typing up my notes. Saturdays are busy for us, and it'd spare me some trouble if I got started then. I was feeding the first fresh sheet of paper into my typewriter when the phone rang. It was after hours, but when we're on a case I answer anytime, day or night.

"Lillian Pentecost's office, Will Parker speaking."

"Will. It's Becca Collins." Hearing my name in that smoky voice was not unpleasant.

"Good evening, Miss Collins. What can I do for you?"

"This is a little . . . I'm not quite sure . . ."

"Just spit it out."

"Are you free tonight?"

"It's after hours," I said. "Ms. Pentecost won't be able to see anyone until tomorrow."

Her laugh was like river water over smooth stones.

"No, Will," she said, her voice buoyed by a smile. "Are *you* free tonight?"

Have I mentioned that I am sometimes a little dull?

"I'm asking because I was going to go to a club and my date for the evening canceled. I know it's last-minute, but you did say you liked dancing."

"Miss Collins—"

"Becca."

"Becca. It wouldn't be very professional. Going on a . . . Going out socially with a—"

Suspect.

"—client."

"Please," she purred. "A singer I absolutely adore is playing at this little hole-in-the-wall club near Columbia and I don't want to go alone. Pretty please? Be unprofessional, just this once."

I told her to hold the line, then I hurried upstairs and poked my head into Ms. P's bedroom.

"Are the scallops ready?" she asked.

"You'll have to ask Mrs. Campbell," I said. "I came up because that phone call just now was one of our clients—the one with the curls and the legs—who wants to take me out dancing tonight."

Both eyebrows, straight up, at least half an inch.

"I don't know what she has in mind, but if the place she's suggesting is the one I think it is, her intentions might go beyond just needing to fill a two-top. I know she's a client, or maybe not technically but the goddaughter of our—"

"You should go," she said.

My mouth made some sort of noise. I'm not sure what.

"We need insight into that family," she declared. "Too much of what we have is from the outside looking in."

I composed myself.

"I'm to take Becca Collins out dancing and try to get a glimpse of her inner workings?"

"Don't be crude." She sniffed and, dare I say it, blushed a little. "I trust you to use your best judgment. Don't do anything you aren't comfortable doing."

"You realize I used to dress up like a showgirl and have knives thrown at my face. My threshold for uncomfortable is pretty high."

She lifted her paper back up, I'm pretty sure to hide a smile.

"I trust your judgment," she said.

I ran downstairs to tell Becca the good news. She said she'd swing by in a taxi in about an hour.

"See you soon, Will," she purred before hanging up.

I sat at my desk for half a minute, vacillating between two kinds of nervous. Then I looked down at myself.

"Shoot," I muttered to no one. "I've got to change again."

CHAPTER 17

Walked up to St. Peter
Said hey what can you do?
He said rejoice
Just stay the course
And you'll be in Heaven, too.
You'll be singing in Heaven, too.

So I went down to the Devil,
Straddled the gates of hell.
What do you say,
I got bills to pay,
My soul's all I got to sell.
It's all I got left to sell.

Times is hard.
Angel, times is hard.

The singer was draped in an ankle-length dress stitched together with sequins and a prayer. She clutched the microphone like it was a lifeline and made eye contact with everyone in the club, even through the thick haze of cigarette and marijuana smoke, wailing about life and death and the tough choices we make in between.

The stage was tight as a telephone booth, but she managed to share it with a drummer, saxophonist, and piano player, along with a string bean of a man plucking an upright bass. The music they created on that scrap of real estate set everybody in the place swaying.

The club was a no-sign basement deal right on the edge of Harlem. The kind you used to find scattered all over the city, but had been forced out by high rents and nosey neighbors.

I had never been to this particular joint, but had heard of it. It was known as a sort of late-night limbo that catered to people of all shades and predilections. All were welcome, as long as you paid the cover, bought drinks, applauded when proper, and didn't attract trouble.

That night most of the crowd, along with the singer and the band, were from the Harlem side of the line. The door and half the bar were going to pay for the funeral of Charlie Silverhorn, the jazz singer who'd been found dead with a needle in his arm earlier that week.

Becca had scored us a corner table in the back. They seemed to know her there. The muscle working the door greeted her by name and all the waitresses smiled big, angling for tips. She looked in her element.

"You clean up nice," she said, sipping the house cocktail, which was basically straight gin with a mixer waved over it.

"Thanks," I said. "You turn out pretty good yourself."

To be honest, it was no contest. Picture Veronica Lake in . . . well, just about anything, and you're halfway to Becca that night. She had on a red satin number that brushed the top of her knees and dropped dangerously low in the back. She finished the outfit off with matching heels and a set of pearl earrings.

In the hour before Becca picked me up I'd gone back and forth on half a dozen outfits. Not knowing what exactly it was I was dressing for made the decision harder than it needed to be. Was it a date, was I playing escort, or was she looking to let slip whatever it was she'd been holding back the other day? Was she looking for sex appeal, or should I butch it up?

I owned a teal wrap dress that had a slit up the side so high it was illegal in some states. It would have blended into any club in Manhattan. But I'd just spent eight hours in a pencil skirt. I was tired of dressing to blend.

I settled on a navy blue, two-button pinstripe tailored by the same transplanted Italian Ms. Pentecost swears by. It was ingeniously cut so as to give the illusion I have hips. I also had him sew a special pocket into the lining on the left just about rib height. It was a perfect size for my .38, which I'd tucked carefully inside. The outfit came complete with a white, open-collar shirt and black leather pumps with two-inch heels. The latter gave me an added boost but didn't interfere on the dance floor. They also did something to my stride that both men and women had found equally appealing.

Turns out I needn't have worried about blending. I wasn't the only woman there in a tailored suit, and Becca and I weren't the only women sharing time at a table. Seems the club really was neutral territory.

A dance floor had been carved out in front of the stage and couples of all persuasions were cutting a rug to everything the singer served up.

But even with the dapper threads, I felt like a sow's ear to Becca's silk purse. I'd made a half-hearted attempt to rouge away my freckles and had gone through four different eye shadows trying to find one that went with mud brown. Finally,

I'd given up, washed the lot of it away, and settled on simple lipstick that I hoped was a bright enough red it would distract from everything else.

"You look nervous." She had to lean nearly all the way across the table to be heard. Her lips were only about a foot and change from mine. I breathed in her lavender perfume. "Is it me or the venue?"

I wanted to ask her if she'd passed a mirror lately. Me being nervous was proof I had a pulse.

Instead I said, "I'm a little on edge because I don't know exactly what this is. I don't usually fraternize with clients."

"Fraternize." She felt the word out in her mouth. "Now, *that's* a five-dollar word that sucks all the fun out of things."

"You know what I mean. What do you want?"

"What do I want?" She said it like it was a foreign question. "I want a night off. I want to stop worrying. Stop living afraid. I want to stop walking on eggshells."

She leaned in even closer. Another three inches and we'd be rounding first.

"I just want to dance," she said.

Oh well. My boss had practically ordered me. And I am, if nothing else, an excellent employee.

I led her through the packed tables to the dance floor just as the singer started in on a jitterbug medley. Becca let me lead, which I appreciated.

I'd learned to dance from spec girls and snake charmers, and I think I held my own pretty well. We shook and twirled through a trio of tailshakers, then the singer switched gears to a slow number. Most of the dancers fled to the bar, but Becca and I stayed put.

For three minutes I forgot all about murder and ghosts and

truth and lies, and maybe she did, too. I don't know about her, but my world had shrunk to my fingers pressed against her bare back, her chin on my shoulder, the smell of perfume and cigarettes.

When the song was over we stumbled back to our table. I was feeling a little high, either from the dancing or the marijuana haze. Becca ordered another gin and nothing, and I topped off my ginger ale.

"Sure you won't have anything stronger?" she asked.

"Afraid not," I said. "I've got a lifetime ticket to ride the water wagon."

"You're missing out on some fantastic gin. They don't have to make it in bathtubs anymore."

"Some days it's tempting," I said. "But my father drank enough for the whole family."

"Does it bother you if I drink?" she asked.

"Not at all. Imbibe away."

She took a healthy sip.

"I probably like it a little too much," she said. "According to Randy, a lot too much."

"It hasn't been the easiest year."

"That's the truth."

"Were you close to your mother?" I asked as nonchalantly as possible.

"Depends on who you're comparing me to," she said. "Were you close to yours?"

"I asked you first."

On the stage the singer went into something I hadn't heard before—a quick number with a good beat. The tables around us emptied onto the dance floor. Suddenly we had a little bubble of privacy.

"How about this?" Becca said, letting the leash slip on a sly grin. "We trade off questions. One for one. We have to answer and we have to be honest."

I was more comfortable digging up secrets than sharing them, but I agreed.

"I asked first, though," I said. "How'd you get along with your mom?"

"All right, I suppose."

"I'm going to need you to fill in that pencil sketch if you want me to play."

"Fine," she said. "I guess I was just closer to my father, that's all."

"Really? I understood he wasn't the . . . warmest individual."

"He was a hard man," she said. "But he had to be, didn't he? To run a company. He had to be cruel sometimes."

I wasn't sure if cruelty was a necessary ingredient in success, but I kept that to myself. Becca took a long sip of her gin and kept going.

"He was never cruel to me, though. He'd let me sit on the floor in his study, reading or playing with dolls or whatever I wanted, while he did company business. I was never his pretty little princess. I was always his smart little girl. Too bright to be some blue blood's showpiece. When I, um . . . When I had my first crush on a girl, he was the only person I told."

I raised my eyebrows at that. So what if he let her draw on his office walls with her crayons? That's not a thing you let slip lightly.

"Well, I didn't really tell him," she admitted. "I talked around it the way you do. But he, um . . . he figured it out. It was this friend from school. I'd had her over, so he'd seen the two of us together. How I acted toward her. He asked if I was talking about my friend. Eventually I admitted I was."

"How did he react?" I asked.

"I expected him to be angry. To tell me I was being foolish," she said. "Instead, he told me to be careful. That the world was not a kind place, and that I would have to keep my heart hidden if I wanted to survive."

She traced the rim of her glass with one long, slender finger, lost in thought.

"So I hid my heart," she said in a voice almost too quiet to hear. "Then he died and being careful didn't seem so important anymore."

I waited a ten count before prodding her. "You never told your mother?"

She snapped out of her reverie and shook her head. "She wouldn't have understood. She really would have called me a fool. She believed the best thing a woman could do was to smile, dress well, and marry up."

I'd met a lot of smart women who'd shoved their light under a bushel in order to marry their way into stability. I didn't know Becca well, but I couldn't picture her hiding her fire for anyone.

"My turn," she said. "How did *you* get along with your parents?"

"My mother died when I was pretty young, so we never got a chance to get along," I said.

"I'm sorry." She rested her hand on mine and the fine hairs on my arms shot up. "How did she die?"

"Pneumonia. Mostly."

"Mostly?"

I pulled my hand away and pretended to be captivated with

a hangnail. "She was never the healthiest. Always walking around with bruises, you know? I was little, so I never understood. Doctor said pneumonia could kill even a hale and hearty woman. But she never got the chance to be hale and hearty."

I could have lied. I'm a good liar. Shoot—I'm a great liar. Not sure why I gave her the truth. To her credit, Becca didn't say she was sorry or pat my hand or anything. She just gave me a moment.

"Anyway," I continued, "after that it was just Dad and me. If we ever got along, I don't remember it. I ran away when I was fifteen and never looked back."

I took a swig of ginger ale and wished it were something stronger.

"My turn," I said. "What do you think of John Meredith?"

"In what sense?"

"Whatever sense you want to take it," I said. "I ask because for someone who's a step above shift manager, he seems to have a lot of access to your family."

"Well, he's been around forever, hasn't he?" she said. "And to be honest, Randy has a little crush on him. Totally platonic, of course. I think he sees John as a role model. A real man's man."

"How do you see him?"

"I don't know. As an employee. He's nice. Kind of . . . I don't know. Rough."

"No grudges against your family?" I asked.

"None."

She said that with a level of confidence that made me raise my eyebrows. Even if Meredith hadn't given off the vibe of being a little too interested in Becca, I'd have been skeptical of any longtime employee who hadn't stored up some grudges against his boss.

"As far as I know, he's harmless," she said. "I swear. Cross my heart."

A manicured nail traced an X across red satin.

"My turn. What's the most dangerous situation you've ever found yourself in?"

If I had kept being 100 percent honest, the answer would have been one of the times my father came home blind drunk and I had to spend the night hiding in a cornfield. Instead, I gave her three-quarters honest and told her about the first time I met Ms. Pentecost. By the time I was pulling the knife on McCloskey, her jaw was half dropped and she was perched on the edge of her chair. Her blue eyes practically vibrated with excitement.

"That is amazing!" she exclaimed when I was finished. "You are, by far, the most interesting person I have ever gone dancing with."

"Thank you," I said with a little bow. "My turn?"

"How can I compete with that?"

"It's not a competition," I reassured her. "Just a friendly game of mutual interrogation."

She downed her gin and waved to the waitress for another. "As long as it's friendly," she said.

I pondered my next question. I figured I'd get one more out of her before she either tired of the game or had one too many gins to make it ethical.

"How far do you trust your uncle Harry?" I asked. "And why?"

The waitress came over with a replacement cocktail, giving Becca some time to chase down that curveball.

"I trust him as much as anyone alive," she said. "He's always looked out for us. My father trusted him, and I trusted my father."

"Did your mother trust him?"

"I never asked," she said.

"But what do you think?"

"I *think* you're trying to sneak in extra questions." Somewhere in the last exchange, something had happened. Her face had been open. Now a mask had fallen over it. I made a mental note to find out why she was protecting trustworthy ol' Uncle Harry.

"Okay," I said. "Your turn."

She narrowed her eyes in thought, then her face broke into a wide grin.

"I've got one," she said.

"Uh-oh. I don't know if I like that look."

"What is the absolute most unforgettable kiss you've ever had?"

I'll admit it. I blushed. You would too with that face grinning at you from across the table. I shuffled through the possibilities, finally settling on one.

"Carmine Vincenzio."

Her smile faltered.

"But it's unforgettable only because he was wearing bright yellow tights and had one leg wrapped around his head."

I briefly explained about my summer fling with the Italian contortionist.

"But if you're talking about the best kiss," I said, "that would be Sarah. No last name."

She put a hand to her mouth in feigned horror. "No last name? How scandalous!"

"I never got a first name, either. I just call her Sarah because she looked like a Sarah," I said.

"Is this another circus story?"

"Afraid so," I said. "It's like this. We were parked for a

weekend gig in some no-horse town in the middle of Ohio. One night I was helping shuffle people on and off the Ferris wheel. There was this girl on a date with a farm boy. Definitely a first date, and she definitely didn't want to be on it.

"She wants to ride the wheel, but he's scared of heights. Doesn't want to go up. She doesn't want to sit alone, but the only other singles waiting in line are men, and farm boy doesn't want her seeing the sights with some other fella. So I volunteer to ride with her. Everyone's happy."

On the stage, the singer brought a song to its finish. I waited for the applause to die down before continuing.

"We get to the top and the wheel pauses. Give everyone a chance to get their necking in. Sarah says, 'At the end of the night, he's gonna kiss me. It'll be my first kiss and I don't even like him.' So I say, 'How about I kiss you? You might still get a peck at the end of the night from farm boy Johnny, but at least it won't be your first.'"

"What did she say?" Becca asked, on the edge of her seat again.

"Not a thing," I told her. "She just closed her eyes and leaned in. So I kissed her."

Becca laughed with delight.

"This no-name girl in the middle of Ohio was such a good kisser she went right to the top spot?" she asked in disbelief.

I counted off on my fingers. "Fifty feet in the air. Hot summer night. Lights of the midway stretching out below us. With all that going for it, you tend to grade technique on a steep curve."

Onstage, the band announced they were taking twenty. Becca and I stood and joined in the applause as the singer took a bow.

"You want to blow this pop stand?" Becca asked. "I've got plenty of gin and a cabinet full of forty-fives back home."

Going out dancing was one thing. Heading back to her place was something else entirely. I wondered how far she'd stray from discretion. But I had my orders, so I said yes. She paid the check and we made our way outside. A light snow had begun to fall and the sidewalks were already covered.

Becca shivered in her backless dress. I deftly transferred my gun to my trouser pocket and draped my jacket over her shoulders. We started walking to the end of the block, where we'd be more likely to catch a cab.

We didn't hold hands, but we were close enough that our respective knuckles brushed against each other as we walked.

We were halfway to the corner when a figure detached itself from the shadows of an alley and grabbed Becca. I turned and stumbled, slipping in the fresh snow and landing hard on my back. My hand dove into my trouser pocket for my gun. I was terrified I was already too late.

CHAPTER **18**

The hammer of my .38 caught on the lining, which was the only reason Randolph didn't get a dose of lead in his gut.

"What the hell, Randy!" Becca said, tearing her hand away from her brother. "You scared me half to death."

"I've been waiting out here for nearly an hour," he hissed.

"That's not my fault," she said, helping me to my feet. "You could have come in."

"And have both of us seen in there?" His face spoke volumes about exactly what he thought of "in there." "What did I tell you about going to places like that?"

"What did I tell you about trying to control me?" she spat back. "Money and appearances. That's all you care about. Don't want me to embarrass the corporate giant in training."

I didn't think his face could get much redder, but he managed.

"If this place was raided while you were in it, your picture would be splashed all over the front pages tomorrow. 'Collins Daughter Arrested at' . . . whatever they call this place. And if they find you with *her*. Jesus Christ, Becca!"

It's funny. A while back I called him one of the most beautiful humans I'd ever laid eyes on. I didn't see it now. His face was an ugly mask of anger and disgust. I'd seen that face before. That face was why I left home.

"I swear to God, Randy! I will do what I want with whoever I want!"

"How much have you had to drink?"

"None of your business!"

"I can smell it on you, Becca! I can smell the gin!"

With every volley more heads turned our way. The muscle working the door to the club began climbing up the steps to see what was the matter.

I took Becca's arm, intending to move the exchange into the alley. Randolph misread the move. He grabbed hold of my shoulder and squeezed.

"Get your hands off my sister," he growled.

I was startled by how strong he was. That swimmer's body wasn't just for show.

"Uncle Harry's going to hear about this," he said, spittle flying in my face. "So will your boss. I'll make sure you don't have a job this time tomorrow."

"You tell whoever you need to tell," I said, conjuring up my meanest smile. "Ms. Pentecost's asleep right now, and she's had a long day, so I'd appreciate it if you could wait until morning."

I reached up to the hand grabbing my shoulder and took his wrist in both hands. Giving a firm yank, I swiveled on my heel and twisted his arm to an uncomfortable angle. Locking his elbow, I bent his wrist forward in a way it was never meant to go.

Randy hissed in pain and I let him loose.

"Next time you do that, I don't stop until something's broken," I told him. "Now, if you're really worried about making the papers, I'd suggest taking this off the street. You've got about thirty seconds before that doorman comes over, and he looks like someone else who enjoys picking on people half his size."

Randolph shot a look at the doorman, who was up on the sidewalk now, watching the scene playing out and wondering if he'd have to get involved before the cops did.

"I'm just worried that—"

"I know," I said. "You're being a good big brother. Give us two ticks."

I pulled Becca into the alley and away from the reach of the streetlights. She bit her lower lip, tears swirling in her eyes.

"I'm so sorry," she said. "We were having such a nice evening."

"It was a great evening. One of the best. Your brother playing truant officer can't take that away. But he's right."

"What?"

"The police have their eye on you. I kept an eye out for a tail on the way here, but they might have somebody watching your place."

She did some quick math and came to the same conclusion.

"No gin and forty-fives?"

"Not tonight," I said. "You should probably go home with your brother."

She wiped her tears away with a gloved hand. "So pragmatic. I thought you were a thrill-seeker."

"I contain multitudes."

That brought a smile, but it was curdled around the edges. She took a breath and found some poise, then called back to her brother. "All right, Randy. You may have the honor of driving me home."

Randy, who had been staring apprehensively at the doorman, breathed a sigh of relief.

"I'll bring the car around," he said before darting down the street.

Becca turned back to me. "Can we see each other again?" she asked.

I cocked a shoulder. "It's a possibility," I said. "There's the matter of a murder to clear up."

"Always the professional."

"Not always," I said. "But I have my moments."

A two-door Lincoln pulled up to the curb, brakes squealing.

"My ride's here," she sighed.

She slipped off my jacket and draped it over my shoulders.

"Good night, Will. You're a pretty good dancer."

"Night, Becca. You're not half bad yourself."

She was two steps from the car before she abruptly turned on her heel and ran back into the alley. She leaned in and kissed me. Not a peck, either. Three full seconds of contact. Not that I was in a mind to time it. My mind had left the building.

Randy yelled something unprintable from the car.

Then it was over. By the time I opened my eyes, she was disappearing into the Lincoln. With a Detroit roar, she was gone.

I tottered out of the alley, yanking my head out of the clouds long enough to look around and see if anyone had eyes on me. The bouncer had returned to his station and nobody was paying me any mind.

I walked south for five blocks before I remembered I hadn't driven. I hailed a cab.

No contest.

She'd knocked whatshername from the Ferris wheel right to number two.

CHAPTER 19

Saturday was a madhouse at Chez Pentecost, but Saturdays usually were. The women started arriving around eleven in the morning and didn't let up until dinnertime. Maids and cooks, students and schoolteachers, barmaids and burlesque dancers from Brooklyn to the Bronx to Harlem. All the neighborhoods people like Randy wouldn't have been caught dead in.

Some came for advice, some with an honest-to-God crime that needed solving. There was a nursemaid who'd been fired because her employer accused her of stealing a diamond bracelet. Two phone calls got us the fence. A third got us the pawnshop owner. A few quick questions and a not-too-subtle threat to pass the owner's name on to the cops for trafficking stolen goods revealed the culprit to be the employer's stepdaughter. The pawnshop owner suspected the girl had put the money right up her nose.

Ms. P promised the nursemaid she'd write a carefully worded letter to her former employer but suggested asking for a month's severance and a glowing recommendation in lieu of her old job back. After the nursemaid walked out leaking tears of gratitude, the boss turned to me and said, "Twenty minutes of my time. And it probably kept that woman and her family out of the poorhouse. Or worse."

She wasn't bragging, or at least not only bragging.

I'd been on her to cut back on the Saturday open house. Cramming two dozen cases into an eight-hour day took a toll. It was a rare Sunday she didn't stay in bed.

She wouldn't have it. Since she spent so much of her time and energy keeping the lights on by helping folks like the Collins family, she wanted to balance the scales.

Every woman in the five boroughs who lived in the bottom tax brackets knew that Ms. Pentecost's door was open every Saturday. Mrs. Campbell made enough food to feed the 401st. Anyone who showed up got a hot meal and twenty minutes of Ms. P's time.

She'd been doing it since long before I came into the picture, and bad days or not, she wasn't about to stop. So I helped any way I could, including poring over my address book for fences, drafting carefully worded letters, and so on.

The nursemaid's case was an outlier. Most weren't nearly so complicated. Most of the women who turned up at our door lived with the people giving them grief. Many sported black eyes and busted lips and the occasional broken limb.

Not long after I started working for Ms. Pentecost, I joked that these women didn't need a detective, they needed a revolver, a divorce lawyer, or at the very least somebody to teach them how to throw a punch. That was before I understood that a useful suggestion, even in jest, was as good as raising my hand.

We cleaned out the basement, which at the time was mostly old furniture, and created a big open space. Then we laid out a bunch of old wrestling mats I'd scrounged from a local high school. The following Saturday, while Ms. P consulted, I invited any and all to join me in the basement to learn some self-defense. I'd picked up boxing from a strongman, wrestling from that ill-fated episode with a contortionist, and more than a few nasty tricks from Kalishenko. I didn't have many takers at first. Then I showed the few women who joined me how to dodge a punch, take someone to the ground, and, if all went well, snap their arm in two.

Word spread.

That particular Saturday I had nearly twenty women on the mat. Inspired by Randy's antics the night before, I was teaching them how to turn the tables on a guy if he put his hands on you.

"Most of the time they'll be big enough to yank themselves free before you can do serious damage," I explained, demonstrating the arm twist on a housewife who'd been coming to the classes for over a year. "But it gets them off you and gives you some space to work with. Follow up with one of the other moves we worked on. If you've got a weapon nearby, use it. If you've got open air, run for it."

I made eye contact with everyone on the mat, making sure they heard this next bit.

"I don't care what tricks you know, if you're up against a guy that has fifty pounds on you, you're going to get hurt. You get a chance to run, you run until you get somewhere safe."

I broke them up into groups according to skill and size and began working through moves. I was showing this five-foot-nothing woman old enough to be my grandmother how to throw a proper liver shot when Mrs. Campbell called from the top of the steps.

"Will! The missus wants you."

I left the room in the hands of the women who'd been coming longest and went up to join my employer in the office. In one of the guest chairs I found a middle-aged woman with beefy forearms and a face like an axe blade—narrow, chipped, and just as friendly.

"This is Mrs. Nowak," my boss said. "Mrs. Nowak, this is my associate, Will Parker."

"Not missus," she said in an accent that originated somewhere east of the Rhine. "I am Ms. Nowak. Or Anna. I was missus when I had a husband. Now I have a drunkard who I will not let into my home."

Ms. P gave her a nod of apology and understanding.

"Anna was explaining how she spent five years in the employ of Vincent and Dianna Lance."

The names failed to throw off a spark of recognition.

"I have to admit, I'm drawing a blank."

"There's no reason you should know them," my boss explained. "Mr. Lance was the vice president of a modest import company that specialized in Asian silks. Mrs. Lance was a homemaker. As Anna describes it, they were comfortable but hardly wealthy."

So well-off but not fodder for the society pages.

"Anna was telling me about the last year she worked at the Lances'. This was about five years ago, is that right?" my boss prompted.

The axe blade nodded.

"Yes," Anna said. "I was a cook. I still am a cook, but different family. I see this woman you ask about many times. She does not like onions. Who does not like onions?"

I felt like I'd missed my train.

"Hold on," I said. "Who didn't like onions? Mrs. Lance?"

"No, no, no," the cook said. "The czarownica. Belestrade."

She turned her head to the side and spat—"ptooey"—onto the carpet, then immediately realized where she was. She started to apologize, but I held up a hand.

"It's okay," I said. "I ptooey on the floor all the time."

I need to make a confession here. Our Saturday program is

as altruistic as advertised, but that doesn't mean we don't leverage it when we need to. If we're looking for information, we get
the word out. The women who come to the open house know
that if they happen across any sundry or sordid details of interest, we might be in the market. They also pass that word on to
their friends and neighbors. The word Ms. Pentecost had sent
out earlier in the week was this: *Willing to trade favors or cash for
any solid intelligence about Ariel Belestrade.*

"Mrs. Lance—she starts seeing this woman. Then she
brings her home. Invites her to dinner. This is when I'm told
no onions," Anna explained. "First time she comes, she makes
nice. Next time, she asks questions. Mrs. Lance says I should
answer. That they are to help . . . something . . . Something
with making good energy."

The way she said it left no doubt as to Anna's opinion of
"good energy."

"What sort of questions did she ask?" I asked.

"All of the sorts. All about Mr. and Mrs. Lance. What food?
How much do I spend? What nights do they eat together? What
nights separate? What are their moods? What do they eat when
they are sad? What do they eat when they are happy?"

Anna threw up her hands in exasperation.

"It was śmieszny. Ridiculous."

Ms. P tossed me a look. I nodded, letting her know I was
seeing what she was seeing.

"Let me take a crack at guessing some of the rest," I said.
"Did she ask if Mr. Lance canceled dinner a lot? What was his
energy the next day? Did he show up for breakfast? Was Mr.
Lance eating new foods recently? Cutting down on sweets?
Trying to lose that spare tire?"

"Yes, yes, yes!" The axe blade was really chopping away
now. "Very much like that."

"How long after these questions did the Lances separate?" Ms. P asked.

Anna shrugged. "I think two months? Three months? Mr. Lance, he became very different. Very unhappy. Shouts at me. Very suspicious. Then Mrs. Lance leaves and I am fired."

Ms. P peppered her with a few more questions. Once she determined we'd gotten the lot, she stood and shook Anna's hand.

"You will help with landlord?" the cook asked. She looked like she wanted to spit again but restrained herself.

"I'm going to pass your name on to a group that specializes in litigation against predatory landlords," Ms. P explained. "You'll hear from them soon. If that is not effective, I will visit him personally."

A smile blossomed across Anna's face and any resemblance to an axe blade vanished.

"Thank you, Ms. Pentecost. Thank you so much. I wish you much luck against the czarownica."

With that, she left, cutting through the kitchen to exit by the back door. No use getting a reputation as an informant.

"That was educational," I said when she was gone.

"You see the pattern." A statement, not a question.

"Sure," I said. "She gets a lead on some marital trouble from Mrs. Lance. She says, hey, you've got bad energy around your house, let me track it down. Then she grills the household until she nails down what Mr. Lance has been up to. Or gets down who Mr. Lance has been nailing."

Ms. P scrunched her nose at the wordplay but didn't disagree.

"Considering Mr. Lance's mood change between the questioning and his separation, especially his newfound suspiciousness, we can infer that Ms. Belestrade put her information to use," she said.

"If by 'use' you mean blackmail, I'm making the same assumption."

"The real question is whether Belestrade employed the same methods with the Collins family. If so, what secrets did she uncover?"

I thought about that for a breath or two.

"Not to pile it on," I said, "but here's another question for the list. How does Belestrade go from some no-name VP like Lance to hobnobbing with the Gramercy Park crowd? That's a lot of tax brackets to leapfrog."

Ms. P leaned back in her chair and closed her eyes.

"Too many questions and not enough answers," she murmured. "But at least we know what questions to ask when we visit Ms. Belestrade on Wednesday."

Mrs. Campbell poked her head into the office. Her cheeks were flushed red and there was a smile playing around her usually disapproving mouth. She complained about Saturdays—the extra shopping and all the cooking and the feet tracking mud every which way in the house—but I suspected she harbored a secret love for our open house tradition. She let the gruffness slip away and allowed herself to play hostess.

"Ya ready for the next one?" she asked. "If you're not, can you get her yourselves? I've got soda bread ready to come out."

"That's quite all right," the boss said, prying her eyes open and resituating herself in her chair. "Send the next one in."

Effectively dismissed, I went back to punches and pressure points. Once class was over and I'd gotten my fill of brisket, I retreated to my room and pulled out the portable Remington I kept stashed in my closet, and got to work typing up my notes from the factory interviews. She wanted the whole lot, not just the highlights, and it took me all the way through to dinner. By then our guests had left, so I took dinner at my desk and finished off my typing there.

For good measure, I included a summary of my night with Becca. With a few judicious edits, of course. For example, I left out the flirting and the dancing and the kiss. But I kept in the encounter with Randy and the likelihood that Becca was no stranger to spending time in smoky clubs with the occasional woman.

If Belestrade had gone digging for dirt, that wouldn't have been a hard nugget to uncover.

I was reading over the last few pages when my boss stepped into the office. In one hand she held a plate. On it was some soda bread, a healthy portion of homemade apple butter, and a spreading knife. The other had a firm grip on a king-size goblet of honey wine.

"I'll be up in the archives if you need me."

"Here," I said, putting the stack of typed notes on her desk. "You can add this to your reading."

She didn't look thrilled at the homework. She'd probably planned to go diving into the Belestrade files again.

"How are you feeling?" I asked.

Saturdays were always strenuous, and she was coming off a bad day. She put down the plate and goblet, spread her arms to demonstrate the absence of her cane, and did a little curtsy.

"Very well, I think," she said. "Less a relapse and more of a hiccup."

I slapped on a smile. "Good," I said. "Don't stay up too late."

She didn't dignify my mothering with a response. She put the notes under her arm, retrieved the goblet and plate of bread, and headed to the stairs. I listened to her slow, careful steps and the mad rattle of the butter knife on the plate.

A thing you need to remember: Lillian Pentecost is a world-class detective, which means she's also a world-class liar.

I'd have to keep an eye out for more "hiccups."

I went to bed not long after, devouring the last story in the latest issue of *Strange Crime* before turning out the light.

Instead of counting sheep, I counted suspects. There was Belestrade and her assistant, Randy and Becca, Harrison Wallace, John Meredith, any of a thousand Collins Steelworks shareholders, not to mention whatever characters were lurking in the dark spots of Abigail's early years. I threw in Dora and Sanford for good measure. And of course there was the ghost of Alistair Collins.

I was sending them over the fence for the thirteenth time when I finally fell asleep.

CHAPTER **20**

Mrs. Campbell was the only one under our roof who was particularly religious, but my boss and I still tried to observe the Sabbath even when in the middle of a hot case. If we didn't, we ended up working a month nonstop, and that was no good for anyone, especially Ms. Pentecost.

I slept until noon, then took a quick jaunt to a Brooklyn barber who kept Sunday hours and knew how to hold my red curls in check. Afterward, I indulged in a midafternoon showing of *Blithe Spirit,* hoping the movie about a skeptical novelist and a hapless psychic would knock some ideas loose. The only ideas I got were about Constance Cummings, the novelist's new bride, who has to deal with the summoned spirit of the writer's dead wife. Unfortunately, none of them were applicable to the Collins case.

I was home by dusk, where I found my employer sipping wine at her desk and catching up on the last month's clippings. Since she had no pressing orders for me, I took my dinner of leftover brisket up to my room. That's where I keep my radio, and I didn't want to miss the latest episode of *The Shadow.*

Knowing what evil lurks in the hearts of men let Lamont Cranston wrap up his case in a tight half hour. The announcer signed off, and so did I.

———

The next morning I came downstairs to find a note on my desk.

"Track down Abigail Collins's family. We know too little of her life before her arrival in New York City."

I appreciated her faith in my ability as evidenced by the lack of the preface "Try to." She wanted Abigail's backstory and I'd been tasked with delivering.

I started with a call to the Collins residence. After some bickering with Sanford, he agreed to transfer me to Becca's bedroom. After half a minute of ringing, she came on the line.

"Hello?" She sounded groggy and hoarse.

"Good morning, sunshine."

She cleared her throat and forced some cheer into her voice. "Hello, Miss Parker. I thought I'd never hear from you again after the way our evening ended."

"I remember it ending quite nicely," I said. "If you mean that little incident with the truant officer, I'd practically forgotten it."

"Are you calling to arrange another date?" she asked.

"As nice as that sounds, this is a business call. You mentioned that your mother came from upstate New York? I don't suppose you know where exactly that might be."

She was silent for a moment. "She didn't like to talk about her childhood. It was something like Prattsville or Pattsville. Something like that," she said, sounding far from certain. "I remember because it was so similar to her maiden name."

"You ever meet anyone from that side of the family?" I asked.

"Never," Becca said. "Her parents died when she was a teenager. She was an only child and she wasn't close to any of her extended family."

I thought for a second, then asked, "What are the chances of Pratt not being her birth name?"

"What makes you ask that?"

"Girl shows up ready to take a bite out of the Big Apple. No family. Starting fresh. It wouldn't be the first time someone like that shed a name along with her old skin." I could have been describing myself, except I'd ended up with an eccentric detective instead of a king of industry.

"Pratt's her real name, as far as I know," Becca told me. "We've been through all her personal papers the last two weeks and everything says Pratt."

That proved nothing. I knew from personal experience how easy it is to get a bogus birth certificate.

"If it's not too much trouble, could you take a run through any photo albums she might have?" I asked. "Let me know if you come across anyone that looks like kin."

"I doubt I'll find much. Mother wasn't exactly a sentimentalist," Becca said. "Why do you need to know about her family?"

"With any investigation, it's good to know everything you can about the deceased," I told her, reading her the boilerplate we handed every victim's family when we went snooping. "You never know what might end up being relevant."

There was a second or two of awkward silence, then she cut in.

"So," she said, "about seeing each other again . . ."

I was about to beg off. A lone night of dancing was one thing; two dates added up to something else. Then I remembered the flyers I'd seen plastered all over the subway the other evening.

"What are you doing Friday night?" I asked.

"Whatever you tell me to do." The line dripped with the kind of innuendo they invented the Hays Code for.

"This time I'll pick you up. Let's say six," I said. "The dress code is decidedly downscale. More a walk in the park than a night dancing."

"*Are* we going for a walk in the park?"

"No peeking," I said. "I give it even money you'll enjoy yourself. Two-to-one that you'll love it."

"I'll take those odds," she purred.

Three minutes after hanging up, I still had a goofy grin on my face. I wiped it off and went hunting for our New York State atlas. Lo and behold, there was a Prattsville. According to the atlas it was about an hour southwest of Albany in Greene County and boasted a population of 848 as of the last census. Not a metropolis, but not exactly a one-horse burg either.

I made a quick trip to the library and found a copy of the Greene County phone book. Because Prattsville was close to Delaware and Schoharie counties, I tracked down those as well. Then I went to work copying the number for every Pratt I could find. There were 294 listings in total. I noted which ones were in towns within twenty miles of Prattsville. That cut things down to 82. Not awful, but definitely a chore.

While I was there, I also copied the numbers for every sheriff's office, town hall, and library in the three counties. Better safe than sorry.

I went back to the office and started making calls.

I knew it was possible that news of Abigail Collins's death had made it back to any family she may have left behind, so I stuck to the truth. I was employed by Abigail's children to track down her kin. I kept the reasons for the hunt vague. The easy assumption was that there was some money in the will, which I hoped might grease the skids.

I made calls all Monday afternoon and all day Tuesday. I did so much dialing, I didn't know what was going to overheat first, the phone or my ear. Ma Bell should have sent me flowers.

For all of you thinking that detective work is a thrilling, glamorous gig, sorry to disabuse you. This is what the job is like nine hours out of ten. It's grueling, tedious, and frequently fruitless. Also, it was a fifty-fifty shot as to whether our Abigail's kin had a phone. If she grew up as poor as she'd reported to Becca and Randolph, it was possible whatever family she'd left behind weren't forking over cash for a home line.

I actually did track down Abigail Pratt. I tracked down seven of them. My favorite was the eighty-four-year-old Scottish immigrant who had an accent so thick I had to get Mrs. Campbell to translate. I was holding out hope that our Abigail was her long-lost granddaughter. No such luck. But Mrs. Campbell did get a recipe for sausage stuffing out of the call.

By dinnertime Tuesday, Ms. P was ready to pull the plug on the endeavor. She'd spent that time making calls to the wives and girlfriends who had been at the Halloween party, a job that was proving as tedious as my own.

"It's possible she changed her name," Ms. Pentecost conceded. "If so, I'm afraid you've wasted the last two days."

I didn't disagree with her. But I woke Wednesday morning with an idea. I might have been going about it all wrong, I thought. I shouldn't have been looking for Abigail Pratt. She might very well have changed her name. But Prattsville was so small that it was unlikely she'd have been able to name-drop it to Becca unless she had some familiarity with the region.

What I should have been asking about was a girl—between seventeen and twenty, blond hair and blue eyes, and probably considered one of the prettiest girls around—who had up and left sometime around 1924.

I started with the town libraries, using the same spiel but adding that it was possible that Abigail had changed her name. Nobody gave me a snap answer, but I didn't expect them to.

Instead, I told them to think it over and ask around, and if they came up with anything to give me a call.

I also asked for the name and phone number of the oldest, most clued-in woman in town. I didn't say "town gossip" but I didn't have to. Every librarian, to a woman, knew what I was asking for. Then I started calling those clued-in women, in one case a very chatty widower.

In the process I gathered a lot of juicy tidbits about the inner workings of Greene County towns, including what sounded like a bed-and-breakfast that doubled as a brothel and the names of several town councilmen open to bribes. By midafternoon, I had her. Specifically I had Mrs. Bettyanne Casey-Hutts of Cockerville, a town about a dozen miles north of Prattsville.

From how Bettyanne described it, Cockerville made its southern neighbor look like Paris, France.

"Town's so small we're buying our first stoplight on layaway," she joked in a cigarette addict's crag. "Can't blame the girl for leaving. Wasn't nothing for her here. Especially after what happened."

"The girl" was Abby Crouch, which—from Bettyanne's detailed description—was our Abigail.

"There wasn't a man or boy within twenty miles that didn't know who Abby Crouch was. I don't mean that in the lewd sense. I just mean she turned heads," Bettyanne told me. "She wasn't the prettiest girl around, but she was pretty enough. She had a look about her. Confidence, I guess it was. Men find that sort of thing attractive until they're up close with it. Then they start thinking they might prefer something a little meeker."

Five minutes on the phone and I was ready to adopt Bettyanne as the cranky grandmother I never knew.

"All that's speculation, mind you," she continued. "My husband and I went to First Methodist, and so did the Crouch family. One Sunday I'd hear that Abby was seeing so-and-so. Two or three Sundays later, I'd hear they'd called it quits."

"Are her parents still around?" I asked.

"No. Her mother died young. Not in childbirth, but soon after, I think," Bettyanne said. "Raised by her father and older brother. Can't recall the brother's name. Something odd. A family name. Orlando? Orren? Something like that."

She trailed off as she tried to pull the name out of her memory. For a second I thought I'd lost her, but she snapped back. "Father ran a small farm. Quiet type. Kept to himself. He died. Can't remember when exactly. After she left, I think. I switched churches after Clarence—that's my husband—after he passed. Haven't thought about the Crouches in ages."

"You mentioned that you couldn't blame Abby for leaving," I said, reeling her back in. "That there was some messy business. What business was that?"

"Awful thing. Just awful." Her pack-a-day voice developed a quiver. "Only time something like that has happened around here. At least with a boy that young. His whole life ahead of him."

"What happened?" I asked.

"Billy McCray. A boy Abby was dating. Or I think she was dating him. They might have been through when it happened. It's been so long. You think your memory is sharp as a knife and then . . ."

If Ma Bell had offered a way to gently shake somebody through the phone, I'd have taken them up on it.

"What happened to Billy McCray?" I prodded.

"Oh, he killed himself, dear," she said, as if that should have been perfectly obvious. "He blew his brains out with his daddy's shotgun."

CHAPTER 21

I eased the Cadillac into a space directly across the street from number 215. I looked over at the park, searching for the babushkas. The sun had set already, and if they'd been there, they'd left.

It had taken me a good fifteen minutes to get Bettyanne off the line. I got the sense she didn't get many visitors and a phone call from a New York City detective was the most exciting thing to come her way in a month of Sundays.

She hadn't been able to tell me much more. Billy McCray had been a bright, handsome lad who'd been expected to eventually take over his father's hardware store. His suicide had come as a shock to the entire town. The McCrays closed up shop not long after and moved south, where the winters were milder and the bad memories not so thick on the ground.

I hit her with a baker's dozen of follow-up questions, but her well had run dry. She said she'd look up the name and number of Abigail's brother and give me a call. If she came through, I'd send her roses. Maybe one of those chatty parakeets to keep her company.

I caught Ms. Pentecost up on developments as we made our way to the Village, tossing the scant details of Abigail's early life into the backseat.

"You think she might have killed him?" I asked. "That can't be a coincidence. Two men shooting themselves."

Ms. P was solidly on the fence.

"A boyfriend of several weeks when she was sixteen. A husband of two decades when she was nearly forty." In the rearview I saw her hold out her hands like scales, balancing those two points on Abigail's biography. "There's undoubtedly a similarity," she said, "but it's difficult to call it a pattern when the skeins are so far separated."

"Sure, it's threadbare," I admitted. "But I know how you feel about coincidences in a murder case."

All I got was a scowl and a grumble. The rest of the ride was conducted in silence, except for the occasional invective spat at my fellow drivers. I didn't want to badger her. She was doing whatever geniuses do to get their heads right when they're about to face an adversary.

That's how I was thinking of Belestrade—an adversary. Smart, devious, attractive—if that kind of thing does it for you—and dangerous. She might not have been a murderer, but she was likely a blackmailer, certainly a fraud, and definitely not someone to be trifled with.

Good thing my boss didn't trifle.

The plan, she told me, was to let Belestrade guide the evening. Give her as much rope as she wanted. Then hit her with the blackmail question at the end.

"The more time we are in the room with her, the more we can glean about her methods," Ms. P explained.

She took a few seconds after getting out of the car to straighten her outfit—a gray worsted suit over a shirt the color of blood, accented by a black tie fixed with a silver tiepin. Her going-to-war ensemble. All her features seemed bigger: her chin sharper, her mouth wider, her nose just a little more hooked. Her eyes, real and glass alike, were shining bright.

She didn't forget her cane tonight. Better to show the prop than wobble when she didn't want to.

We knocked on the door.

SEEKERS INQUIRE WITHIN

A moment later, it was opened by Neal Watkins—raven hair plastered in an impeccable wave and wearing a suit an undertaker would have put back on the rack for being too grim.

"Good evening," he said. I think he was going for his boss's hypnotic tone, but it came off more as sleepy. "Ms. Belestrade will be ready in a few minutes. If you don't mind waiting."

He sat us in a narrow room with padded benches on either side and a pair of heavy oak doors on one end. Ms. P and I took one bench. After asking if either of us would like something to drink—neither of us did—Neal perched on the other.

"Ms. Belestrade has been greatly anticipating your visit," he said.

"Really? Why is that?" Ms. P asked.

"I think she sees you as a challenge," Neal declared. "A non-believer who, nonetheless, has the same goals as her."

"And what are those?"

"Providing assistance for those who need it."

"Is that what drew you to her employ?" she asked. "She provided an opportunity for altruism that a university history department did not?"

If Neal was flustered by that nugget we'd picked up from Dr. Waterhouse, he didn't show it.

"That was part of it. Also, it's interesting work. And Ms. Belestrade pays well. More than any teaching assistantship," Neal said, brushing his flop away from his forehead again. "The answer to your other questions is uniformly 'No, I'm afraid not.'"

"My other questions?"

"No, I did not get out of the car the night of the party. No, I didn't see anything suspicious. No, I'm afraid I don't know who murdered Abigail Collins." He gave what he probably thought was a charming smile, which made him look like exactly what he was: a wannabe academic training to be a second-rate con man.

He didn't get the chance to foretell our follow-ups. A soft chime rang from behind the double doors.

"She's ready for you," Neal said, standing.

We followed his lead. With a flourish, he flung open the oak doors.

We crossed the threshold into what looked like the kind of parlor you'd find in any well-to-do New York brownstone: a half-dozen softly upholstered chairs, a chaise longue against one wall, a scattering of end tables and Tiffany lamps, and a small electric chandelier that reflected pleasantly off the wood. The paintings on the walls were tasteful nudes and American landscapes. I'm not an expert, but I'm pretty sure I spotted an original Hopper in the mix.

No draped silks. No esoteric symbols scrawled on the walls. Also no windows or curtains for Neal to hide behind.

The only thing in the room that lived up to my expectations was our hostess. She stood barefoot in the center of the room in a white silk number that was half evening dress, half nightgown. She had rings on every finger and her black bob was fixed with a piece of jade shaped like a spider.

The smile on her face when she greeted us was wide and sincere. I didn't trust it for a second.

"Ms. Pentecost. Miss Parker. Welcome to my home," she said. "Please sit wherever you're most comfortable."

I was tempted to go outside and sit in the car, that being the most comfortable of available options. But Neal had closed the doors behind us, so I followed Ms. P's lead. She took one of a trio of armchairs, and I grabbed the one next to her. But not before shifting it a few degrees so I was facing the closed double doors. I wasn't really expecting anything to burst through and try to do us in, but I also hadn't forgotten my .38 tucked away in a holster beneath my vest.

Belestrade looked amused by my chair choreography.

"You're safe here, Miss Parker," she said. "You have nothing to fear."

"You said 'comfortable,'" I reminded her. "I'm never comfortable with my back to a door."

The smile faded and was replaced by a look of pity.

"I find that very sad," she said. "Your experience with the world has taught you that doorways are things to fear rather than opportunities for wonder and adventure."

I came up with half a dozen quick retorts, but all involved language unfit for nice parlors. Besides, this was Ms. Pentecost's show. So I just smiled politely as our host took the third seat. The clairvoyant made herself comfortable, crossing her legs and showing off matching silver toe rings.

For a good five count, no one in the semicircle spoke. Ms. P and Belestrade looked at each other—my boss's mouth a straight line, our host's a gently curving grin. I was considering telling a joke I'd heard about a postman and a farmer's daughter when Belestrade broke the silence.

"I'm not unaware of or ungrateful for how unique this

experience is. For both of us," she said with equal parts honey and spice. "I've invited skeptics to my home before. Dr. Waterhouse, for example. But only as observers. Never as a spiritual focus. Just as I'm sure you are always the one in the room seeking answers, not the one whose soul is being exposed."

I don't know how Ms. Pentecost felt about that, but I certainly bristled. If there was any exposing to be done, it'd be my boss pulling back the curtain.

"I don't mean that in a threatening sense," Belestrade said. "To you, 'expose' has harsh connotations—revelations of misconduct and murder. To me, exposure is light and air—bringing things out of the dark so they can grow and bloom."

Ms. P laid one hand, palm up, on her lap. "How do we proceed?" she asked.

"Close your eyes," Belestrade instructed. "You, too, Miss Parker. Don't worry. Nothing will harm you here."

Seeing Ms. P close her eyes, I did the same. But you better believe I kept an ear cocked for the creak of a door or the faintest click of a toe ring.

"Empty your mind of the day," the spiritualist said. "From morning until this moment. All the events, the encounters, the chores, the thoughts, the desire—take it all in your arms, hold it tight to your breast, then let it go. Breathe deep, and let it go."

She repeated that last again and again until it became a chant.

"Breathe deep, and let it go. Breathe deep, and let it go. Breathe deep, and let it go. Breathe deep, and let it go."

The words began to blur together until it was a single chain of syllables. When I'd closed my eyes, my nerves were practically vibrating. But that woman with her voice and its cadence was actually making me relax.

"Breathe deep, and let it go."

I heard a faint and muffled ticking beneath her words. Like a clock was hidden somewhere in the walls. Or the deathwatch beetles my grandmother told me about at my mother's funeral. The ones that gather in the walls when death gets near.

"Breathe deep, and let it go."

I began to float in my chair.

"Breathe deep, and let it go."

She was quiet for a long stretch. All I heard was the faint ticking. Tick, tick, tick, tick. Time was getting blurry around the edges. How long had we been sitting in that room? I didn't know.

Tick, tick, tick, tick.

"I want you to tarry a moment in this empty space, this warm hollow in your heart," Belestrade said. "I want you to listen. Listen for the voices of those who have gone beyond the veil. Not gone forever. Just obscured. Muffled by the desires of daily life. Listen. Listen for their voices. Their whispers."

I listened.

Tick, tick, tick, tick. Was there something else beneath that sound?

"There are so many around you," the spiritualist whispered. "You carry so many spirits in your wake. *Listen.*"

I almost heard them. Or imagined I did. The soft murmuring.

Faces started to swim up out of the darkness behind my eyelids. My mother's. My grandmother's. Lovely Lulu, who'd died in a pneumonia ward two months before I left the circus. McCloskey, his face a mask of pain and confusion, trying to pry the knife from his back. A girl I'd seen stabbed to death in a dockside bar. All the bodies I'd seen spread out on Hiram's cold table.

I saw each of them for a fleeting moment before they sank back into the darkness.

"Now open your eyes."

I did. The clairvoyant hadn't moved, but something was different. The rest of the room was shrouded in darkness and the light seemed to be focused in a narrow circle around our chairs, like reality itself was condensing around us.

While our eyes were open, Belestrade's were closed, her head cocked as if listening.

"So many," she whispered. "So many dead trailing behind you. A retinue of the lost."

I glanced at Ms. P. She had a new line carving across the center of her brow. I wondered whose faces she'd seen.

"You hear them, don't you?" the spiritualist asked. "You hear them crying out—in your dreams, your quiet thoughts— but you can't make out what they're saying. You think they're calling for vengeance, for justice, but you don't know."

Belstrade's fingers gripped the arms of the seat, nails digging into the soft upholstery.

"I hear her," she hissed, writhing in her chair. "Calling to you. You're afraid that her death will go unavenged. She's saying that you . . . you . . . You should let her go. Let her go. Do not clasp her death to your heart. It only brings her pain. It only brings *you* pain."

Out of the corner of my eye I glimpsed Ms. Pentecost's lip curl into the slightest of sneers.

"If this is a gambit to convince me to drop my investigation into the murder of Abigail Collins, it is misguided and beneath us both," she said.

Eyes still clamped shut, Belestrade shook her head.

"Nooooo." The word escaped her lips like a dying breath.

Quick as a snake, her hand darted out and grabbed my wrist. I tried to pull away, but her fingers were like steel.

"You have to let it go, Willowjean. You have to let me go." Belestrade's voice was different. It had an oh-so-familiar Midwestern flatness with hints of the Deep South. I knew that voice.

"You were right," she said. "What you always thought. It was him that killed me. He didn't pull a trigger, but it was him all the same."

Tears were streaming down Belestrade's cheeks. Her eyelids fluttered open, showing white.

"You have to let me go," she croaked. "You couldn't have done a thing. You have to stop blaming yourself. You were just a child. You were just—"

There's a blank space here. Drunks would call it a blackout, except I don't drink. All I know is that one moment I was hearing my mother's voice being parroted by that fraud, the next I was standing, pointing my gun at her head and yelling.

"Shut up! Shut your goddamn mouth!"

My chair was tipped over behind me. Tears were streaming down my face. Neal was standing in the doorway, mouth open in shock. And Belestrade was silent, utterly calm as she stared down the barrel. There wasn't an ounce of fear in those wide, dark eyes. Only triumph.

Very slowly, Ms. Pentecost placed her hand over mine—the one holding the pistol.

"Will," she whispered. "Put it away. She's not worth it."

Breathe, and let it go.

Whatever had possessed me retreated. I lowered the gun and slid it back into my holster.

"I'm sorry," I said, though I wasn't sure who I was apologizing to.

"It's all right," my boss told me. "We're leaving."

She turned to our host and in a voice as cold and level as a coffin she said, "You've made a grave mistake tonight. To challenge me is foolhardy. But to taunt my companions?"

Ms. Pentecost rapped the end of her cane hard into the floor. Her knuckles were white around its brass handle.

"You might wish I'd let her shoot you."

Ms. P took my still-trembling hand in hers and led me out.

CHAPTER 22

Ms. Pentecost wanted us to get a cab, but I refused to leave the Caddy in front of that woman's house.

Somehow I got us to Brooklyn. I started the journey dazed and numb, but as thought and feeling worked their way back into my brain, numbness turned to anger. Either Belestrade was channeling the spirit of my dead mother, or someone had given her enough personal information about me to allow her to turn me into a mark.

There was only one person in recent memory to whom I'd let slip details of my mother's death.

When we got back to the office, Ms. P suggested I go to my room and rest, or at least let Mrs. Campbell make me some rice pudding, which always helped when I was in a mood. Instead, I asked to be left alone in the office.

I picked up the phone and dialed. Becca answered on the third ring. She barely got out "Hello" before I tore into her.

"Did she pay you for the information, or did you just hand it over?"

"I don't know what—"

"I hope you got something out of it," I snarled. "A C-note, a kiss. Something."

"Will, what's going on? What happened?" she pleaded. "I don't understand. Is this about my mother?"

"It's about you slipping details of my mother's death to that . . . to Belestrade."

"Why would I tell that woman anything?"

"I don't know. Maybe you were drunk." My voice dripped with bitterness. I barely recognized it. "Maybe that's how she gets all her good blackmail dirt. She feeds pretty little girls gin until they tell her whatever she wants to know. Maybe the only reason you asked me to dance in the first place was to crack me open. If that's the case, well played."

There was silence on the other end. I wondered if she'd disconnected.

"Will, I'm going to hang up the—"

I beat her to it.

I stared at the phone for a good minute, waiting for my heart to slow to jogging speed. I looked up to see Ms. Pentecost standing in the doorway.

"I know I flubbed it, okay? I let both of them play me and . . ."

I started leaking tears for the second time that night. Ms. P came around her desk, put an arm around me, and led me upstairs to bed. She walked me into my room and waited as I went into the bathroom and washed my face and changed into pajamas.

"I'm not a child," I told her as she saw me into bed. "You don't need to treat me like one."

She looked surprised.

"I don't think you're a child," she said. "I think you're my associate and my friend, and that you have helped me into bed more times than I can number."

Then she left, and I slept. Or I tried to. I couldn't get those words out of my head.

You have to stop blaming yourself.

Because I did.

The rational part of me knew that I was just a kid back then. There was nothing I could have done to keep my father from whaling on my mother. I didn't have a gun holstered under my arm, no knife strapped to my calf. No words to convince her to leave him while she could.

But the part of me that had pulled the gun on Belestrade? The part that twists my stomach into knots whenever I think about those days? It doesn't listen to reason. It still thinks I should have done something. And if I just save enough women, help put enough killers behind bars, maybe the guilt will go away.

The next morning was bog-standard, as Mrs. Campbell would say. Wake, breakfast, correspondence, phone calls, patient waiting for my boss to come downstairs.

I hadn't forgotten the events of the night before, but they felt less immediate. The anger had mostly receded.

The only aberration was a certain nagging guilt about how I'd exploded at Becca. I still figured her for being the leak. But what if Belestrade had used some kind of trick to pry the information out of her? Had hypnotized her somehow?

Either way, Becca was a main character in an active case and she didn't deserve me spitting curses in her ear. I figured I'd wait until early afternoon when I was sure Becca would be awake, and call and apologize. Or head over in person if she'd agree to see me.

Ms. Pentecost came downstairs around two—a little later than usual. Maybe she wanted to give me some more time to myself. I didn't ask and she didn't offer. I was about to request the day's orders when there was a knock at the door—five raps hard and fast.

"I know that Morse code," I said, getting up to answer. I was surprised to find that Lieutenant Lazenby wasn't alone. He was accompanied by two uniformed sergeants.

"Parker," he said in a voice like a mine collapse. "Is she awake?"

His abruptness startled me. It was a lapse in cordiality that was unlike the burly policeman. And his face had a bit of the granite I'd seen the first night we met.

"I'm sure she'll be delighted to see her favorite public servant."

I led the three into the office. Lazenby immediately pulled a folded document from his coat pocket and handed it to Ms. P.

"This is a warrant for any and all firearms on the premises."

He waited as she read it top to bottom. Then she gave me a nod.

I had a lot of questions, but I took my .38 from my desk drawer and retrieved a .45 from the safe.

Ms. P pulled a two-shot derringer from her own desk. It was only accurate to about six feet, which was all she'd need if somebody ever got into the office with mischief on their mind.

Lazenby directed the narrower of the two sergeants to take the weapons.

"That's all?" Lazenby asked.

"You think we have an arsenal?" I quipped.

That earned me a look I didn't like one bit. Once the first sergeant had left with our cache of shooters, Lazenby pulled out a second paper.

"This is a material witness warrant for Willowjean Parker," he declared.

Ms. P shot to her feet and snatched it out of his hand. Her eyes flickered down the document. I peeked over her shoulder.

A material witness warrant allows the police to take a person into custody and requires the individual to provide information about a crime. If they refuse, they'll be held in contempt. It wasn't rare for the cops to use them as a prelude to an arrest warrant.

I noticed a conspicuous blank space on the document. As usual, my boss got there first.

"There's no crime mentioned here. What is she suspected of having knowledge of?"

"We're not required to provide that information," Lazenby said.

Ms. Pentecost's eyes would have burned a hole through a lesser man. Lazenby might as well have been made of stone.

She saw he was resolved, and her face relaxed.

"Nathan," she said in a gentle voice. One word. Very calm.

He gave a nod and turned his dark eyes to me.

"The murder of Ariel Belestrade."

CHAPTER 23

It was the exact same interrogation room. No foolin'. Same cheap metal table. Same wobbly chair. Except this time, I didn't have to work my way up the ranks. I got the big guy right off.

"We've got you dead to rights, Parker," he growled. "It's not a matter of guilty or innocent. It's murder or manslaughter. If we can show you were provoked, maybe we can keep you out of the chair."

He leaned across the table, his voice soft and low.

"What Belestrade did to you was awful," he said. "To use a personal tragedy, to play you like that. If she had done the same to me, I might have killed her then and there. You had more restraint than me. So what I've got to know is—when you went back to her house last night, what did she say? Was it more of the same? More lies and voodoo?"

Every detective has his or her own interrogation style. Ms. Pentecost's is to be everyone's second-favorite aunt—not the cheery one you can have a drink with, but the no-nonsense one you turn to when you need serious advice or serious money.

Mine leverages people's misconceptions. If they look at me and see a little girl playing detective, I use it. If they see a glorified secretary, I use that. In between I give people the character from all those pulp novels I was weaned on, all hard-boiled charm and acerbic wit. Or at least I try. Like Kalishenko used to say: Every act is a work in progress.

Lazenby's style is the father confessor. Maybe he figures that since he looks like a sixteenth-century friar, he should play the part. Every question is couched in an offer of understanding, of absolution. Not being on the receiving end too often, I tend to forget how good he is.

Unfortunately for him, I knew his tricks. Even if I didn't, I was too steamed at him for them to work on me. I'd always hoped his comments about my not putting any more knives in people was just play. Harmless jabs between professionals. This wasn't playing. He'd gone to a judge with a warrant and gotten him to sign it. Maybe he didn't really think I offed Belestrade and he was just covering his bases, but that meant he considered me a base that needed covering. That no matter who did my tailoring these days, I was still a cirky girl with a body to her record.

I was tempted to answer his questions with a few single-syllable answers. Then I thought about how Ms. Pentecost would handle things. I hadn't spent three years in her company for nothing. She wouldn't let Lazenby get under her skin, and if she did she sure as hell wouldn't show it.

I thought about my dime-novel heroes, leaned back as much as the wobbly chair would allow, and put on a grin.

"That's a nice yarn," I said. "I prefer Hammett myself. Gardner if I'm in a pinch."

"I'm dead serious, Will," he said. "This isn't a joke."

"Do you see me laughing?"

I recited a name and number I had long since memorized—the lawyer Ms. P had on permanent retainer. Not that it was necessary. I was sure both he and Ms. P were somewhere in the building working to break me loose.

Apparently Lazenby realized that, guilty or innocent, I wasn't going to bite on his usual line, so he started asking the useful questions. The when, where, how, and so forth. I gave him the basics of our trip to Belestrade's the night before, glossing over the juicier details.

To my surprise, he pushed in every puzzle piece that I held back.

"You pulled a gun on the woman," he declared. "Your boss actually threatened her life."

"You know you can't take Neal's word for anything," I said. "Whatever schemes Belestrade was up to, he was part of it."

"We've got a lot more than his testimony."

A lot of confidence in that line. I believed him. Combined with everything else he'd let slip, it could only mean one thing.

"It's on tape," I said—a statement not a question. "The room was wired for sound."

Hardly a Pentecost-level feat of deduction. Not with the questions he was asking and his ability to quote Belestrade verbatim. Also, I remembered that soft ticking I'd heard. Not a clock, but the reeling of a hidden tape recorder.

"How far back do the recordings go?" I asked. "Did she record everything in the room? Do you have the entire catalog?"

The detective's poker face was good, but I caught the flicker of frustration.

"You don't, do you? You don't have the lot."

His face got that fun shade of crimson I enjoy so much. "I'm asking the questions!" he shouted.

"Of course you are," I said. "Never any doubt. But still . . . If she recorded last night, she recorded every night. Why wouldn't she? Which means she'd have her sessions with Abigail Collins on tape."

I set the gears in my head into motion.

"Somebody gave you the tape of last night. I'm guessing Neal," I said. "So the question becomes, did Neal hold back the rest? Or did he never have them? If he didn't, who does?"

To his credit, the lieutenant applied the brakes. After a moment of fuming silence, he returned to the nuts-and-bolts questions of my contact with Belestrade. This time, I held nothing back, including my first botched surveillance of the clairvoyant.

All in all, it took about two hours from start to finish. By the time we were done, I was a limp rag. Lazenby wasn't looking so starched himself.

He leaned back in his chair, which creaked under his weight.

"We'll get ballistics back soon," he said. "Anything you want to add to your tale?"

I leaned back as well. Since I had the chair with the wobbly leg, it didn't have quite the same effect.

"Not a thing," I said. "Bring on the ballistics."

He nodded. If I had to make a bet then, I'd have put his inner scales tipping in favor of innocent. It was a very mild tip, though.

"So," he said, "why do you think Belestrade had such a fix on you?"

I shrugged. "I wouldn't call it a fix. She had her sights set on my boss and I was the next best thing. She happened on some information about me and decided to pull her trick."

The big policeman chuckled. It's a disconcerting sound, hearing a statue laugh.

"She didn't just happen on anything, Parker. We found a whole file in her office," he said. "Interviews with some reporter cronies of yours. People you've had relationships with. Looks like she was even able to get some of your old circus friends on the phone."

My stomach dropped. There were plenty of folks at Hart and Halloway who knew about my early years. I'd torn into Becca for nothing.

"Looks like she's had her eye on you and your boss for a while," Lazenby continued. "A lot more on you than Pentecost, but Lillian's always been one to cover her tracks. Believe me, I've pried. Makes me wonder what Belestrade was planning on doing with all that information. Other than piss you off."

It made me wonder, too.

Had she known Ms. P had been investigating her these last few years? Had she been gathering nuggets to use against us if we got too close? If that was the case, she hadn't done a very good job of it. The scene in her parlor? That late-night tour around New York? They were beyond showy. It almost assured we'd keep our eye on her.

I was still pondering this when the door opened. The narrow sergeant who'd confiscated our firearms walked in with a note. He handed it to Lazenby, who read it. He waved a hand and the sergeant scurried back out.

"Ballistics," he said. "Last chance to change your story."

For a quick, panicked moment I tried to figure the odds of someone sneaking into the house, borrowing one of our guns, going off and shooting Belestrade, then returning the gun so as to frame yours truly. But, as Ms. Pentecost would say, that was pulp mystery thinking.

"You've got all the news that's fit to print," I told him.

He stared me down for a long few seconds, then stuck a thumb in the direction of the door. "You're done here," he said. "Your boss is waiting."

I evacuated my wobbly chair and cracked my back.

"Ballistics were negative?" I asked, already knowing the answer.

"Just go. And try and not point your gun at anyone in the near future."

"Can't," I said. "You've got my gun. Speaking of which . . ."

"You'll get them back. Eventually. Paperwork, you understand?" I suspected a grin underneath his beard, but I didn't stick around to check. The door had been left unlocked and I walked through it.

CHAPTER 24

When he'd said my boss was outside, I hadn't expected immediately outside, but there the lady detective was, waiting on a bench in the hall.

"He held out for a long time, but I eventually got him to crack," I told her as she collected her coat and cane.

"Good," she said. "I would like to leave now. I find myself incredibly angry with Nathan. I'm afraid I might say something we'll both regret."

We caught a taxi out front and compared notes on the way back to Brooklyn. I gave her the rundown of my interrogation, including my surmise that Belestrade had recorded her clients and that somewhere there were recordings of Abigail Collins talking about . . . what? I didn't know. If she suspected, Ms. P wasn't saying.

The lady detective hadn't been loafing, either. While our lawyer was attempting to poke holes in the warrants, Ms. Pentecost had taken a trip to the morgue. Hiram hadn't been there, and there had been a uniformed sergeant on guard. But it was a sergeant we were familiar with. He was far from friendly but knew the value of a dollar. Or a hundred dollars, as the case may be.

"So there's no doubt?" I asked.

"None. Ariel Belestrade is dead."

"You know, I read that there are drugs that can slow the heart down so much that it can mimic death."

Ms. P shook her head. "Unless these drugs can mimic two bullets to the skull, I think we can rule out fakery."

Damn. Belestrade had been shaping up to be a good fit for Abigail Collins's murder. If the message from the late, lamented Jonathan Markel was to be believed, Belestrade was a good fit for a lot of other shady business as well.

"Hang on," I said. "She could still be good for the murder. This could be blowback from something else. The woman probably made a lot of enemies."

"Perhaps," Ms. P conceded. "Though the timing suggests a connection."

"The word 'connection' covers a lot of territory. Mastermind, accomplice, witness, blackmailer. Any idea where to start?"

Ms. P sank into quiet thought. The silence lasted the rest of the way home. Back at the office, I sat at my desk and dialed the Collins residence. This time, my second-favorite Collins sibling answered.

"She doesn't want to speak with you," Randy said. "I don't know what you said to her yesterday, but she locked herself in her bedroom and didn't come out all night. She's still in there."

"Fine," I said. "I'll be there in half an hour. Less if traffic is accommodating."

"I told you. She doesn't want to—"

I hung up. I'd let him finish his sentence in person.

"I've got an apology to deliver," I told Ms. P. "Not sure if they've got the news about Belestrade or not. Want me to let it drop and watch the ripples?"

"Use your best judgment," she said. "But keep the details to yourself. We don't want to be accused by the lieutenant of interference."

I took the sedan and, thanks to Midtown traffic, made it to the Collins manse in something closer to fifty minutes than thirty. Randy met me at the door. He adjusted his shoulders to fill the frame and played linebacker.

"I said she doesn't want to speak to you," he said. I wondered if he'd practiced that haughty look the mirror.

"Have you asked her that?"

"I don't need to ask her. In case you haven't forgotten, this is my house and if I don't want you to enter—"

He was interrupted by a shout from the sitting room.

"Who's that at the door?" Wallace came around the corner. "If it's the police again, I—"

He was surprised to see me but not unpleasantly so. The lawyer looked wrung out. The stoop in his shoulders was even more pronounced, robbing him of a few inches. His thinning hair fell limply across his high forehead.

"Miss Parker."

"Mr. Wallace. I'm sorry to disturb you."

"Quite all right," he said. "Is your employer with you?"

"Afraid it's just me."

"Let the girl in, Randy."

Randy did the math of letting me in versus having to explain to his godfather exactly why he didn't want me to. The latter would open a can of worms I was guessing dear Uncle Harry was blissfully unaware of.

Begrudgingly, Randy stepped aside.

"Is there news?" Wallace asked, leading me into the sitting room where my boss had interviewed them a few days before.

"There is, though not what you might expect," I said, claiming a spot on a particularly uncomfortable chair. "You'll want to sit down."

It wasn't that I thought either man would go weak in the

knees. I just wanted both of their faces in my line of sight when I dropped this particular stone in the water. Both perched on an overstuffed sofa—Wallace nervous, Randy sullen and simmering.

"So," Wallace said, pushing his half-moons back up his nose, "what's this news?"

"Ariel Belestrade was murdered last night."

I wanted a reaction, and I got it.

"Murdered? How? By who?" That was Randy, his face a perfect mixture of surprise and confusion.

"That's awful . . . I mean, she was . . . not a pleasant woman. But that's still terrible. When was this?" That was Wallace. He was also working with surprise and confusion, but there was some other ingredient in the mix. Fear, maybe?

I was about to answer as many of their questions as I could when I heard footsteps on the stairs. Becca descended from the landing, where I guess she'd been eavesdropping. She was awake and properly put together in a blouse and slacks—very Kate Hepburn in *The Philadelphia Story*. No makeup, though. Her eyes looked puffy, like she'd spent too long crying. A sliver of guilt slid into my heart.

"That woman is dead?" she asked.

"Last night. Shot," I told her, keeping one eye on her and one on Wallace's face.

"Good."

"Becca!" Wallace exclaimed. "That's terrible."

"*She* was terrible, Uncle Harry. You said so yourself."

"Yes, but . . . No one should be . . ." He hopped off that train and switched to lawyer mode. Turning to me, he asked, "What does this mean for us? Does that woman's death have something to do with Abigail's? Do the police think it was the same person?"

"It's a fool's errand to say for sure what the police think," I said. "It's possible that Belestrade ticked off a lot of people, and I'm sure they're following up every lead."

Using my best judgment, I neglected to mention I was one of those leads.

"You can be sure that if the police don't drop by tonight, they'll be here first thing in the morning."

"What would the police want with us?" Randy asked.

"I'm surprised they haven't been here already," I told them. "Belestrade was a suspect in your mother's death. All of you were vocal in your dislike for her. The cops would have to be dull, lazy, or both not to want to spend a few hours tacking down your alibis."

All three shuffled a little, Becca on her feet, the two men in their seats. Nobody likes to hear they're a suspect in a homicide, much less two homicides within a fortnight.

"I was at the office until nearly midnight," Wallace said. His fingers twitched in his lap and he stared at them rather than at my eyes. "After that, I went home."

"I was here all night," Randy added. "So was Becca. The servants can vouch for us."

Lazenby had asked me about midnight until two in the morning, so I was guessing that was when Belestrade had died. The butler and cook would have been asleep by midnight. And Wallace's alibi was so flimsy I wouldn't blow my nose with it.

I decided to go for a kidney punch.

"One question the police will be sure to hit you with is what dirt Belestrade had on your family."

Becca and Wallace looked blankly quizzical. Randolph, on the other hand, boiled over.

"I'm sick of these insinuations!" he snarled. "First from the police, and now her? Our family, our mother, is the victim here!"

I'd seen his take on sputtering rage before, and this version seemed somewhat counterfeit. But not so put-on that I didn't follow the advice I gave my basement students—look for exits or weapons.

Wallace put a hand on his godson's arm. "Randy, calm down."

Randy found the brakes and tapped them. He was still simmering but managed to spit out the question he should have started with.

"What do you mean 'dirt'?"

I explained what Ms. Pentecost and I had discovered about Belestrade's operation, or at least what we surmised. How she abused her clients' confidences to ferret out secrets she could then use for blackmail.

"The police are going to start flinging open closets," I said. "If you have any skeletons, they're sure to come tumbling out."

None of the three looked particularly enthused by that, but who would?

"Anyway, you might want to call your lawyers tonight and have them ready to go, just in case the police try and get you down to the station."

Wallace nodded and got up. "I'll get Simpson on the phone now."

He left to make the call and I looked back to Becca.

"Do you have a minute?"

Randy started to stir again, but Becca shot him a look that nailed his tongue down and sent him fuming into the next room. I wondered how much of his outburst had been an act and what he really knew about what Belestrade might have had on his mother.

While I pondered, Becca led me through the house and out onto the veranda. The sun had set and a chill wind was blowing what little snow was on the ground. White, swirling devils twisted around our ankles. I could see goosebumps pebbling the flesh of her arms. I resisted the urge to put an arm around her.

"Aren't you cold?" I asked.

"I need some air. I've been cooped up all day."

Without lipstick or eye shadow, her features tended to disappear into her pale face. She resembled one of the marble statues nailing down either corner of the veranda. But those statues weren't shooting blue daggers at me from between narrowed eyelids.

"I'm sorry about last night," I said. "You didn't deserve that."

"No, I didn't," she said, thrusting her chin out. "I would never have told that woman anything."

"I know that now."

I gave her the basics of what I'd learned from the police—that Belestrade had a file on me.

"Why would she target you?"

I shrugged. "Probably as a way to get to my boss. Or to get me angry enough to do something stupid. Like call you up and let go with both barrels."

She reached out and took my hand. The goose bumps on her arm spread to mine.

"I forgive you," she said, gracing me with a smile.

"We still on for tomorrow night?" I asked.

"Of course. But I'm going to have to insist you tell me where we're going. If only so I don't turn up in the wrong shoes."

I told her.

Her smile got much bigger.

CHAPTER 25

Ms. Pentecost's answer to my question of "Where do we start?" was "At the beginning." Friday morning we began sorting through everything we'd learned to date. Common practice when a case stretches out and we can't get traction.

Ms. P is fond of saying, "If we never go back and examine what we have as a whole, we might not see the pattern that exists in the chaos." She's equally fond of the corollary "Spend every moment gnawing on the things you know and you might miss a new morsel that comes your way."

The former sounds like her. The latter like something she picked up from someone a lot more homespun.

Ms. P was downstairs by ten-thirty and we ate a quick breakfast, then retreated to the office. Mrs. Campbell had been up before the sun making a batch of homemade sausage. It was an all-day affair and the thick scent of pork and pepper saturated the brownstone.

At two, we were still at it, so we lunched at our desks. The kitchen had been given over entirely to sausage manufacturing, so I called to the deli around the corner and had them send a boy with sandwiches and a couple of greasy bags of French fries.

I was on my second egg salad on rye when I noticed one of those patterns in the chaos. I had just finished my third pass through the interviews from partygoers. It was the first time I'd taken in my factory interviews and Ms. P's calls to the wives and hired help all as a single piece.

"Nobody's accounted for," I muttered to myself.

My boss looked up from her own homework, her toasted pastrami still untouched.

"There's not a single major player in this little drama whose whereabouts are accounted for continuously from the moment the séance is over until the body is found," I said. "There are gaps everywhere. Not to mention all the company people who had a bone to pick with Abigail making waves with the shareholders. Not a decent alibi for anybody. Except maybe Dr. Waterhouse, who left early."

My boss didn't blink.

"You already clued into this, didn't you?"

"It was to be expected," she said with a shrug. "At a party of so many people, it would have been unrealistic for anyone to be fully accounted for. Add in the presence of alcohol, and things become even cloudier. I've put in another call to Mrs. Buckley—the woman with the Kodak. She said she'll have the film developed right away and send over copies. That might help provide clarity. Even then, it's likely there will be gaps in people's movements."

"How about a twenty-minute gap?"

That raised an eyebrow.

I showed her the pages I'd dog-eared. "Wallace said he talked to the board president, Henry Chamblis, then went out onto the veranda to pass a couple words with Randy. But Chamblis said that after he talked to Wallace, he said some long goodbyes to a few board members, then headed for the veranda to say farewell to the one Collins sibling still circulating."

I flipped some pages to Ms. P's interview with the Collins clan.

"Look at this." I pointed to a passage in the center of the page. "Randy says Chamblis came out, said goodbye, and left. About ten minutes later Wallace came out on the veranda."

Ms. P leaned back, closed her eyes, and double-checked my math. "Long goodbyes with board members and then a farewell to Randolph Collins. Yes, I can see that fifteen minutes actually being as long as twenty," she said, half to herself and half to me. "Or as short as ten if Collins is mistaken about the time."

"Ten minutes is still ten minutes," I said. "We might be able to track him if we piece together enough interviews. Hard to lose sight of a sparkly Uncle Sam."

"We could," my boss admitted. Then she opened her eyes, picked up the phone, and dialed. After a moment . . .

"Mr. Wallace, please. Tell him it's Lillian Pentecost."

A pause, then . . .

"Mr. Wallace, good afternoon . . . No . . . Yes, I'm concerned about that as well . . . Yes, I think that was wise. . . . Mr. Wallace, the reason I'm calling is to ask a question. The night of the party you said you spoke to Henry Chamblis, then immediately joined your godson on the veranda. Is that correct? . . . Are you sure you weren't delayed? . . . Ah . . . Yes . . . Yes, of course . . . Absolutely understandable . . . Which one, might I ask? . . . Thank you. I will be in touch."

She hung up, cutting off what I'm sure would have been a load of time-consuming questions from Wallace.

"He says that the police interviewed him and Randolph at the office and Becca at their home this morning," she said. "Also that he was in the bathroom."

"Ah . . . Can't imagine why he didn't mention that the first time around," I quipped.

"Hrrrmmm."

"What do you mean 'hrrrrmmm'?" I asked. "What's wrong with him visiting the can?"

"He says it was the second-floor bathroom."

It took me a second, then it clicked. I shuffled through the pages until I found the right interview.

"Conroy was 'indisposed' in the upstairs bathroom from the séance through the fire. Pretty sure he didn't make up that little nugget."

That meant Wallace had just lied. But why?

"He couldn't have done it," I protested. "He's the one who hired us. That's his personal cash in the safe."

"People do many strange things for even stranger reasons," said the genius behind the desk. "If you recall, he told us that first day that I had been suggested by the board. Perhaps strongly suggested. Perhaps over Wallace's objections."

I tried to imagine that prim pigeon of a man bludgeoning Abigail Collins but came up blank. Still, there was his reaction when I announced Belestrade's death. Maybe the mystery ingredient had been guilt.

We spent another few hours on it, but nothing else leaped out. At six o'clock I excused myself and went upstairs to change.

For this second time out with Becca, I leaned toward comfort, passing an iron over some pleated trousers and buffing my brown oxfords. However, I did opt for my sheerest blouse, a silk number in pale green that Mrs. Campbell referred to as "a scandal waiting to happen."

I tried to hammer my red curls into something closer to Carole Lombard than Harpo Marx but eventually gave it up for lost. I slipped a peacoat over my silk scandal before telling Ms. P that I'd be back but didn't know when.

"Be careful," she said.

I turned, surprised. She was still at her desk, surrounded by precarious towers of paper. "Worried mother" wasn't her usual manner, but I guess with one woman bludgeoned and another with two bullets in her, it wasn't unreasonable to be a little concerned.

"Don't worry," I told her. "Where I'm going, I'll practically be at home."

I gave a little curtsy and walked out into the night.

CHAPTER 26

The woman plummeted through empty air as the ground reached up to meet her. The crowd gasped. Becca held her hands over her mouth, eyes wide. A man swooped in out of nowhere, his hands clasping tight around the woman's wrists. The swing continued in its arc, the man's legs wrapped tight around its bar as he held fast to the woman dangling beneath him.

The crowd at the Garden erupted in cheers, Becca and myself included, as the husband-and-wife team arrived safely on a platform four stories above our heads.

After the aerialists came the lions, and after them a trick horse rider who galloped a pair of white stallions full speed as she did flips, rode backward, and leapt between the animals with ease.

Darning Brothers wasn't the biggest circus going, but they were impressive enough to draw a hearty Friday night crowd to Madison Square Garden.

"So this was your life before detective work?" Becca asked as they led the horses off and replaced them with a group of clowns riding a twenty-foot tricycle.

When it came to her wardrobe, she'd opted for capricious coed—black A-line skirt over white stockings and a red pullover tight enough it made imagination obsolete.

"H and H was rinky-dink compared to this," I told her. "We

were plenty good for what we were, but that was mostly the
county cornfield circuit. When we came to the city, we played
Long Island or set up in an empty lot in Brooklyn. We made
half our nut on midway games and rides. Put us in here, we'd
have been a joke."

However, Darning Brothers didn't have a sideshow, which
I held against it. No Human Blockhead, no Tattooed Woman,
no sword-swallowers and fire-eaters. Just big-top razzle-dazzle.

Becca plucked a piece of cotton candy from the cone in my
hand. "I'd still have paid my two bits to see you in rhinestones."
Her tongue lapped the pink sugar into her mouth.

With great difficulty, I turned my eyes back to the center
ring.

The clowns wheeled off to laughter and applause, and the
aerialists returned—this time the whole family, a dozen strong.
They waved to the crowd as they climbed the ladders. With an
ominous roll of drums, the net was lowered to the ground and
pulled away. The crowd watched as the first flier leaped, then
three. Soon the full dozen men and women in red were flying
across the empty air in defiance of death and gravity.

I glanced over at Becca, who was rapt, staring up at the fli-
ers with wide eyes. I could see the pulse in her neck throbbing
with fear or excitement or both.

No one fell.

Everyone cheered.

Becca slipped her hand into mine and squeezed.

We had the cab drop us off ten blocks south of her house.
We wanted the stroll. As we walked, I told her more about my
unlikely education at Hart and Halloway.

"Do you miss it?" she asked.

"Some of it. I miss the people. I miss the travel. Or at least I miss some of the people and some of the travel."

I didn't miss living hand-to-mouth, struggling to make our nut at every town. Or the parade of red-faced church deacons who beat a Bible with one hand and squeezed my ass with the other.

I didn't say any of that. It was too nice an evening.

"It sounds wonderful, the way you grew up," Becca said as we crossed a vacant intersection.

"I must not have mentioned shoveling the tiger cages."

"You had a whole circus family who loved you for who you are," she said. "It's worth shoveling a little shit."

I was about to make a quip about tigers not doing anything in moderation, but I curbed myself. Her head wasn't in a place for jokes.

"And look how your life ended up," she continued. "Doing good. Helping people. A real detective."

The laugh came out before I could stop it.

"What's so funny?"

"You might be the one person aside from my boss who thinks of me as a real detective," I said. "Pretty sure most people think of me as a sidekick at best. A wannabe at worst."

She stopped in the middle of the sidewalk and turned to me. "Is that how you feel about yourself?"

I shrugged, wishing I hadn't said anything. "I don't know. Sometimes."

She arched a perfect swoop of eyebrow.

"Okay, maybe a lot of the time," I admitted. "Standing next to Ms. Pentecost, it's hard not to feel like I'm just playing a part. A little girl trying to learn her lines."

She took both my hands in hers. I looked up and down the street. It was late, and there was no one in sight.

"I never thought you were anything but the real deal," she said. Her mouth curved into a wicked little grin and she added, "And I definitely don't think of you as a little girl."

She started up the block again but kept one of my hands in hers. We walked like that the rest of the way.

As we approached her house, I kept an eye out. I was curious if the police still had them under surveillance. Sure enough, I caught the shadow of a man stepping deeper into an alley farther down the block. I guess there was overtime to go around in the NYPD. I gently shook Becca's hand loose.

We stopped in front of her door. It was only ten and light still shone bright from the windows.

"You know," she said, "I still have those records."

"Kind of late to be playing jazz, don't you think?"

She reached out and brushed a red curl away from my forehead.

"We don't need to play jazz," she whispered.

I felt her long fingers idly play with the bottom buttons of my blouse. Simple things like breathing and thinking suddenly became very difficult.

One button came undone.

Then a second.

A third.

A sudden gust of wind came roaring down the street, shaking snow off the stone eaves and pressing ice cubes against my bared stomach.

In a flash I could think again. While Ms. Pentecost might say things like "use your best judgment," I didn't think that leeway stretched as far as hopping into bed with the goddaughter of a paying client.

"Sorry," I said, gently pushing her hands away and rebuttoning my blouse. "Maybe once this is all wrapped up."

Her face fell. She immediately tried to jack it back up. "Tonight was the most fun I've had in ages."

"Me too," I said. I wasn't lying.

Then, because I'm only human, I pushed her into the shadow of the doorway, out of sight of peepers and policemen, and kissed her.

When I came up for air and watched Becca disappear inside her house, I was flying higher than that family of daredevils.

I turned on my heel and started south again to where I could find a cab. I was nearing the end of the block when I caught a movement out of the corner of my eye. I was turning into it when the punch hit me square on the left side of my head.

I stumbled into the brick wall of a house. By the time the second punch came, I had my hands up. What would have been a cross to my nose hit my left wrist. Pain exploded down my arm. I got off a weak jab, then a solid cross that landed squarely on the man's face, which was covered by a sheer stocking mask.

He grunted and I heard something crack. I didn't know if it was his nose or my fingers.

He came in toward me. I reached into my jacket for my gun, remembering too late that my pistol had been confiscated. I tried to retreat but forgot there was a wall behind me. My head wasn't working right. He let a shot fly into my kidneys.

I crumpled forward, then snapped back up, arm bent, elbow aiming for his chin. I missed by a mile. Another shot to the stomach and I went down.

What I tell my students in the basement is to run if you can, find a weapon if you can't, and if worse comes to worst, protect your head.

I curled into a ball on the ground, arms wrapped around my head, as he kicked me—once, then twice. A third kick got through my arms and connected square with the side of my face. I tried to yell for help, but I couldn't get air into my lungs. A wave of sickening blackness advanced from the edges.

I looked up to see the man looming over me, a hulking monster in the dark. Somewhere I heard footsteps running and somebody crying out for the police. The man pulled back his foot for another kick.

Then darkness swooped in and swallowed me whole.

CHAPTER 27

I woke to white walls and starched sheets and the unmistakable smell of a hospital—that horrible mix of sterile and sick. Sunlight streamed through a narrow window. A nurse was adjusting something at the foot of my bed.

There was no pain, which surprised me. To be honest, I wasn't feeling much of anything.

"Back with us, sweetheart?" the nurse asked, coming to the head of the bed and leaning over me. "She'll be pleased."

The nurse threw a nod over her shoulder. The "she" in question was asleep in a chair in the corner. I know she was asleep because the great lady detective's head was propped back against the wall and she was not-so-softly snoring.

"She's been on the doctors something fierce."

"How long?" I asked. Or tried to. What came out was more a croak than a question, but she got the gist.

"You came in Friday night. It's Sunday morning."

A whole day unconscious? That wasn't good. Then it started to come back to me—flashes of lucidity. A careening ambulance ride. Being propped up for X-rays. Groaning in pain as cold, gloved hands prodded my ribs.

As the nurse took my vitals, I took inventory. My left wrist was in a cast. Two fingers of my right hand were splinted. I felt stiff bandages around my rib cage and my head felt enormous—like an overstuffed pillow. I lifted a hand to my face, but the nurse stopped me.

"Don't do that," she said, gingerly forcing my hand back to the bed. "Everything will be tender for a while."

"Numb," I croaked.

The nurse nodded. "We gave you some pretty strong stuff so that you could rest," she said. "It'll wear off after a bit. You'll feel plenty then."

"Will?" Ms. P was looking at me from her chair, eyes wide and bright.

"Present . . . and accounted for."

"I'll leave you two alone," the nurse said. "The doctor should be back in a bit to check on you. He'll want to check on you, too, Ms. Pentecost." She leveled a look at my boss before continuing her rounds.

I tried to say, "Why does he need to check on you?" but my tongue wasn't up to the challenge. Ms. P stood and walked carefully to my bed. Her legs were unsteady and her hands were shaking. That was all the answer I needed.

She took a glass of water from my bedside table and maneuvered a straw into my mouth. I took a few long sips.

"Tall. Strong. Dark clothes. Work boots. Stocking over his face," I said. "Waiting for us."

Ms. Pentecost held up a hand but I kept going.

"I got a good one to his face. Think I did some damage. He should show it."

"You don't have to worry about that right now."

"Get the description to . . . to the cops. Get them looking."

"They are looking," she assured me. "Ms. Collins gave the police the man's description."

Had Becca been attacked, too? I thought I'd seen her go inside her house, but the drugs were making everything dim and foggy. My confusion must have showed.

"Ms. Collins came back outside and saw the man standing over you," Ms. Pentecost explained. "She called for help. That's likely the reason the attack ended when it did."

I remembered the footsteps and someone yelling for the police. So things could have been worse if not for Becca. I owed her another kiss. Once I could feel my lips again.

I noticed for the first time that my boss was wearing the same outfit I'd last seen her in.

"Have you been here the whole time?" I asked.

"I did not want to rely on the doctors or the police to keep me abreast by phone," she said. "That chair in the corner is not as uncomfortable as it appears."

I gave her a look. Or I tried to. I was having difficulty knowing what my face was doing. She apparently got the hint.

"I had an incident in the downstairs cafeteria," she said, managing to look a little sheepish. "I was trying to balance a tray and my cane at the same time and I fell. It alarmed some of the doctors more than it should."

I didn't have the strength for a lecture. The nurse—I'd need to get her name—seemed capable enough. I figured she had it in her to get my employer to sit still for a checkup.

Ms. P was saying something about decent food and a good night's sleep taking care of it, but her words were wobbly in my ear. With no warning, sleep dragged me back under.

When I woke, it was late afternoon. A different nurse told me that Ms. Pentecost had run home for a change of clothes and would be back later.

My head felt clearer, which I chalked up to the drugs starting to wear off. With that came the pain, and boy, was there plenty. Everything ached, from my curls to my toes, some of it with an intensity I'd never experienced before. It even hurt to breathe, which I was informed by the nurse was due to two cracked ribs.

"Great," I groaned. "I've been meaning to give up breathing."

I was awake half an hour before a doctor who looked about two weeks my senior came to check on me. He gave me the full tally.

"You've got a broken wrist, two dislocated fingers, two cracked ribs, a bad laceration on your face that we stitched up, and a ruptured eardrum," he said with the prescribed amount of somberness.

The eardrum explained why I was missing every fourth word.

"You know, it's a miracle you don't have a skull fracture. You were lucky. You should be more careful," he said.

He let me know I'd be in the hospital for a few days and that he'd get me on a regular dose of morphine. I told him I'd settle for some low-octane stuff. I wanted to keep my head clear.

"I think you're going to regret that," he said. "Probably around two in the morning when you're trying to sleep. When you change your mind, ring a nurse."

After he left, I thought about what he'd said. That I "should be more careful." Like it was my fault I'd ended up there.

Then I started thinking that maybe it *was* my fault. Carrying on with Becca like I had. A public street on the Upper East Side isn't exactly an after-hours club. Then I started to get angry at myself for thinking like that. And at the doctor. And at the guy who beat me up.

By the time Ms. Pentecost got back, dressed in her going-to-war grays, I was ready to pick a fight with the world.

"Any word from the police?" I asked.

"Nothing yet. The lieutenant told me they are pursuing leads."

"Lazenby's got a hand in it?"

"He's taken over the investigation," she said, settling down in the corner chair.

Lazenby must have thought my attack had something to do with the murders. But if it was all the same person, why didn't he just shoot me? Why leave me alive when a bullet could have done the job quicker, easier, and a lot more permanently?

The idea sent a shiver through me. Even my goose bumps hurt.

"Can you lend me your cane?" I asked. "I want to make a trip to the bathroom and take a look at the damage."

She hesitated. "Perhaps it would be best to wait for some of the swelling to go down."

That told me more than any mirror ever could, but I needed to see for myself.

"I also need to visit the bathroom for another of its intended uses," I lied. "I know this is a full-service hospital, but I don't want to impose that far."

I tried to smile, but that hurt, too.

Instead of her cane, Ms. P lent me her arm. My legs seemed to be working all right. Nothing in my lower half was broken and the drugs had worn off. I shut the bathroom door and looked in the mirror.

I'll spare you the details. Needless to say, it was not pretty and wouldn't be for quite some time. The swelling and bruises would fade, but the jagged cut across my cheek would leave a scar. It cut right through my thickest cloud of freckles.

I cried. Which hurt, but not as much as smiling.

When I opened the door, Ms. Pentecost was standing where I'd left her. She wrapped her arms around me and squeezed. It hurt my ribs, but I didn't complain.

CHAPTER 28

I was in the hospital a total of three days and four very sleepless nights. The smug young doctor had been right. Morphine in the wee hours would have been nice, but I held out and managed a couple hours every night.

Four notable incidents occurred while I was stuck in my starched white prison. The first was that Becca visited me. She cried. I managed not to. Her presence made me strangely uncomfortable.

At first I thought it was how I looked. There she was, tear streaked but still ready for the cover of *Vogue*. While I resembled something you'd see at a creature feature matinee.

When I caught myself looking at the open door for the fifth time in a minute, I realized what was really wrong. Part of me was worried the masked man would come in to finish the job.

Lazenby had assigned an officer to patrol my floor, so my fear was irrational. Still, I couldn't shake it.

I put a pin in the psychoanalysis and asked Becca as politely as possible not to visit me at the hospital again. I didn't want her to see me like that. She said she understood, and maybe she really did.

The second notable incident was a visit from Lazenby himself, who arrived with a bag of paperback detective novels.

"I was here three weeks when I was shot. You can go out of

your mind without a good book. Though I wouldn't call any of these good," he said.

I let the literary criticism slide and thanked him. Then we got down to the real reason for his visit—to get the events of Friday evening from my own lips. I gave him the lot, including a couple of details that hadn't registered when the hits were coming, and a few ideas on where he could start. He didn't give me false hope, but he didn't brush me off, either. To his credit, there was none of the blame and shame the doctor had snuck in.

I took the opportunity to ask how the police were faring with the Collins case.

"Even laid up, you don't quit."

"Like you said—lot of time here to keep a person's brain going," I said. "Any new leads?"

"Nothing you need to worry about," he said. "Stick to your Raymond Chandlers and let the police worry about the real criminals. We do manage to get one occasionally."

With that as his exit line, the policeman left.

Something about our chat bugged me. I replayed the exchange and eventually realized what was off. He was calm. There was none of the usual teeth-grinding. He had something.

I didn't have to wait long to find out what.

Later that afternoon, a nurse came in to change my dressing and said, "You work for Lillian Pentecost, don't you? I just heard on the radio they arrested somebody in that Collins murder."

She didn't know who. All the radio had said was that "an arrest had been made in relation to." There wasn't a private phone in my room, so I slipped on a robe and made my way down to the basement cafeteria, where there was a pay phone.

It took ten minutes and three tries to get through to the office.

"What's this about somebody getting pinched for the Collins case?" I demanded as soon as Ms. P got on the line.

"I just got off the phone with Randolph Collins," she said. "Lazenby arrived at the Collins Steelworks offices around noon and arrested Harrison Wallace."

"For murder?"

"Embezzlement," Ms. P declared. "Apparently they have considerable evidence that Mr. Wallace has been siphoning money out of the company. Their theory is that Mrs. Collins discovered the crime and Wallace killed her so she wouldn't talk."

That threw me hard. Wallace seemed so vanilla. I had as difficult a time imagining him engaged in thievery as I did imagining him killing Abigail Collins.

"How sure are they about the money angle?"

I needn't have asked the question. Lazenby wasn't going to make a move like this in such a high-profile case unless he had everything crossed and dotted.

"The lieutenant sounded very confident about the embezzlement," my boss said. "He disclosed that it has been going on for at least a year. At least two hundred thousand dollars over that time. Though they are still tracking where all of the money ended up."

Two hundred grand wasn't much considering Collins Steelworks had annual profits in the eight-digit range. But it wasn't chump change. The New York cops' money men had cut their teeth tracking mob-laundered dough and knew their stuff. It didn't look good for Wallace. I wondered whether the stack of bills in our safe was part of the lot.

"Anything else to tell?" I asked. "What about Belestrade? How does she figure into it?"

According to Ms. P, Lazenby hadn't let anything slip on that angle, but it wasn't hard to connect the dots. Abigail had told her pet clairvoyant what she'd found out and somehow Belestrade had let it slip to Wallace. Maybe she'd tried her old blackmail trick with him.

"What do we do now?" I asked.

"You recover," Ms. P said. "I attempt to get in to see Mr. Wallace. His bail hearing is being delayed since a separate murder charge is expected."

First-degree murder and hidden cash would mean big-time flight risk, which would mean the DA would contest bail.

I signed off and let my boss do her job. I made a few more calls to some friends at the *Times* and the *Mirror* but they had more questions than answers. Eventually I gave up and went back to my room. I briefly entertained checking myself out against doctor's orders but realized that if I showed up back at the townhouse, I'd be press-ganged right back to the hospital.

I'd rarely felt quite so useless.

The last notable thing to happen came on Tuesday morning. I was due to head home and had everything packed and ready to go, but Ms. P was late in arriving. I was left sitting in the corner chair, my clothes and books and a paper bag filled with pills packed away in a small suitcase.

As far as I knew, Wallace was still locked up. Ms. P hadn't gotten in to see him. The murder charge was still looming.

When my boss finally walked in, she looked as close to flustered as she gets. Her braids had suffered some sort of structural collapse and were sitting lopsided on her head.

"I'm sorry," she said, perching on the bed and tending to her hair. "We were on our way out when we received a call. It was Mr. Wallace's personal attorney."

"Let me guess—he wants everything we have on the Collins killing and he wants it yesterday."

"No," she said with a scowl. "He wanted to thank me for my efforts to date and told me that my services will no longer be required."

We had been fired from the Collins case.

CHAPTER 29

What followed were three of the more frustrating days I've ever slogged through. As expected, the murder charge came down for Wallace on Tuesday night. Unexpectedly, it was for Belestrade, not Abigail Collins. Apparently, some intrepid officer had found the murder weapon in a storm drain a few blocks from Belestrade's place. It was a Colt .38 automatic registered to Harrison Wallace.

We learned all this along with the rest of the city in the Wednesday morning papers. No one was returning our calls. Not Lazenby, not Wallace's attorney, and not the Collins family. The one time I got through to somebody it was Sanford, who said that the household "did not wish to speak to anyone at this difficult time."

I was tempted to go over in person and toss stones at Becca's window until she opened up, but that would have been difficult. The doctors had prescribed bed rest for my ribs. While Ms. Pentecost could not legally confine me to bed, she could at least make it difficult for me to wander far.

The sedan was off-limits, and Mrs. Campbell had stepped into the role of warden. Any time I went for the door, she'd intercept me.

"Where do you think you're going?" she bellowed. "Ms. Pentecost gave you a job and a bed and a roof and the least you can do is take care of yourself like she asked you, and if you believe I'm above twisting your arm and marching you upstairs to bed, you've got another think coming."

And more along that line.

So I stayed put and healed and ate my weight in homemade sausage. I spent hours in the basement throwing knives into a block of wood, first with my right hand and its two splinted fingers, then with my left with its broken wrist.

The first day I was lucky to come within two feet of the target. By the second day, I was still lacking power, but my accuracy wasn't too bad. With each throw I pictured my attacker's masked face.

Sleep came hard. I kept running through the facts of the case over and over again. When I finally got my mind to quiet down, my wrist or my ribs or my head started screaming at me. The doctors had given me painkillers. I tried them once and they gave me nightmares. Hulking shadows lunged at me from dark corners.

I opted for five good hours instead of eight dream-plagued ones.

Apparently Wallace's lawyer was tired of getting a dozen calls a day from us. On Thursday, we received a certified letter in the mail signed by Wallace officially relieving us of our duties. This was followed up by a call from Lazenby, who said, in no quibbling terms, that we no longer had a client or a case and therefore had no reason to stick our noses into the Collins business.

This echoed what we were reading in the papers. The *Journal* had a piece about how Wallace and Collins Steelworks were distancing themselves from each other, with both the company and Wallace's attorney stating that he had been a caretaker CEO and that the business remained in the hands of the family. Various Wall Street know-it-alls were quoted as saying this tactic would help ensure the company would be able to re-up its military contracts.

Apparently you had to do a lot worse than embezzlement and murder to turn off the U.S. government.

Speaking of which, there was no statement from Wallace contesting the allegations of embezzlement or murder. From where we were sitting, it looked like he was going to roll over and play dead for the prosecution.

After the call from Lazenby, Ms. P leaned back in her chair and closed her eyes. After a few minutes of silence, I broke it.

"If we can get to Becca or maybe even Randolph I bet we could get them to hire us on. We don't even need to charge them, since we have Wallace's retainer. Until they tag Wallace with Abigail Collins's murder, the case is still open."

She opened her eyes. They were red-veined and carrying heavier luggage than usual.

"Wallace's guilt in both murders is certainly the intimation," she said, "whether or not the police will ever have enough evidence to charge him with Abigail's."

"Whether Wallace did it or not, if we can get signed back on, at least we can help put the pieces together," I argued. "Let me try to get to Becca again. If I go over there, I'm sure—"

"No!" she snapped. "You will not approach Miss Collins. You will do no more work on the Collins business. Our role in the affair is done. We have other cases to attend to."

I was stunned. I'd seen my employer bend every rule and regulation on the books in the interest of truth. It'd be like walking away from a puzzle with half a dozen pieces missing.

"I don't buy it," I said. "You're not going to drop this. Two murders—including a woman you've been tracking for years. And you let it go just like that?"

She shrugged. "I've warned you before about becoming emotionally involved in the work."

"Bullshit!" I jumped out of my chair. "Emotionally involved? This from the woman who spends whole days and nights poring over her files, desperate because she's afraid someone's going to get away with something. You make yourself sick doing it. And you're telling me not to get emotional?"

I realized I was yelling, but I couldn't stop myself. Mrs. Campbell appeared in the doorway, but Ms. P waved her off.

"You can't tell me this was just another case. Belestrade was personal for you. You know it was. I know it was. Don't pretend Jonathan Markel was just another source. Or that . . . that . . ."

I ran out of steam. Which was well enough. Any farther and I would have crossed a line, and I couldn't see what was waiting on the other side.

I fell back into my chair, breathing hard, ribs aching. It was a while before she spoke. Her response came slow and measured, like she was tiptoeing through a minefield.

"My work does not make me sick. My passion for the job does not make me sick. The multiple sclerosis makes me sick," she declared. "If I push myself farther than I should, it is because I know I will not be able to do this work forever. That is why I value your safety, physical and emotional. So that you may pick up the load when I am no longer able to lift it."

It was the first time she'd ever come right out and said it. I wasn't just her assistant. Someday, I'd be her replacement.

The anger drained out of me like so much venom.

"You have been grievously injured," she continued. "I am your employer and not your mother and I cannot force you into any course you do not wish to run. But as your employer, and hopefully your friend, I wish you would put this case aside and take time to heal."

Looking into her eyes, I wondered how I could have ever mistaken them for cold. I couldn't think of anything else to say. I was so tired. The words wouldn't come. I nodded. I excused myself and went up to my room to lie down.

But don't think I didn't clock the fact she'd never answered my question about whether she was really done with the Collins case.

CHAPTER 30

I woke the next day to find Ms. Pentecost gone.

"She hired a driver—one of the services she used before you came along," Mrs. Campbell told me over breakfast. "She had her suitcase—the smaller one—and she said she'd be gone at least one night but no more than three. Said she'd call tonight so we know she arrived safe."

"Arrive safe where?" I asked.

"She didn't say."

Ms. P had gone off by herself in the past on one or another of her pet cases, but she'd always given me a general idea of where she was headed. To keep mum about her destination meant only one thing: It had to do with the Collins case and she didn't want me chasing her.

I was equal parts angry and worried. Angry for the obvious reasons. Worried because I got that way whenever she went off on her own. What would she do if she had a bad day? I looked around her bedroom and the office and was comforted to see that at least she'd remembered to take her cane with her.

I sat down at my desk and tried to work. There were notes from previous investigations that needed filing, contact lists that needed updating, plenty to do. After an hour, all I'd managed was to turn one pile of paper into five smaller piles. I was actually considering getting out the Murphy's and polishing my desk when the phone rang.

"Thank Christ," I muttered, sure it was Ms. P. Instead, I was greeted by a panicked Olivia Waterhouse.

"Is what they're saying true?" she asked. "Was Ariel black-mailing people?"

Once Wallace had been charged with Belestrade's murder, everything had begun spilling out. The papers were there wait-ing with cupped hands. They hadn't gotten the exact details of what went down at the Collinses' Halloween party, but they had the gist. The more enterprising reporters had tracked down previous clients of Belestrade and they, or their spouses, were starting to talk. Among the five piles on my desk were several requests from reporters asking for comment. I'd have to feed them something eventually, but I still wasn't up for chatting.

Since Dr. Waterhouse had helped us get the background on Belestrade, I figured I owed her the bad news.

"I'm afraid so, Professor. At least, that's how it's shaping up."

"That's awful!" she exclaimed. "That she would use her tal-ents to hurt people in that way."

I was tempted to ask her why she was so surprised. Surely someone who would lie about being able to speak with the dearly departed would be willing to take it a step farther. In some ways, coming right out and blackmailing her clients made Belestrade a more honest specimen than her peers.

I kept all that to myself.

"Yeah, it's a big shock to everyone," I lied.

"I've had to ask my publisher to hold off sending my book to press. I can't have a whole chapter on Ariel and *not* mention this. I'd be laughed at."

"Was your publisher ticked?"

"On the contrary. He said that a chapter on Belestrade that includes her murder at the hands of . . . of one of her victims . . . Well . . ." She trailed off. I could imagine her removing her glasses, squinting, putting them back on.

"Adding her murder would sell a lot more copies?" I offered.

"Essentially," she said. "I find it grotesque. This is an academic book, not a pulp magazine."

I didn't argue, but not because I agreed. Academics, in my experience, enjoyed blood and intrigue as much as the great unwashed. Also, while Waterhouse might have found it grotesque, she made no mention of not complying.

I figured since I had her on the line, I might as well do a little digging.

"Did you have any idea this was going on?" I asked.

"The blackmail? No. None," Waterhouse said. "I thought the worst that was happening was that—well, that she was like the rest of them. Reading her clients and giving them what they wanted."

"When you sat in on those séances at her office, you never saw anything out of the ordinary? Any notion that she was recording people so she could blackmail them?"

"Is *that* what she was doing?"

The details about the recordings hadn't made it into the papers.

"That's what it looks like," I said. "She'd probably get them on tape admitting something about themselves or a loved one, then use it to pry some cash loose later."

There was silence on the other end of the phone.

"Doc? You still there?"

"Yes, I'm here," she said in a near whisper.

"Did you have any clue?"

"I . . . I knew about the recording."

"Really?"

"I saw her retrieve the tape. The recorder was in a false panel in a bookshelf," Waterhouse said. "She told me it was so she had a record of what she said when she was channeling."

"You didn't find that suspicious?" I asked.

"I didn't at the time, no."

Which meant she bought that Belestrade wasn't aware of what she was saying when she was "channeling." I started to suspect that not only was Waterhouse a little smitten with the late clairvoyant, but was a secret believer, as well.

Then I had another thought.

"What did she do with that tape?" I asked.

"I don't know," Waterhouse said. "She went upstairs. Then I heard this rumbling sound."

"Rumbling?"

"I thought it might be a train going by, but there's no train near there."

I made a note of that for later.

"Is that helpful?" the professor asked.

"Maybe," I said. "I'll pass it on to the police. Ms. Pentecost is officially done with the case."

"Oh. So, this man they have in jail. She thinks he did it?"

"She's keeping her options open," I said.

"What should I do about my book?" she pleaded. "I can't wait until a trial. That could take months."

Considering how little resistance Wallace was putting up, I didn't know if a trial would take all that long.

"Borrow a trick from the newspapers and use the word 'alleged' a lot," I suggested. "Besides, the juicy stuff is what Belestrade was up to. Not who did her in."

She thanked me and said she'd be sure to send a copy over whenever her book hit the shelves.

No sooner had I hung up the phone than there was a familiar knock at the door. I opened it to find Lazenby's storm-cloud face.

"I'm afraid you're out of luck," I said. "The lady of the house has gone adventuring and I know not where."

"That's all right. It's you I've come for."

I was about to yell for Mrs. Campbell to call the lawyer when he added, "We got him."

I didn't have to ask who. I rode with Lazenby across the bridge to a station house south of Midtown. Once there, he escorted me to one of its less hospitable interrogation rooms.

He pounded on the door and yelled, "Turn the light on him!"

A voice called from inside, "It's on!"

Lazenby opened the door.

Sitting on a metal chair, a handheld interrogation light shining into his eyes, was John Meredith.

He had a bandage on his nose that looked a few days old. Apparently that right cross had broken more than my fingers. I couldn't take credit for the rest of it, though. His lip was busted in two places, one eye was swollen shut, and he was listing in his chair, like it hurt to sit straight.

Lazenby nodded to his sergeant, who shut the door again.

"He didn't come easy," he said, reading my mind.

"Is he talking?"

"He didn't at first. So we started tallying up the evidence: his nose, the blood on his boots, the metal splinters."

The splinters were my find. When I was in the hospital, my young smug doctor mentioned that he'd tweezed a number of sharp metal filings from my face where my attacker's boot had hit me. I'd had to pry identical splinters from the soles of my shoes after my visit to Collins Steelworks.

That made it a coin flip between Meredith and Randolph Collins, or the former working on instructions from the latter, or a third-party factory employee on instructions from someone. I'd told Lazenby about my deductions when he visited me in the hospital.

"That's not a lot of evidence," I noted. "And it's all circumstantial."

"True," Lazenby said, a smile shaping under his beard. "Then I told him about our witness."

"Witness?"

"The little old lady who was looking out her window just in time to see Meredith slip on the stocking mask. Sweet old bird. Everybody's favorite grandma. Told him she'd be a wonder on the stand, nail the coffin down on attempted murder. He broke and said he found out about your . . . appointment . . . with Rebecca from her brother."

"Did Randolph sic him on me?" I asked.

Lazenby shook his head. "Not according to Meredith. He says he did this on his own. Guess he has a thing for the girl."

I thought about how Meredith had talked about Becca during our interview. I'd pegged him as having the hots for her. Seeing her stepping out with me must have sent him over the edge.

"Little old lady?" I asked. "Were you telling a fib?"

Lazenby shrugged and did his best at looking innocent. "I'll talk to the DA. Make sure he pushes hard for attempted murder, then cut a deal for aggravated assault. Save the city the money of a trial."

Between the lines: I wouldn't have to parade my and Becca's private life in front of a jury and roll the dice they didn't vote not guilty by reason of I was asking for it.

We shared a look, and I nodded a thank-you.

I turned down the offer of a ride home, made my way out of the station, and began walking. Winter had arrived in force the last week, and the wind cut through my coat like a knife. At least it took my mind off my ribs and arms and face.

And everything else.

I took a meandering way home, stopping at my favorite corner diner for a hot turkey sandwich I barely touched and a bookstore where I wandered up and down the aisles for the better part of an hour.

I found myself going down the romance aisle for the fifth time and realized I was just putting off going back to the empty office. I didn't want to face my uselessness and the waiting.

As soon as I recognized that, I high-stepped it out of the store, flagged down a cab, and was back at the office in fifteen minutes.

Mrs. Campbell came out of the kitchen, arms covered in flour up to the elbows.

"You were gone so long, I was worried."

"I was with the police. How much trouble could I get into?"

She gave me a look that said "plenty."

"I'm making raisin nut bread. I'll be at it a while. There are sandwich fixings in the icebox if you're hungry," she said. "And a package was delivered for you. I put it on your desk."

She returned to her kneading and I went to my desk to find a thick, flat envelope from Liberty Developing. Inside were two dozen snaps taken during the Collinses' Halloween bash.

As promised, most were off-kilter, out of focus, or both. But there were a few good ones in the lot.

There was Wallace chatting it up with a flock of executives, all looking a little sloshed. Abigail Collins, in a white gown and mask, posed on the stairs, no clue she was living out her last hour. There was Dr. Waterhouse, looking uncomfortable and out of place. And there was Meredith, smiling, laughing at something.

Becca and Randolph were caught candidly in the study in the minutes prior to Belestrade's show: Randolph in a tailored tux, Becca in a hip-hugging black number that was accented with elbow-length white gloves and a sequined cape. Both sported matching Harlequin masks.

Even half-masked and in celluloid, her face made my heart flutter. I thought about calling her. Then had second thoughts. And third and fourth and so on.

Eventually I shoved the photos back into their envelope and went to put them in a drawer of Ms. Pentecost's desk. As I did, I noticed a yellow legal pad tucked inside. On it was an address scribbled in my boss's chicken scratch.

Orly Crouch

#213 Rte 5 (Old Wallace Drive)

Cockerville, NY

That answered that. Mrs. Bettyanne Casey-Hutts had come through. Ms. Pentecost was out hunting down Abigail Collins, née Pratt, née Crouch's past.

Why for? I didn't know. But at least I had a sense of where she was. A weight lifted from my heart.

When she called that night, I answered the phone with "How's Nowhere, New York? Did you find a place to stay in Cockerville or are you commuting from Albany?"

"I am staying at the Driftwood Inn, a small rooming house in Prattsville. Which as you know is not so far from Cockerville."

"You're doing a fine job of hiding your admiration for my detective skills, but I'm sure they're present," I quipped.

"I assume you found someone at the car service who could be bribed for information."

I think I've mentioned how I sometimes can't stand my boss.

"Have you talked to Orly Crouch yet?" I asked, changing the subject.

"He would not open his door. I will try again tomorrow."

"Why?" I asked. "We have been discharged, remember? And as avenues of investigation go, this one seems the least scenic."

"You said it yourself. I don't like coincidences."

That was all she'd expound on that.

I filled her in on Meredith's arrest. She seemed pleased but not surprised.

"You noted in your report that you felt uneasy in his presence," she said. "Your instincts, especially around people with the potential for violence, are not to be dismissed."

I asked if she thought she'd be home tomorrow. She said she didn't know. If she struck out with Orly Crouch, she'd probably be back in the office by early evening. I wished her luck, and reminded her to get some shuteye and eat her Wheaties.

"You do realize I survived for a number of years without your assistance," she said.

"I know. It's a miracle."

I hung up before she could get in the last word.

CHAPTER 31

The Saturday morning paper delivered another bombshell.

MURDER SUSPECT HAS TUMOR, NOT EXPECTED TO LAST UNTIL TRIAL

Wallace had collapsed in his cell the day before. A specialist had been called in. The verdict was stomach cancer—something Wallace had apparently known for months. I'd noticed how ragged he'd looked but had chalked it up to stress.

A sidebar noted that the police had finally released Abigail Collins's body and that the funeral would be held on Monday. Hiram would free up a slab, and the Collins family could start putting all this behind them.

Though I knew they wouldn't. Not with dear Uncle Harry slowly dying in a cell.

I put the paper on my desk and looked outside to a world smothered in white. There were three inches on the ground and it was still coming down strong. On the radio, the announcer said we could expect as much as two feet by Sunday. I started lowering the odds of Ms. P getting home that night.

Our usual Saturday morning open house had been canceled and all the chores that needed doing had been done. I was left to sit in my chair and stare at the picture above Ms. Pentecost's desk. For the thousandth time I wondered who the girl in the blue dress was. What was she doing beneath that lone yellow tree in the middle of nowhere?

When the phone rang, I nearly toppled out of my seat.

"Pentecost Investigations, Will Parker speaking."

"Ms. Pentecost. Please, I need Ms. Pentecost." The accent sounded familiar but I couldn't place it.

"I'm sorry, but Ms. Pentecost isn't here at the moment. Can I take a message?"

"Please tell her I need her help. She has to tell him."

"I'm sorry," I said. "Who is this? Tell who what?"

"This is Anna. Anna Nowak." The penny dropped. The hatchet-faced cook who'd given us the lowdown on Belestrade. I hadn't recognized her voice, it was so distorted by panic.

"Ms. Nowak, it's Will Parker. We met last Saturday."

"Yes. Yes, I remember."

"What's the matter?"

"My husband. He comes back," she said. "He finds out I go to Ms. Pentecost. He thinks she pay me. Give me reward for information. I tell him no, but he does not believe me."

"Where is he now?"

"Outside. He will not leave. He will not let me leave. He . . ."

There was the sound of wood splintering. Anna cried out and the line went dead.

I fumbled through the notebooks on my desk until I found the one I'd been using when we interviewed Anna. Inside I found her address.

I picked up the phone and started dialing the number of the Brooklyn precinct, then froze. What were the chances they'd get there quicker than I would? Or even take it seriously enough to send a patrolman? I sure as hell knew there'd be no beat cops out in this weather. And definitely none in Anna Nowak's neighborhood.

I put the phone back in its cradle. Then I stood there, unmoving.

Before the attack, before the hospital, I'd already have been out the door. Doing what my dime-store detective heroes would have done—handling the matter myself.

Now I was a quivering ball of hesitation.

Who was I to pretend I knew what I was doing? That I could make the right call?

Then I thought about the panic in Anna's voice. How scared she'd sounded. And the call she'd made had been to us. Not the police. Us.

I might have been playing at being the hard-boiled hero, but that's who she needed.

I grabbed my coat and hat and was halfway to the door when I had a second thought. I didn't know what I was running into. Better to be a little delayed but prepared.

I ran upstairs to my room, opened my chest of drawers, and pulled out one of my knives from underneath a pile of underclothes. Then I had a third thought and decided to grab a couple other things as well.

One of those things I found in the same drawer. For the other, I ran into the kitchen. I found Mrs. Campbell hunched over the table culling old spices.

"What devil's got ahold a ya?" she asked as I began rummaging through the dry goods cabinet.

"We've got a client in trouble."

"Then call the police."

"They won't do any good. Not in the long run," I said. "Maybe not the short run, either."

I found what I was looking for, shoved it into my pocket, and ran for the door.

"You're supposed to be resting!" she called after me. Or at least that's what I assume she said. I was already down the steps and stumbling through the snow.

Ms. Pentecost had the sedan and the snow had thinned taxis out, so I ran for it. Nowak's tenement building was a good twenty blocks away, but I slimmed that by cutting through a few alleys.

As I plowed through the snow, I tried not to think about how foolish this was. I tried to conjure up the voice of my father. He was a son of a bitch, but he was a son of a bitch who never questioned what he was doing. He just did it, for good or ill.

Twenty minutes after I hung up the phone, I was flying up the five flights to Anna's apartment. It wasn't hard to locate her place. It was the one open door on the entire floor. The frame around its lock was splintered.

Before I stepped in, I took two things out of my pocket. I slipped one into the other, then hid both up my coat sleeve.

Cautiously, I stepped inside. It was a tidy place—kitchen, dining, and living area squeezed into a single room.

Or at least it had been tidy.

The kitchen table had been overturned and shattered dishes littered the floor. What I assumed had been a potted plant was spilled all over the woven rug. A man was leaning against the door to the only other room. He wasn't much taller than me but he was twice as wide. His once-white undershirt strained across an ample gut, and his dungarees had slipped halfway down the crack of his ass.

I stayed well away from him and called out, "Anna, are you in there?"

The man swung about, nearly losing his balance. His face was all red nose and pockmarks.

"Who are you?" he slurred. "Get out. Mind your business."

No accent, unless you consider whiskey an accent. The stuff was coming off him so strong I could have gotten sloshed just standing there.

"I'm Will Parker, an associate of Lillian Pentecost. So I'm guessing this might be my business."

His livery lips curled into a smile.

"You bring the bitch her money?"

"I don't know any bitches, Mr. Nowak. And I don't have any money."

"You're lying," he said, letting out a boozy burp. "That why somebody went at your face? Teaching you not to lie?"

My hands and face went cold. That feeling you get when you know a fight's coming and you can't avoid it.

"You should really go," I told him, making one last attempt to head off what was about to happen.

"My brother told me she went to that Pentecost bitch. Spilled her guts and they put that guy in jail. Don't tell me there wasn't a reward. Rich people die, there's always rewards."

He pointed a meaty fist at me, and I saw why his pants were at half-mast. A leather belt was wrapped around his fingers. The silver of the buckle was stained with blood.

"Sorry, Mr. Nowak. No reward for you," I said, flashing him my very meanest smile. "But if you walk out right now, I might let you keep your front teeth."

He let out a roar and charged blindly. It was exactly what I'd wanted.

I let the wool stocking drop out of my coat sleeve, the can of cranberry sauce inside pulling it tight at the toe. I swung the homemade sap straight up.

It hit Nowak right under the jaw. He kept stumbling forward, but I sidestepped like a matador and sent him crashing into the far wall. He bounced backward, and before he could gain his bearings I swung again. The can slammed into the side of his head with a loud crack.

Nowak went cartwheeling over a chair and landed hard on the floor.

His head was covered in red gore. Had I brained him that hard? Then I realized that both stocking and can had split open. It was cranberry sauce. Mostly.

He stumbled to his feet, wobbled, then spat out a mouthful of blood.

"Leave off if you know what's good for you," I said.

He rushed at me.

I went low, plowed my shoulder into his belly, and used his momentum to flip him over my back. He landed hard on the overturned kitchen table, splintering its legs.

He tried to get up, then collapsed with a snort.

I kept an eye on him as I walked over to the bedroom door and knocked.

"Anna? It's Will Parker. You can come out now."

I heard a rumbling as heavy furniture was pushed away. The door opened and Anna peeked out. Her hatchet of a nose was bloody, though it didn't look broken, and she had the makings of a black eye.

I told her to pack some things, then waited while she threw some clothes into a battered suitcase. When she was finished, I led her into the hallway. As we passed her husband she paused long enough to ptooey into his half-conscious face.

Safe in the hall, I asked her, "Is there someplace you can go?"

"I have friends from church. I can stay with them."

"Good," I told her. "I saw a pay phone outside. Go to that, and I'll join you in a jiff."

Once Anna started downstairs, I went back into the apartment. Her husband was where I'd left him but starting to stir. I pulled my Kalishenko knife from inside my coat, then dropped to my knees on Nowak's heavy stomach.

He screamed as splintered table and broken crockery ground into his back, but he choked off his squeals when I pressed the blade against his throat.

"You know what this is?" I asked.

He tried to nod but came up against the knife's edge. "Yeah," he croaked.

"And you know who my boss is? The Pentecost bitch? You know all about her, right?"

"I know."

"If I tell you something, are you sober enough to remember?"

He said something impolite and I pressed the blade harder. A line of blood formed under the edge.

"Yeah. Yeah, I'll remember," he said.

"Good," I said. Then I asked him if he'd heard of a certain gentleman—the head of a particular fraternal organization who held a lot of sway in the neighborhood.

"I know him."

"Ms. Pentecost and I did him a favor once. Helped solve the murder of a member of his family. He was very grateful. He said if we ever needed anything—anything at all—to let him know."

I brought my mouth right up to his ear for this next part.

"You ever come near Anna again—you even get within shouting distance of her—I will call in that favor," I whispered, pressing the knife good and hard against his neck. "I'll ask him to take care of you. And I will ask him to do it slow."

His eyes were quivering saucers. Sweat and blood were pouring off him.

"You understand?"

He mouthed a silent "Yes."

I moved to get up but stopped.

"I almost forgot."

I brought the heavy hilt of the blade down onto his mouth. His lip split open and his front teeth disappeared down his gullet.

I stood and walked out.

Outside, I found Anna standing next to the phone booth, shivering in the snow. I called her a cab and when the taxi showed, I gave the driver a five and told him to make sure she got in the door.

Then I began the long walk home through the still-falling snow.

My ribs were killing me and I was pretty sure I'd rebroken at least one of my fingers. The adrenaline had run its course and left me cold and sore and shaking.

I felt better than I had in days.

CHAPTER 32

That was incredibly foolish. You should have called the police. You could have been seriously injured. You're *already* seriously injured!"

And so on. This from Ms. Pentecost, who was berating me long-distance from her rented room in Nowhere, New York.

I traced circles on my desk with a splinted finger and waited patiently until she ran out of steam.

"I know," I said. "It was foolish and dangerous and anyone with an ounce of common sense would have rung up the cops."

I heard her take a breath to respond, but I barreled over her.

"But I'd like to point out that the two of us are blessed with a helping of uncommon sense. We both know what would have happened. The cops *maybe* would have showed. They'd have broken up the fight and sent the husband on his way. Maybe he spends a night in the clink. Then he's back tomorrow. Or the next day. And this time he wouldn't give Anna a chance to get to the phone."

Silence from the other end.

"You realize your threat was a bluff," Ms. P finally said. "We already called in that particular marker."

"I know that, but Nowak didn't."

"He believed you?"

I thought about the look of terror in the man's eyes as I crouched on top of him.

"Oh yeah," I said. "He swallowed it."

A pause and then . . . "Good."

My boss and I shared a lot of things, and the pragmatic philosophy she'd mentioned that first day in her office was one of them.

Though I didn't know what was pragmatic about spending another night up in Greene County. Orly Crouch had refused to see her for a second time, but Ms. P didn't feel like giving up.

"Third time's a charm?" I asked.

"I'm going to try another tack," she said. "If I fail again, I will write the endeavor off as a lost cause and return home."

"I don't know about that," I said. "You might be stuck up there awhile."

Night was falling outside, and the snow was still piling up.

"The weather is not as bad here," my boss said. "The locals I've spoken with don't expect it to accumulate much."

"Well, I hope you brought a book or three."

"Do you have any further adventures planned during my absence?" she asked with only the lightest dash of sarcasm.

"Just one," I said. "I have an idea and I want to test it out."

I told her what I was thinking. I expected her to say something about not wanting me to take any more risks.

Instead, she reminded me, "It will be Sunday. You will need to be careful with your timing."

Like I said—pragmatic.

———

By the time the bells at the church down the block from Belestrade's chimed for the noon service, I'd been planted on the corner for the better part of an hour.

I'd made three forays down the block so far. Each time, staying a step behind groups of people, most of them kissing cousins of the Russian babushkas I'd seen the first time I was there.

Each time I passed number 215, I glanced at the windows. Each time, a light shone in a window on the second floor. On one trip I saw the shadow of a figure moving behind the curtain—tall, slender, male.

Neal Watkins. It had to be. He must have had his own room. Either that, or he was disposing of evidence. But if that was the case, I figured he'd be a little more subtle.

The last of the bells echoed out and the milling babushkas filed into the church. I decided I'd give it another hour.

The snow had slowed to a light flurry, but nearly two feet were on the ground. My feet had long turned to ice.

Also, I was self-conscious about my face. Running to help Anna the day before, I hadn't had time to think about it. Now I felt like everyone's eyes were on me when they passed.

There were Frankenstein stitches pulling my cheek tight, and while the swelling had gone down some, most of my face was still shades of black and purple with a few yellow highlights thrown in for variety. No amount of makeup was going to help. I'd pulled my hat down tight around my ears and wrapped a scarf around the rest so only my eyes showed.

One hour. Then I'd go home and beg Mrs. Campbell for some hot chocolate.

My patience paid off.

About twenty minutes after the service began, the door to number 215 opened and Neal Watkins stepped out. He'd traded his undertaker's suit for a wool coat, a hat, and what looked from that distance to be a university sweater. He headed off down the street in the other direction with a canvas grocery sack swinging from one hand.

Grocery shopping. Which meant he could be gone for half an hour or ten minutes, depending on the day's menu. I decided to chance it. As soon as he'd turned the far corner, I hurried through the snow to Belestrade's front door.

I knocked loudly. "Delivery!"

Now if any neighbors glanced out, they'd think I was a delivery boy leaving a note.

From an inside pocket, I took out a long wallet filled with picks. A quick look in either direction, then I went to work on the lock. I was inside in under a minute. Not a personal best, but pretty good considering I was working with two broken fingers and a busted wrist.

I stepped inside the dead woman's house.

What I'd come for was upstairs. But I couldn't resist walking into the parlor. It smelled like a room where someone had been killed—blood and bowels and stale air. Nobody had bothered cleaning up after the cops had been through, and fingerprint powder was everywhere. With those black smears as a guide, it didn't take long to locate all the gimmicks.

There were microphones secreted in strategic places, all of which led to a reel-to-reel behind a slab of fake books. It was a professional rig using magnetic audiotape, which wasn't something you saw much of in those days outside of the military or certain government acronyms.

There were also dials that controlled the lights and hidden speakers that, I discovered after some testing, produced a limited variety of sounds: waves, wind, footsteps, and voices whispering words too soft to hear.

She really was no better than Madame Fortuna. It was comforting and disappointing at the same time.

After I was satisfied I'd located all the tricks, I went up.

On the second floor I found a bathroom, an office, and what I assume was Neal's bedroom. The office had been picked clean by the police. The desk and filing cabinet were empty. Even the typewriter ribbon had been taken. All that was left were a few innocuous notes scribbled in a decidedly masculine hand.

I made my way up to the third floor.

There I found a lavish bedroom done in dark silks. It had an attached master bath that featured a claw-footed tub that could have fit three with room to spare. The bed was equally oversized—an enormous, four-poster, oak-framed thing that could have played host to an orgy.

It was exactly what I'd been hoping to find.

The incident at the Nowaks' had put something Dr. Water-house had said in a new light and I wanted to test my theory.

There was no carpet on the floor. Not even a rug. Just the original hardwood. It didn't take me long to find what I was looking for—long, faint grooves leading in a semicircle out from the footboard of the massive bed.

I bent down and discovered scraps of fabric tied to the four feet of the bed frame. I leaned against the footboard and began to push. It was as heavy as it looked, but the fabric allowed the massive bed to slide with relative ease.

The fabric didn't stop it from making a loud rumbling—the sound Dr. Waterhouse had heard from two floors below. The sound I'd heard when Anna had moved the furniture away from the door to let me in.

Once the bed was angled out, I got down on all fours and examined the floor beneath. There I found a hidden compartment in the floorboards, not unlike what concealed the safe at our office, only more cleverly constructed.

In the compartment, I found a flat, heavy metal box. It was the type a paranoid millionaire might use to stash their greenbacks when they didn't trust banks. There were scratches around the lock, and I wondered if I wasn't the first person to go at it with a pick.

It took about ten seconds to crack.

The only thing inside the box was a single round metal case containing a ten-inch reel of magnetic audiotape. On the case was a piece of tape and the penciled notation: "*A.C. 10/20/45.*"

AC? Abigail Collins? And if the date was right, it was less than two weeks before the Halloween party.

The box had almost certainly held dozens of such tapes. Who had taken the rest? Why leave this single reel behind?

Never one to look a gift horse in the mouth, I slid the reel into the pocket of my coat, closed the box and its secret compartment in the floorboards, and moved the bed back into place. Once I was satisfied that everything looked more or less as I'd found it, I headed back downstairs.

As I hit the last step, I heard a key in the front door.

Damn! I'd been in there too long.

Hiding was no good. Who knew how long he'd be there. I decided to play it a different way. I hurried back into the parlor, found a chair facing the door, and sat down.

By the time Neal walked in, I was settled into what I hoped passed for nonchalance.

In his threadbare overcoat and university sweater, he looked more like the promising grad student he used to be than an archvillain's assistant.

"What are you doing here?" he demanded.

"Just following the invitation on the door."

He looked confused.

"'Seekers inquire within'? I was seeking, so I came in."

"I'm going to call the police," he declared, making a half-hearted start toward the phone.

"It'd be an interesting coin-flip to see whose side the cops take. The nosy detective, or the blackmailer."

That set him on his back foot.

"I never blackmailed anyone," he said, jutting out his chin. "I was just an assistant. I told the police that."

"And the best researcher the history department ever saw, according to Doc Waterhouse," I mused. "I wonder how much your boss relied on you to fill in the blanks on her clients. Did you get to listen to her tapes? Or were those for her ears only?"

He wasn't even looking at the phone now.

"Like I said, I already talked to the police," he said. "They've been through the whole place, top to bottom. They found no evidence of wrongdoing."

"Sure," I said with a dollop of sarcasm. "Just hidden mics and the trick lights and sound effects. But they didn't find the stash of tapes, did they? Guess they didn't bother looking under the bed. Was that your handiwork on the lock?"

Neal arranged his features into what he must have figured was a poker face. "I don't know what you're talking about," he said.

"I don't know what game you're playing, but if you're thinking of picking up where your boss left off, I wouldn't recommend it. You don't want to get on Ms. Pentecost's radar. With your boss dead, I think she'd settle for second fiddle."

He threw his shoulders back and struck a pose. "If you and your boss want to come after me, go ahead. I've got nothing to hide," he declared. "Not like some people."

I gave him what my grandmother used to call a "send-'em-to-the-graveyard grin." "What are you referring to, Neal? That I keep the company of women as well as men? Or that I saw *Follow the Girls* three times on Broadway? Because I'm only ashamed of one of them."

I stood up and walked past him out of the parlor. I was reaching for the knob when he finally spoke.

"I don't want any trouble, okay?" he said. "She gave me assignments. Specific assignments. I didn't always know the details. So I don't know anything."

It was a good monologue. But he'd apprenticed with the best.

"I almost believe you," I said, then walked out the front door and into the snow.

CHAPTER 33

I found a pay phone and called the office to check in. Mrs. Campbell answered on the fifth ring.

"Any update from the missus?" I asked.

"No, but there was a call for you. A Hollis Graham said to tell you he was back in the stacks today, whatever that means."

"It means I'll be out in the elements a little longer," I said. "Hold the fort down."

Despite the snow, the library was bustling. Every loafer or weekend bibliophile within thirty blocks was wandering up and down the stacks.

I bypassed the crowd and headed down to the basement archives, where I found my quarry sorting through a table piled high with magazines.

Hollis wasn't much to look at. Short, squat, with a pair of thick cheaters perpetually sliding down his nose and a pile of bushy steel-gray hair sitting precariously atop his head. He was wearing his usual uniform of a painter's smock and dusty boots. He would have preferred to dress up—I've been to his house and have seen his impressive collection of Savile Row suits. But he ends every day covered in the dust of disintegrating newspapers, many of them with his byline somewhere between the folds.

I peered over his shoulder at the magazines he was giving the stink eye.

"French?" I asked.

"Belgian."

"What's the difference?"

"Coinage, kings, landmass, history, and where they get filed," he said. "I wouldn't bother filing them at all, except they were part of a donation and— Moses on a broomstick, what happened to your face!?"

"You should see the other guy."

"Was the other guy Sugar Ray Robinson?"

I gave him the rough sketch of the events. He shook his head, sending his steel-gray curls bouncing. "You gotta be more careful, girl. This city's full of monsters, thieves, and assholes. And that's just City Hall."

"Yeah, yeah," I said, waving off his concerns. "You got my message?"

"I did. I'm still catching up on the Collins stuff. I was down in Panama City Beach. They didn't carry the New York papers. Can you believe it?"

"Heathens."

"You have no idea. Anyway, what are you looking to find out?"

"Anything that you know that hasn't made it into the record," I said. "We've got a dead socialite who came to New York under a pseudonym. Whose husband up and shot himself for what most people agree was no good reason. Not to mention the blackmailing—now murdered—clairvoyant who may or may not have had a hand in picking the pockets of the Gramercy Park crowd."

"Your boss doesn't think this Wallace guy is good for it?"

"What my boss thinks, I couldn't tell you. She's out of town following strings of her own," I said. "Speaking for myself, there's a lot of blank spaces in this puzzle and I'd love to fill some in."

He gave me a look I couldn't decipher, then asked, "You eat lunch yet?"

I shook my head.

"Let's get out of this dungeon," he said. "I'll be down here all day and I'd like to see the sun. Also, I've got two assistants who are great at filing and better at eavesdropping."

He unzipped his smock, revealing a wool sweater and trousers in complementary shades of blue, and swapped his dusty boots for a pair of brown leather brogues. He grabbed his coat and we made our way up into the light and cold, then trudged through the snow to a little Italian place on Forty-eighth that I'd passed but never eaten at. The maître d' smiled and called Hollis by name before seating us at an isolated booth in a corner where we could watch the snow and talk without anyone's overhearing us.

A waiter who looked like he could remember when the Brooklyn Bridge was still a pipe dream took our order. I went for the meatloaf; Hollis opted for pasta primavera. After delivering a glass of red wine for him and water for me, the waiter made himself scarce.

"Been here before?" Hollis asked.

"Never had the pleasure."

"Good place. Good food. Same family running it since the turn of the century. Used to be it was the only place within twenty blocks that served a full menu until two in the morning and stocked something better than bathtub gin."

"Must have been popular with the journos and the cops," I surmised.

He shook his head. "Too pricey for working stiffs. During normal hours, it catered to the wannabe-titans-of-business crowd."

"And during abnormal hours?"

"It was the first stop for anyone who was out late, could afford a ten-dollar meal, and wanted some privacy," Hollis said. "I was here the first time I ever saw Al Collins close up. I was out to dinner with a friend who was treating. It was late—well after midnight. Place was full, though you wouldn't have known it. All the booths had curtains back then, and there was a big upstairs room for private parties.

"Anyway, a couple of suits come in, three sheets in and laughing their guts out. I look over and catch the eye of one of them—tall, older, kind of grim-looking. He seems to make me as a reporter and he grabs his friend and hurries upstairs. I asked the friend I was with who that was. He says, 'Oh, that's Al Collins. You should keep an eye on him. He's gonna be one of the string-pullers in this city one day.'"

The waiter arrived with our meals and we dog-eared the conversation. Having grown up where money was scarce and so was the meat, I'd developed an affinity for meatloaf. Mrs. Campbell couldn't seem to get it right, insisting on throwing big hunks of vegetables into the mix. This place got close, though.

"Did you keep an eye on Collins?" I asked after we'd gotten a few bites in.

"I kept an eye on a lot of people," Hollis said. "Though Collins wasn't much of a mover and shaker until a lot later."

That threw me some. "He seemed to have done okay for himself from the jump," I said. "He might not have been a Rockefeller, but he was in the ballpark, wasn't he?"

Hollis shook his head. "I'm not talking money, Will. Lots of men in this city have that. Only a handful really make the decisions. Who gets appointed to what? Where does the city put its dough? What neighborhoods get developed and which get forgotten? In his early days, Collins was on the outside of that clubhouse."

"Maybe he didn't want to be a member," I suggested.

"Never known a rich man to turn down a chance to make himself richer. Especially not one as cutthroat as Collins," he said around a big mouthful of pasta.

That begged a follow-up, but I waited until we'd cleaned our plates to toss it.

"What kept him out of the big boys' treehouse?" I asked. "And you said most of his career. Which means he eventually got let in. What changed?"

Hollis dabbed some sauce off his chin, then gave a quick look around the mostly empty restaurant. Whatever he was about to say, he didn't want any eavesdroppers.

"It wasn't until a couple years after I first saw him that I thought about Collins again. I was busy digging up dirt on the people who really mattered. I couldn't spare the time for an also-ran," he said. "Then I heard he was marrying his secretary. Big news because of the class difference and the fact that she was pregnant. I was onto the City Hall beat by then, so I was only sort of following it. But one night me and the woman who covered the society beat were sharing a typewriter getting last-minute stories in. She—this reporter—said she was real surprised Al Collins was getting married. I said something about him doing right by the girl and she laughed. I asked what was funny. And she said she knew for a fact he was a confirmed bachelor."

Hollis looked at me, waiting for a reaction.

"What?" I asked. "So she lost the bet on him getting hitched."

Hollis laughed, a big, loud, rolling laugh out of proportion with such a squat frame.

"Honey, sometimes I forget how young you are," he said, still grinning. "I'm saying that he was a confirmed bachelor in the way I'm a confirmed bachelor."

"Hang on." I struggled to get my bearings. "You're saying Alistair Collins was . . . ?"

"As a three-dollar bill."

I took half a minute and let the implications sink in. There were too many dominoes to track. Hollis kept going.

"Suddenly Collins not being in the upper echelons made sense," he said. "Back then things weren't as bad as they are now, but they were bad enough. With the Committee of Fourteen going after everyone they could get their hands on. But things changed for Collins when he got married. He started flexing his muscles, put down those labor strikes. There were rumors he had some people disappeared. After that, he started getting the government contracts. He moved up to the big leagues."

Hollis downed the rest of his wine.

"Anyway, she told me about Collins and I remembered the first time I saw him here in this restaurant. Shone a whole different light on him. That look he gave me. How he grabbed his friend and hurried upstairs."

"Any idea who the other man was?" I asked.

"Funny you should ask," he said. "I never saw him before. Never saw him again. Not until yesterday."

"You saw him?"

"Yep."

"All right," I said. "Spill it. Where'd you see this guy?"

So he spilled it.

And a whole lot of puzzle pieces fell into place.

CHAPTER 34

I walked Hollis back to the library. The flurries had finally stopped.

We said our goodbyes under the steely gaze of one of the library's lion sentries. Hollis left me with a parting thought.

"I wasn't kidding when I said things are getting bad. The war put a pin in it for a while. But now that everyone's not so distracted, they'll get back to it. Anyone who can't be easily categorized and shelved is gonna get tossed."

I gestured at my battered face. "You think I don't know, Holly?"

"I think you're young. Despite everything you've been through—maybe because of it—you think you're immortal."

"I've got no misconceptions of that." I threw him a grin, but he didn't return it. Instead he scowled and ran typewriter-callused fingers through his hair.

"Not only do you not fit, but you're not afraid of standing out," Hollis said. "You and your boss both. Nails that stick out get hammered down, Will. Just be careful is all I'm saying."

His words stuck with me the whole way home. Once upon a time, Hollis was the best reporter east of the Hudson, or so I'd been told by people who'd know. I thought about how, at that moment, he was losing himself in the stacks. Far out of sight of anyone with strings in their hands. Keeping his head down. Staying alive.

I didn't think it sounded much like living.

Back at the office, I went to put the reel of audiotape in the safe and saw a message on my desk from Mrs. Campbell. The boss had phoned. Weather permitting, she expected to be back later that night.

The intensity of my relief startled me. I wanted her back for her sake, but also for mine. She might have been a nail that was sticking out, but she held an awful lot together.

I spent the rest of the afternoon and early evening attending to leftover paperwork and looking out the window every few minutes. Eventually Mrs. Campbell emerged from the kitchen and told me, "If she can't make it, she'll stay put and call. Stop pacing and have a bowl of lamb stew."

I had two bowls, and a piece of raisin nut bread and coffee. It was ten P.M. and I was on my fifth cup when I heard a car pull up in front of the house. I looked outside to see a familiar figure limping up the front steps. I ran out and grabbed the suitcase out of my employer's hand.

"Thank you," she said, following me in. "I was afraid I wouldn't make it back tonight and would have to take shelter in a roadside motel."

There were dark circles under her eyes and her skin looked dry and parchment thin. Like she could crumble to pieces at any moment and blow away.

I waited as she got settled behind her desk with a glass of honey wine. When the pink finally started coming back to her cheeks, I asked her if she'd had any luck getting in to see Orly Crouch.

"I did," she said. "I noticed on my first attempt to see him that his farm was showing neglect. I suspected he'd fallen on hard times and that he would be open to a financial incentive to speak with me."

"You bribed him."

"I bribed him," she said, taking a sip of wine.

"Did you learn anything interesting?"

"Quite a bit, though a few questions remain."

"Before you start on that, maybe I can answer a few."

I filled her in on the results of my day's adventure, starting with my visit to Belestrade's lair and my confrontation with Neal.

"I told you to be careful. You shouldn't have let yourself be caught."

"Yeah, that's on me," I said. "Curiosity and the cat and all that. But we got the tape of Abigail Collins's session out of it."

"Or so you assume."

"It's a good bet. Before you ask, we still have the gear from the McGinnis job, so we can listen to it at our leisure," I said. "But the tape is just the icing on a very rich cake. Wait'll you hear the rest."

I told her about my conversation with Hollis and what I'd learned about Al Collins. None of it seemed to surprise her.

"Why do I have the feeling you already knew all this?"

"On the contrary, I did not," she avowed. "But it fits very nicely with what we know so far, and with what I learned in Cockerville."

Mrs. Campbell delivered a steaming bowl of lamb stew, which Ms. P promptly tucked into. She talked as she ate. Later, she handed me a notebook full of shorthand to type up for our files.

What follows is the bulk of her conversation with Abigail's

brother, along with occasional observations I've cribbed from Ms. Pentecost's notes.

NOTE FROM LP: I met with Orly Crouch in the kitchen of his farmhouse about five miles outside of Cockerville. My driver waited in the car. He held the second half of the money I was paying Mr. Crouch to speak with me. I do not believe he would have done so if I had not provided the incentive. He is a rangy, fair-haired man at least six feet in height, though his bent back belies his size. His face and hands are raw and weather-beaten and he appears a good decade older than his fifty years. His resemblance to Abigail Collins is unmistakable.

From the kitchen window I could see pigs and sheep, as well as a chicken coop. The coop, pens, and fences were all in a state of disrepair. Several outbuildings were falling in on themselves. The house itself was ill kept. Weeds grew up through the floorboards of the front porch. There were cracks in the plaster of the ceiling and the walls. While inquiries among residents of Cockerville suggest this level of distress is common for farms in the area, the Crouch farm seemed to be in a worse state than its neighbors.

All in all, it felt like a homestead slowly being reclaimed by the land around it.

LP: *Thank you for agreeing to speak with me, Mr. Crouch. I hope it will prove beneficial for us both.*

OC: It's your money. And it doesn't buy you all day. I've got work to get to. This farm don't run itself.

LP: *Then I will be direct and brief. When was the last time you communicated with your sister?*

OC: Not since she left home.

LP: *You received no word from her at all?*

OC: Got a postcard a few weeks after she left. Had the Chrysler Building on it. Wasn't signed or nothing. But I figured that was her. Letting me know she was alive.

LP: *That was a concern? Her safety?*

OC: It's New York City. She was only nineteen. Lord knows what can happen to a girl alone in that place.

LP: *And that was the last you knew of her? . . . Mr. Crouch?*

OC: This fellow. Friend of mine. He's got a good-size pig farm. Sells to some restaurants in the city. Better believe he greased some palms to get that setup. Anyway, he was making a delivery and he saw Abby's picture in the newspaper. She was getting married. He brought me a copy.

LP: *So you knew she had changed her name to Pratt?*

OC: Yep.

LP: *And that she had married Alistair Collins?*

OC: Yes.

LP: *Did you reach out to her?*

OC: Nope.

LP: *I find that surprising, Mr. Crouch. Your only sibling getting married. And to a wealthy man.*

OC: What are you saying?

LP: *That you could have used financial assistance.*

OC: I was doing fine. I'm doing just fine. . . . I mean—I didn't need so much assistance then.

LP: *But later?*

OC: My sister wasn't one to . . . She wasn't the charitable sort.

LP: *Even for family?*

OC: She wasn't big on family.

LP: *How do you mean?*

OC: I mean she never much cared for farm life. Always had one eye on the door.

LP: *What was Abigail's home life like?*

OC: Her life was fine.

LP: *But she kept one eye on the door?*

OC: It wasn't glamorous like maybe every girl would want. But her life was all right.

LP: *Surely not every girl runs away to New York City and changes her name and cuts all ties with her family.*

OC: I don't know what to tell you. It's what she did.

NOTE FROM LP: Mr. Crouch's posture changed here. He became stiff and withdrawn and he would not meet my eyes.

LP: *Please remember, Mr. Crouch, that the second half of your payment is dependent upon full, honest answers.*

OC: Fine. Okay. Maybe she had it tough.

Our mother died when Abby was only three or so. Our pa, he . . . Well, he was an old-fashioned sort. Didn't expect to have a hand in raising a girl. Didn't know quite what to do with her. I had to help with the farm a lot. Abby had to see to herself.

LP: *That must have been difficult.*

OC: Sure it was. And when she got older, she and Pa butted heads more.

LP: *In what ways?*

OC: Little things to start. Money mostly. She wanted a new dress or bows or books or whatever girls want. Pa had to keep explaining how we couldn't waste money on things like that. It was the times Pa kept her out of school to help on the farm when things got real heated. Screaming fights in the front yard. Neighbors could hear it a mile away.

LP: *Did he discipline her?*

OC: Sure. But only when she deserved it.

LP: *Did she deserve it often?*

OC: She was stubborn. Pigheaded. She wouldn't learn.

NOTE FROM LP: Mr. Crouch's body language suggested that he was uncomfortable with this line of questioning. I chose not to follow it further in the fear that he would end the interview prematurely. But, in your parlance, Will, I'd put it at even odds that Abigail Crouch was physically abused by her father.

LP: *I understand that your sister had a number of suitors.*

OC: That's real sharp. Real sharp way of putting it. You've been talking to those little gossips at the church, haven't you?

LP: *I've made a number of inquiries.*

OC: Well . . . Yeah, she was a pretty girl. She had fellas interested. But she didn't lead them on, all right? Church women making things more than they are. She didn't even go on a date until she was seventeen. There were other girls around that were up and pregnant by then. She was a saint compared to some of them.

LP: *But she did not remain with one suitor for very long.*

OC: She was always finding something wrong. Never satisfied.

LP: *She was a romantic?*

OC: I don't know about that. She wasn't . . . I don't think she was . . . She wasn't that kind of girl.

LP: *What kind?*

OC: The kind that gets wrapped up in people.

LP: How do you mean?

OC: I mean . . . The reason she kept dropping these boys. One was too poor. Another she said was too dim to amount to much. One boy—she didn't get along with his sister and she said she wasn't going to chain herself to a family she couldn't get along with.

LP: Very practical.

OC: Yeah. That was Abby. Practical.

LP: Did any of these relationships ever progress? Did she ever say she loved any of these boys?

NOTE FROM LP: Mr. Crouch did not answer this question. He excused himself to visit the outhouse. He was gone for nearly a quarter of an hour. When he returned there was the smell of whiskey on his breath.

LP: Tell me about Billy McCray.

OC: What's to tell?

LP: Your sister dated him for several weeks.

OC: She dated a lot of boys for several weeks. Billy wasn't special.

LP: He was special in that he took his own life.

OC: He and Abby called it quits by then.

LP: Was the breakup at her insistence?

OC: She was always in charge.

LP: Do you believe Mr. McCray killed himself because he was spurned by your sister?

Mr. Crouch?

OC: I'm getting a little tired of you poking into my family. You're trying to make my sister sound like . . . like . . .

LP: I assure you, I'm only interested in the truth.

OC: The truth!

LP: *Yes.*

OC: The truth is Billy McCray eating a shotgun didn't have nothing to do with my sister.

LP: *What do you mean?*

OC: Billy liked to gamble. Cards, mostly. He'd make these buying trips to Albany for his dad's hardware store. Supposed to stay at a hotel at night, but he'd use that money to play cards at this place he knew. He lost a lot. Borrowed money from some guys he shouldn't. Got in pretty deep, from what I hear.

LP: *Did your sister know?*

OC: Who do you think I heard it from? Shoot—that's why she dropped him. Said men like that were weak. Said he'd leech his parents' store dry feeding his habit. Anyway—you see how his death didn't have anything to do with her.

LP: *Yet she left immediately after he killed himself.*

OC: I think I'm done.

LP: *Might I remind you that the other half of your payment is contingent on—*

OC: Maybe I don't want your money.

LP: *I can also inform your sister's estate of your existence. She was a very wealthy woman. There might be contingencies in her will. For next of kin.*

NOTE FROM LP: What followed was several minutes of silence. I could see some sort of struggle playing out on Orly Crouch's face. When he continued it was without prompting and his mind seemed far afield.

OC: That was a strange summer. Pa and Abby were fighting more. She was like a hen that just won't settle. Keeps trying to get out of the coop.

There was that damn girl.

Neighbor up the road had a cousin visiting from somewhere down south. Don't remember her name. Something unusual. Younger than Abby by a few years, but they hit it off. Some of the men at the feed store said this girl's mom was a whore and was in jail, and that's why she was staying up here. Think half the reason Abby made friends with her was because it set Pa off.

This was maybe a month after Abby had stopped seeing Billy. She'd seemed pretty set on not getting back with him, but then I walked into the hardware store one day and saw Abby with Billy in the back. Not . . . not like that. Just talking. He looked . . . scared. They shut up when they saw me.

Later I saw Abby and her friend out on the porch talking all serious. Then not long after that, I caught Abby in the old tool-shed. We didn't use it except to store junk. She was in there with one of the floorboards pried up and a wad of bills in her hand.

I asked where she got it. She said it wasn't none of my business and not to tell Pa. She, um . . . she gave me a few dollars. Said there'd be more if I kept my mouth shut.

End of the summer, this friend of Abby's goes back to wherever she came from. Then Billy shot himself. Not two days after, Abby was gone. No warning.

Money was gone, too. I checked.

Good riddance. She was dead weight, you know? Pa died a year after. Facedown in the hog pen. Stroke.

I think I'm done.

Keep your money. Leave it. I don't much care.

But if you're not off my property in five minutes, you're gonna regret it.

Because Ms. Pentecost plays square, she left the money. More than a man like that deserves, but the information was worth it.

After Ms. P finished giving me the abridged version, I made a couple of informed guesses that my boss agreed with. Then she clued me in on a few things I'd overlooked and made a few informed guesses of her own.

I dragged the tape player out of the basement and had it nearly set up when Ms. P found the packet of photos in her desk. She took them out and studied them. She'd never seen a lot of the cast of characters, so I stood over her shoulder and played pin the name to the face.

Looking at one particular photo—a group shot with everyone in the frame—I noticed something that I hadn't before. I pointed it out to Ms. Pentecost and she confirmed my suspicion. Then she pointed out something else. A little detail that I'd overlooked. The rest of the pieces slid home.

By that point, we didn't really need to listen to the tape, but we did anyway. It was well past midnight by the time the reel ended.

There was some hashing out about what should be done and how we should do it. But for all intents and purposes, we knew who had killed Abigail Collins and Ariel Belestrade. More important, we knew why.

CHAPTER 35

Back at the beginning of this thing I told a fib. Let's be honest, I've told a lot of fibs. Some were for my benefit, some for yours, none so big that they changed the heart of the thing.

The fib I'm thinking of is when I said that Lillian Pentecost doesn't work like detective novels, that she doesn't go in for dramatics, for getting all the suspects into a room and holding a show where she fingers the killer.

That was only half true. She does like to put on a show, even if it's for an audience of one. Technically, two, but I didn't really consider myself audience. I was the backstage help.

Settled behind her desk, glass of honey wine within easy reach, Ms. Pentecost focused her good eye on the person sitting in the chair across from her. She looked just like she had that first night I met her.

Resolute. Leaning into the storm.

"The roots of this case extend back at least twenty years, perhaps longer," she began. "Abigail Pratt, who was born under another name, grew up in rural poverty and was likely the recipient of regular abuse at the hands of her father. She learned at a very early age that if she was to survive and thrive, she would have to fend for herself. She learned to view her relationships—especially those with men—in terms of who could benefit her and who couldn't. Those who were not wealthy or ambitious were discarded. As was the boy who had a gambling problem and was stealing from his parents to pay off his debts.

"Then she met a girl—a visitor to her rural county. This girl's mother had raised her daughter to flourish on the fringes of society. The girl had learned how to leverage people, especially vulnerable men.

"Abigail and her friend blackmailed the boy with the gambling problem, threatening to tell his parents he had been stealing from them. The boy acquiesced, stealing even more to pay Abigail and her friend. Eventually he descended into despair and took his life. The girl returned south and Abigail took the money she'd extorted and fled to New York City.

"She'd learned much from her friend, including how to procure false documents. She changed her name. Possibly because she was worried that the boy's family would discover what she'd done. More likely because she wanted to sever ties with her own family."

Ms. P reached for her glass, but her hand was shaking, so she pulled it back. It had been a late night, preceded by a long journey. I knew she was teetering on the edge of exhaustion. I'd argued holding off a day, maybe two. No doing. She wanted to end this. Honestly, so did I.

She shifted in her seat, took a deep breath, and continued.

"But people contain patterns just as crimes do. Abigail—now Pratt—would not stand for feeling trapped. Being a mere secretary would have been just a different kind of cage for her. First she sought comfort, becoming pregnant in the process. Then she sought leverage, as her friend had taught her. She discovered a secret about her employer. Something that would have ruined him, had it been known. But she'd learned from her mistakes. Instead of merely seeking money, she approached him with an offer. Marry her, claim her children as his own, and he could carry on his secret life in perfect camouflage. Alistair Collins accepted the offer. He likely had little choice, though he was able to exert some control by placing Abigail under a strict allowance. So Abigail Pratt became Abigail Collins. And Alistair continued his decades-long affair with his old friend and now business partner, Harrison Wallace."

Hollis Graham had seen Wallace's photo in the paper after his arrest and recognized him as the man who'd followed Al Collins into the upstairs room of the restaurant.

"I do not know how content Abigail Collins was in her new life. People who grow up as she did—deprived and abused—are suspicious of comfort. It's very possible that she was incapable of love, at least selfless love. Whether or not she was content, her life for the next two decades was stable.

"That changed when she attended a charity ball where one of the entertainments was a medium. Both women had changed since that summer, but Ariel Belestrade recognized her summer friend, the one she'd talked into blackmailing her ex-boyfriend. How exactly their partnership was rekindled, I don't know. For someone of Belestrade's skills, I don't think it would have been difficult to feel out the fractures in Abigail's life and marriage. Either way, before long the clairvoyant had . . . awakened that old feeling of discontent in Abigail. That . . . feeling of being trapped. The idea to use . . . Alistair's secret to extort him . . . would not have been so hard a sell. For Abigail, it would have been . . . less about money. And more about . . . freedom."

That hitch was starting to creep into Ms. Pentecost's voice. I knew she hated it, because it took attention away from her words. She was nearing the heart of it, though.

She soldiered on.

"Whether it was the cumulative effects of . . . hiding his true self and of . . . being blackmailed, or whether there was . . . an inciting incident that propelled Al Collins to take . . . his own life, I do not know. Perhaps both. He had ended his . . . relationship with Harrison Wallace that year. He even . . . moved Wallace's office to the other side of the building. So he would . . . see him less. A person . . . forced to deny who they are can easily bow under the . . . weight of their unhappiness."

Ms. P's eyes drifted my way. I'd told her what Hollis had said about nails being hammered down. "Be as circumspect as you feel is needed," she'd told me. "But do not deny who you are. There will always be someone looking to beat you down. Do not do their job for them."

I tried to take the advice to heart, but it didn't make me feel much better. Especially considering what we had ahead of us.

"How long . . . Abigail and Ariel waited . . . until . . . until . . ."

I stood up and grabbed a tall, lidded stein from one of the bookshelves. I poured Ms. P's wine into the stein and handed it to her. She nodded her thanks and managed to take a sip without spilling. While she gathered her strength, I picked up the story.

"Maybe they waited a decent amount of time after Alistair's death to start putting the pinch on Wallace, but I don't think being decent was on the top of their to-do list," I said, reclaiming my seat at my desk. "Belestrade was used to walking a high wire when it came to blackmail. She figured that now that her friend had voting shares, she had the kind of leverage that could get Wallace to fork over six figures. Maybe more if they were smart about it."

I looked to Ms. P. She nodded at me to continue.

"Wallace proved to be a harder squeeze," I said. "He suspected why his friend and lover had killed himself and that put some steel in his spine. Also, he wasn't rich like Alistair. And he was married. He had a wife who saw their bank accounts. She'd notice if chunks started disappearing ten thousand at a time.

"But there was his friend's legacy to consider," I said. "Abigail had enough voting shares to hold the company hostage. That whole shtick about not wanting to be a war profiteer was for show. I'm guessing that's what did it. Wallace was always loyal to Alistair and to the company. He eventually found a way to get the money by siphoning it out of company accounts. This goes on for about a year. Then his doctor delivers the bad news. Cancer. He did some soul-searching and turned off the faucet. No more embezzling. No more payments.

"The average criminals probably would have cut the cord. They'd gotten plenty of dough off of Wallace. But these two women—they weren't average. For Abigail, it was as much about power as it was money. Having Wallace shake off his harness only made her more determined. She had her clairvoyant friend send him a message. That whole Halloween party show was directed at him. What was it Belestrade said? 'Please, just let me be at rest. Don't betray me, my love'? In other words, just because your lover is dead, it doesn't mean his reputation can't still be ruined."

I flashed to sitting in Belestrade's parlor as she aped my mother's voice and just how easily she'd been able to push my buttons.

"We're not so sure it got the job done, though," I said. "Wallace snuck away during the party to powwow with Abigail in the study. There were bruises on her wrist that she picked up right before her death. If I had to lay money I'd say Wallace dug in his heels, said something nasty, she slapped him, and he grabbed her wrist. Something along those lines, anyway.

"Lazenby and his crew don't have that yet. Wallace going back up to the study. Eventually they'll get there. Maybe Wallace will tell them himself. Add in how he got angry and picked up the crystal ball, et cetera. The district attorney will probably overlook the locked door. Lazenby will chafe, because he hates not crossing all the Ts, but he's got to do what his bosses tell him."

My boss held up her hand, signaling that she was ready to take the baton. I gratefully passed it back to her. I didn't want to be the one to say what came next.

She went slowly, taking every word with care.

"Until her death, Ms. Belestrade was the most obvious suspect, though not necessarily one supported by the immediate facts. Something that I stubbornly refused to see," Ms. Pentecost said. "As it had been in their youth, Abigail was her intermediary in the scheme. It . . . buffered her against reprisals. Mrs. Collins's death did her no favors.

"But because of other facts—ones unrelated to this case—I remained focused on her," she admitted. "John Meredith tried to contribute to that belief in Ariel Belestrade's guilt. He lied about seeing her when the body was discovered. But no one else had seen her, and she was someone who would surely be noticed. It was only after Ms. Belestrade's murder that I managed to clear my head enough to see the significance of that lie.

"One of the details I am lacking—and it's a minor one, really—is whether Mr. Meredith glimpsed you through the smoke, already standing in the room. Or whether he saw your bedroom door open and made the correct conclusion."

Becca sat like a statue on the other side of the desk. The

funeral had been the day before, but she'd come dressed for mourning—a slim black dress, black stockings, black gloves. She wore it like armor. There were no tears, no lip-biting. She didn't even blink. It was like she'd seen this speech coming.

"No matter," Ms. P said. "It's a small detail. What matters is that he knew or strongly suspected the truth. That you had killed your mother that night."

CHAPTER 36

If you were expecting Becca to crack once the finger was pointed at her, you haven't been paying attention.

That makes two of us.

Maybe you tumbled to Becca a while ago. Maybe you've been yelling at me this whole time—"It's the dame! Don't trust the dame!"

But you weren't me. I can follow a queen right up the sleeve of any three-card monte dealer in the city, but I couldn't see Becca. Call it love or lust, or just some stupid cliché about falling for the damsel in distress.

I told you before that I was going to be honest with my mistakes. Becca was the biggest one of all.

The boss and I would have a lot of long, late-night conversations about that.

"Ms. Collins was exceptional," Ms. Pentecost would assure me. "In a better world, she would have been the one we were assisting."

In the world we had, I waited for Becca to say something. A confession. A denial. Anything. She just sat there, still and silent. Her baby blues were fixed straight ahead, waiting for Ms. P to go on.

She did.

"I don't believe you knew about the blackmail that led to your father's death. I think if you had, you would have acted sooner," my boss said. "But I imagine you suspected something. Something that began to eat at you. You drank more. You went out to clubs. You took chances. You did your best to escape."

Tears started racing down Becca's cheeks. I had to grip the arms of my chair to keep from going to her. Even knowing what she'd done, she still had a hook in me.

"Then your mother began pushing for the company to forgo its military contracts, saying it was their moral duty," Ms. P continued. "It was so out of character for her. You began to ask questions. About your mother's actions. About why your father killed himself. About why your godfather seemed so haggard and sad."

This we had gotten from the recording of Abigail's last visit to Belestrade's parlor. It didn't spill everything, but it gave us enough to know Becca's curiosity hadn't gone unnoticed. During the visit, the two laid out their plan for the séance—to use it as a way to jolt Wallace to cough up the dough. The idea to use Becca as the "volunteer" had been Belestrade's. Her mother had provided the detail about the stolen perfume. Apparently her father hadn't kept it a secret after all.

"The part of the crossword I can't fill in is the killing itself. How you found yourself picking up that crystal ball. I just can't see it," I admitted. "We know it wasn't planned out. If it was, you'd have kept your gloves on."

I leaned over and took the wheel.

I saw the question in her eyes.

"Your fingerprints were on the crystal ball," I explained. "But you were wearing gloves at the party. The police found smudges they figure for glove prints. Which means you were wearing them during the séance but not when you came back. If you'd known what was going to happen, you wouldn't have taken them off."

I watched as she took that little detail in. It wasn't exactly a keystone clue. If the cops got their hands on the party snaps and noticed the gloves, she could say she'd touched the crystal ball after they discovered the body. Or had taken her gloves off during the séance. And if anyone said otherwise, it'd be she said, they said.

For that matter, she could have clammed up and walked out and there wouldn't have been a thing we could have done about it.

Instead, she said, "I heard them arguing. Uncle Harry and . . . and my mother."

"This was in the study after the séance?" Ms. P asked.

Becca nodded. "I didn't hear the words. But I recognized the voices. And the anger," she said. "I opened my door a crack and saw Uncle Harry walk out. He looked so . . . broken."

She stared down at her hands. Her fingers found a loose thread in the seam of one of her gloves and began picking at it.

"I went to the study and found her there. She was sitting at the desk, staring at her reflection in that crystal ball. I told her . . . I told her I knew something was going on. Something with Uncle Harry and something . . . Something with my father. And that I wouldn't . . . I wouldn't stand for it. Whatever was going on, I wouldn't stand for it."

She'd worked the thread loose. She pulled at it and tore a hole in the palm of her glove.

"She laughed. She laughed at me and said I didn't know what I was talking about. That it wasn't any of my business. I told her if it was about my father, then it was my business. . . . Then she told me."

She yanked off the ruined glove, then the other. Her finger-nails were chewed to the quick.

"What did she tell you?" I prompted gently.

She looked up and met my eyes. What I saw there was hard and cold, like ice rimming the Hudson.

"She told me about my father and Uncle Harry," she said. "That their entire marriage was a lie. That it had always been a lie. That he had used her. That he'd used me. That he . . . that he'd owed us. The money she'd . . . that she'd gotten from him. It was what she was owed."

"You never suspected about your father?" I asked.

"I should have," Becca said. "When I told him about that first crush and he saw right through me. The advice he'd given me. About keeping your heart hidden. I should . . . I should have known he was speaking from experience."

Something ignited in the pits of her eyes.

"That makes me so . . . There I was, telling him my secrets and . . . And he didn't feel like he could do the same. He had to hide. Him and Uncle Harry both. Even from me. The biggest part of his life and . . . I never knew. And now he's dead and we can never . . . I hate her for that. I still hate her."

"Is that what did it?" I asked. "Is that why you picked up the crystal ball?"

She shook her head, her lip curling in disgust.

"No," she said. "It was starting to sink in that this was the reason he'd killed himself. The pressure of hiding. Of . . . No. It was when she said that he wasn't even really my father. He was just . . . He was just an old queer and we were his props."

She took a deep, shaky breath.

"By the time I knew what I was doing, it was already done."

"And the fire?" my boss asked.

"I threw the crystal ball into the fireplace," Becca said. "It caught on one of the drapes and knocked it into the flames. The room began to fill up with smoke. I just sat down. I didn't think about . . . about anything. There was pounding on the door. I ignored it, but it kept going. I got up and went to answer it. Then the door burst open and John Meredith rushed in. He saw everything. He must have figured out what had happened. He grabbed me and threw me to the side and into the drapes. Then everyone else was there. In the smoke and confusion . . ."

She didn't have to finish. Becca might have been bruised and battered on the inside, but her gears could still spin when they needed to. The "I was alone in my room" alibi was good enough as long as she stuck with it and Meredith kept mum.

That must have been a dreadful couple of days. Waiting for Meredith to spill. Then wondering why he hadn't. Maybe thinking he had some blackmail of his own in mind. When really it was love.

Who knows if she'd have been able to keep it buried forever. Even with Meredith keeping his mouth shut, even if the police couldn't pin it on her—killing your mother is a heavy load to carry.

Then fate intervened by way of Lillian Pentecost. Maybe it really was because of the board's urging that Wallace hired her. More likely it was because he was afraid a prolonged police investigation would turn up his secret relationship. He needed a detective who would answer directly to him, get the solution quick, and keep the past under wraps.

"I've got a question," I said. "When you asked me out, were you just fishing for answers on where we were at, or were you hoping to get in my head and short-circuit things?"

Becca answered immediately. "It was just fishing at first," she said. At least she had the decency to look ashamed. "Then it became something more."

"When?"

"About three minutes after we started dancing."

She smiled. I didn't.

I don't know if she was answering straight. I didn't want to know. I nodded to Ms. P to get on with it.

"Your mother's murder was in the throes of rage. Ariel Belestrade's was not," Ms. P declared. "You might have suspected she was involved in the blackmail scheme that led to your father taking his life. But it wasn't until Will called you—angry and accusing you of betraying a confidence—that you knew for sure."

Yeah. I'd set that particular row of dominoes falling. I'm not too proud of it, and I've never dialed a number in anger since. Belestrade wasn't going to be citizen of the year, but her death had slammed shut doors that Ms. P had spent years trying to pry open.

"You knew where you could find a gun. Perhaps it was a gift from Mr. Wallace to your father. Or maybe to yourself or your brother," Ms. P said. "You went to Ms. Belestrade's home. She gladly let you in, perhaps seeing you as her next target. Her skills at reading people failed her that night. She failed to realize that she was the target, and you shot her. Then you left, disposing of the gun in a sewer grate, and returned to another uncorroborated but suitable alibi."

Becca got unlucky, though. The gun was found and traced, and Uncle Harry put two and two together. He might not have known it was Becca, but he probably had a good idea it was one of Alistair's children.

So he decided to be a good godfather. He clammed up, told his lawyer not to fight the charges, fired us, and decided to sit in the Tombs and wait for the cancer to put an end to the whole thing.

"What now?" Becca asked. She sounded like a woman on the edge of the world, staring out into the abyss.

"That is very much up to you," Ms. P told her.

"You have to tell the police, don't you? You said so that first day. If you have evidence of a crime, it's your duty."

Ms. P spread her hands, open and empty, in front of her. "I have no evidence," she explained. "Only suppositions and inferences."

"But I . . . I confessed. I told you—"

"Very little, really. Bits and pieces of the night your mother died. You never said explicitly that you killed her. And you never admitted to shooting Ms. Belestrade," Ms. P said. "Unlike the late clairvoyant, I have not seeded this room with microphones, and Will is taking no notes. Besides, our testimony of this conversation would be deeply suspect. Ms. Parker is still recovering from a head injury and I have a degenerative disease that, in advanced cases, affects the memory. A district attorney would be brave or foolish to build a case on either."

We'd talked it over the night before—how we should approach it; wrestling with the moral implications and all that. For me, it was a one-sided fight. For Ms. Pentecost, it wasn't quite so easy. In the end, we found ourselves standing in the same corner.

Becca was blinking, confused. Now she didn't even have the abyss in front of her. She didn't know where she was standing.

"What should I do?"

She sounded so lost. My heart cracked.

"I cannot tell you what to do, Miss Collins," my boss said.

"What would *you* do?"

Ms. P leaned back in her chair. She raised her hands to her head and smoothed back the loose strands that had escaped her braids. That streak of iron gray looked a mile wide.

She looks so old, I thought. Much older than when I met her. Older than when we started this case.

"What would I do?"

Emotions flitted across her one good eye faster than I could follow. I knew she was exhausted and on the edge herself. I also knew she wanted to choose her next words perfectly.

"I would . . . I would manage to get to women like Abigail in time. Before they learned to trade one pain for another," she said. "I would find a way to turn the gifts of women like Ariel Belestrade toward better ends. I would find a way where your father could be free and happy and you were not left to avenge him.

"I cannot do any of those things. Instead, I would sever the chain of these events so that no one else need suffer from them, innocent or guilty."

For the next half hour, Becca and Ms. P talked through options. I threw in some ideas of my own. When Becca finally left, it was still up in the air exactly what she would do. We had an awkward moment at the door as I let her out into the winter darkness.

No kiss. No words. Just a look.

Part of me worried she'd go home and take the same quick exit her father had taken. I wanted to say something, but I didn't. Instead, I watched her walk away on unsteady legs. I kept my eyes on her until she was in a cab and out of sight.

CHAPTER 37

We learned how the Collins case wrapped up the same way the rest of the city did—in the pages of the daily papers. Though we did supplement that with a few discreet calls to our contacts.

Two days after that meeting in our office, Becca and Randolph convened an emergency, closed-door meeting of the Collins Steelworks board. Nobody leaked what was said behind those doors, but considering what followed, I could hazard a guess.

That same day, the board talked with the DA and the embezzlement charges were dropped. The company, it seemed, was refusing to cooperate with any prosecution of Harrison Wallace. Later that day, Wallace's lawyer finally applied for bail, which was granted. Becca and Randolph paid it. A few days after that, on page 2 of the *Times* business section, I read that the siblings were selling their shares in the company. At a steep discount.

Here's my guess about that board meeting. A threat was made and a deal struck. Help get Wallace out of jail and you get the reins of the company. Or let the prosecution go forward, risk a whole lot of dirt going public, and have the largest shareholders as enemies going forward.

The board made the easy choice.

The case against Wallace for Belestrade's murder floundered. No prints were recovered on the gun, and the lack of other evidence made the district attorney balk. The police tried to build a case against him for Abigail's murder. Even after they pieced together the partygoers' testimony like we had, and figured out he'd gone back to the study that night, it still wasn't enough. Expensive lawyers can work miracles.

The deal would come back and bite the board, though. A few weeks later, it was announced that the military would be going elsewhere with their big contract. The ups and downs at Collins Steelworks had been too much, even for the U.S. government.

Lazenby made a couple of visits to our office looking to pry some information loose. He wanted anything we could give him on Wallace. We kept mum and said we had nothing. It crossed a line, but I've crossed plenty. He left frustrated, sure we knew more than we were telling.

The police were also keen to find Neal Watkins. He'd vanished from his room at Belestrade's, leaving behind empty drawers and an empty bank account. He also took, I guessed, a few dozen audiotapes filled with blackmail material. Why'd he leave behind Abigail Collins's tape? Because he felt some loyalty to his old employer and thought it would point us in the right direction? I didn't know.

The tape was eventually filed away on the third floor with the rest of the notes from this case. You never know when things you thought were dead and buried will come back to haunt you.

———

Shortly before the holidays, John Meredith pleaded guilty in front of a judge and got four years. I wasn't in the courtroom. By then we were in the middle of another case—a missing persons thing—and it was getting messy.

The guilty plea didn't come as a surprise. Not to me, anyway.

The week before, I'd taken a field trip to the Tombs. Fifty dollars slipped to the right guard got me ten minutes in an interview room with Meredith. Another fifty ensured the guard wouldn't have his ear to the door.

By then my bones and bruises had healed. The only reminder of the attack was the scar on my cheek that I was trying to convince myself gave me an air of danger.

Meredith hadn't healed quite so well. His nose had never been set properly and his left eye drooped, giving him a perpetually sleepy look. Seeing me walk in instead of his lawyer woke him up, though.

"What are you doing here?" he snarled, pulling at the cuffs chaining him to the table. "I don't want to talk to you. Guard! Guard!"

"The guard's taking a walk."

"I ain't talking to you."

"I don't need you to talk," I told him. "Just listen. Five minutes and you'll never see me again."

He didn't like it, but he settled down. I sat down at the table across from him.

"My boss and I—we know everything. We know who killed Belestrade and Abigail Collins. We know why you lied for her."

His features twisted, fear and rage warring with each other.

"And we're not going to tell a soul," I said. "Nobody knows. Nobody needs to know. Everyone thinks Wallace did it, and he'll be dead soon. There's no reason for any lingering questions not to go in the ground along with him."

His face settled, but he looked at me warily. Like he was waiting for the other shoe to drop. I dropped it.

"You plead guilty, there's no trial and no questions about why you did what you did. You take it to a jury, there's no telling where the DA will start digging or what will come out. I just wanted you to know that. In case you were weighing your options."

I stood up and pounded on the door to let the guard know I was ready to leave.

"Does she know?" he asked, his voice thick and trembling.

I turned. Tears were streaming out of his wounded eye.

"Not from me," I said. "But she's smart. She knows Collins isn't her real father. She knows you kept silent about seeing her in the study that night. She might put it together. All it took for me was seeing a photo of the three of you in one place. They got their beauty from their mother. But your bone structure's there. If you look close enough."

"But you're not going to tell her?" he croaked.

The heavy lock turned and the door swung open.

"She's had enough pain when it comes to family. I don't see any reason to add to it."

I turned my back on him and left.

We celebrated Christmas in our own way. No decorations aside from a wreath on the door. I bought Ms. P a new cane— one with a two-foot blade hidden in the handle.

"Do you really think I'll have cause to use this?" she asked.

I reminded her of her own advice. "Better to be prepared than found wanting."

She got me a first edition of *Evil Under the Sun* to replace my tattered paperback copy. On the title page was an inscription: *"Will, Keep up the fine work—Agatha."*

I might have squealed with joy, but you'll never prove it.

Christmas afternoon we went with Mrs. Campbell to her church and served dinner to those who didn't have the home or the dough to make it themselves. We did the same thing on New Year's Eve. Not a bad way to greet 1946.

In the second week of January, I opened up the *Times* and was greeted by Harrison Wallace's obituary. They used a cropped photograph. In it, a man's arm rests across Wallace's shoulders. He's smiling.

I half expected Becca to get in touch that week, but she didn't. I considered calling her, but every time I reached for the phone, something stopped me. It wasn't anger. Or not anger alone.

I'd come to the conclusion that maybe she did have feelings for me. That she wasn't just playing me. I also decided that I had feelings for her, too.

If it had been garden-variety lust, I might have called her. Asked her if she felt like dancing.

But I was still healing. And some wounds hadn't quite closed.

It would be a while before we saw each other again.

By spring, the Collins case had more or less receded into memory.

One thing about life in the Pentecost household is that you never have too much time to mull over the past. The first months of 1946 saw us embroiled in a slew of cases. Some came with paychecks, others we'd come across during our Saturday open houses.

There were a few loose ends that bugged us. According to

my sources, there was a good chunk of embezzled money that the police had lost track of. Something in the six-figure range. If Neal Watkins had it, I figured we wouldn't be seeing him again. Five zeroes buys you a long, anonymous life.

Also, why did Belestrade start researching us so early? And how did she figure into those cases that Jonathan Markel had been looking into?

That's the way it is with most mysteries. There are always more questions than answers. Few things wrap up nice and tight like they do in my dime-store novels. That's probably why I like reading them so much.

CHAPTER 38

One warm March day, a package arrived. I opened it to find a copy of Olivia Waterhouse's new book, *Speaking with the Dead: Spiritualists in the Twentieth Century.* She'd inscribed the title page with a short note.

"*To Lillian Pentecost. A fellow seeker of truth. I hope the chapter on Ariel Belestrade meets with your approval. —Olivia Waterhouse.*"

I reached across Ms. P's desk and handed it to her.

"Some light Sunday reading if you're interested."

She cracked the cover, read the inscription, and froze. She stared at it for so long, I was afraid she was having some kind of seizure.

Finally, she spoke. "Please phone Dr. Waterhouse. Tell her I'd like to meet with her here at her earliest convenience."

Her earliest convenience turned out to be three days later at noon.

"Thank you so much for inviting me over," the petite professor said as she crossed the threshold into our office. "To be honest, I was overjoyed. To see where the greatest female detective in the country makes her home. It's thrilling."

She was dressed in her lecture-hall duds: off-the-rack jacket and skirt in bland shades of brown and gray. Her brown curls still needed combing, and her wire-rim glasses sat low on her nose.

I kept my face as expressionless as possible as the professor took a seat in the nicest of our yellow chairs. She was so small that the chair practically swallowed her.

Ms. P slid the book across her desk.

"Oh good, it arrived," Waterhouse said. "I hope you find it interesting. Or at least not terribly boring. The publisher pushed me to include more lurid details than I would have liked, but he knows better than I do what sells, I suppose."

A full ten seconds ticked by. Ms. P just looked—examined, really—the unprepossessing woman sitting across from her.

Finally, she asked, "Who are you?"

"What do you mean?" the woman who called herself Waterhouse responded, the look of confusion on her face a perfect forgery.

"I mean that until you took your post as a lecturing professor, you did not exist."

Or at least she didn't exist on paper. I'd spent three days pushing every resource I had and making half a hundred phone calls to source Dr. Waterhouse's résumé. Phone numbers were defunct, previous employers unreachable or deceased, college records lost to a fire. While all her ID would stand up in court, I couldn't find a single person who knew Olivia Waterhouse before 1938.

Meanwhile, in our office, Waterhouse hadn't let the mask slip an inch. She removed her glasses, squinted, put them back on.

"I'm afraid I don't understand, Ms. Pentecost," she said. "Is this about the book? Did I get something wrong?"

Ms. P reached across and opened the cover of the book to reveal what she'd used to bookmark the title page with the inscription. It was a thin slip of paper with the name "Ariel Belestrade" written on it in tight, elegant handwriting.

"Handwriting analysis is an imperfect science," Ms. P said. "And there are forgers who are expert at re-creating an individual's script. But even when concentrating on deception, there are certain tics of the hand that are difficult to obscure. Especially when one is working quickly. This upstroke of the 't.' This narrow loop in the 'd.'"

I was staring right at Olivia Waterhouse's profile while Ms. P talked. No tells. Just a slight tightening around the eyes, but I might have been imagining it.

"I do not know the exact order of events, but I can surmise. You tasked Robert McCloskey with waylaying Jonathan Markel as he walked home from his club. McCloskey bludgeoned him and dragged him into the building site, where you were waiting. You replaced the message hidden in his watch—something you must have done out of sight of McCloskey, since he later decided to steal the watch. Likely because he was being blackmailed to do the job rather than paid. You somehow discovered he had committed such crimes before. The watch was his recompense. Fortunately for you the message eventually reached its destination and McCloskey died before he could describe you."

"That is . . . fantastic," Waterhouse declared.

My boss shook her head. "Not fantastic," she said. "Merely the explanation best supported by the facts. I might be mistaken on a few of the details, but they lead to the same conclusion. I tasked Jonathan Markel with finding a link. Someone to connect a series of crimes—some not even crimes, merely strange occurrences. I was looking for a single hand behind these events. He was successful. He found you."

Waterhouse shifted in her seat and crossed her legs. The

sudden movement caused my hand to slip half an inch closer to the .38 holstered under my armpit. Maybe I imagined it, but I thought I saw the professor's eyes flick toward me, followed by the very slightest uptick of her mouth.

"I'm afraid you're going to have to elaborate, Ms. Pentecost," she said. "What exactly is it that this person found?"

"Someone who pries out secrets—indiscretions, crimes—and uses them to leverage people of power and influence. Frequently these incidents have ended in disappearance or death." My boss listed the cases in her file—the bank president, the zoning commissioner, the garment tycoon, and others. "You did not limit yourself to people of influence. Mr. McCloskey is an example. Though men such as him have their purpose."

Waterhouse pushed her glasses up on her nose and leaned forward, like one of her own students. My boss continued the lecture.

"With Belestrade, you found someone you could not only leverage but also use to ferret out the secrets of others. You were the reason she was able to elevate to the circles of the city's elite. You were the reason she was so prepared for my attention, how she knew so much about myself and Will."

The mention of my name caused Waterhouse to look my way. I searched her face for some hint that my boss was hitting pay dirt. Nothing. Just my own reflection looking back at me from her spectacles.

"By replacing your name with hers, you'd made Belestrade your stalking horse," Ms. P continued. "You could watch me watching her and learn what you could about my methods. That Abigail Collins's murder brought you into my orbit was merely ill luck. Though perhaps it was inevitable."

"Are you accusing me of having something to do with Abigail Collins's murder?" Waterhouse asked. "With Ariel's?"

"Oh no," Ms. P said. "I know you're not responsible for their deaths. But I believe you arranged the events that triggered those killings. You discovered Ariel Belestrade's former relationship with Abigail Collins and directed her to make contact. That led to all that followed."

Waterhouse shook her head. "Incredible," she said, though I wasn't sure what mast she was nailing that adjective to. "These things you're saying I did. What advantage could I possibly gain from them?"

"That is the question I am still wrestling with," my boss admitted. "With the Collins case, there is still a large amount of money unaccounted for. The police believe Neal Watkins has it, but I'm beginning to suspect otherwise. As for these other cases, we have yet to uncover how you financially benefited. But we have had only three days."

For a solid half minute, there was barely a blink from Waterhouse. I imagine there were wheels turning in there. But her insides were a safe, and I couldn't see the gears.

She removed her glasses, squinted, and . . . tucked them into her breast pocket. When she spoke, it was slowly, carefully, like she was feeling her way through a dark room.

"These . . . cases . . . you mentioned. The bank president? If I remember correctly, he was later discovered to have been embezzling funds from a number of charities he was tasked with overseeing. The zoning commissioner was taking bribes to rule in favor of developers and allow for the desolation of poorer neighborhoods. The garment tycoon . . ."

She said "tycoon" like most people say "rapist."

"Wasn't it one of his factories that caught fire several years back? The one where all those seamstresses died, trapped, screaming? And so many more were burned."

With each word, she grew more confident. Like she was slowly finding her footing.

"I imagine you've met some of those women," she said. "Perhaps during your Saturday sessions. When you've opened your doors. You've seen the scars they carry. He was leading the fight against new safety regulations, this man. Thirty years since the Triangle Shirtwaist and it's like we've learned nothing."

Here was the real Olivia Waterhouse, if that was even her real name. There was a fire in her eyes and in her voice, like a street-corner preacher. She leaned in with each word, keeping time with a conductor only she could see.

"And consider Alistair Collins," she said. "A man who earned his prestige by ordering the brutal beatings of labor organizers. Beatings that sometimes ended in deaths. Who bribed and backstabbed and bartered his own soul. Long before Germany's surrender, he was making inquiries with the military on where the next big war would be. And how he could make money from it."

"What are you suggesting?" my boss asked.

"That not everything is about money," Waterhouse declared.

I let that sit for a second, then chimed in. "That's why you called me about the tapes."

She looked over at me again. Without her glasses, I could see her eyes. They were dark pits that I could have slipped and fallen into if I weren't careful. I had to concentrate to keep my hand from moving toward my gun.

"When it looked like Wallace was going to take the fall and the company was cutting ties with him, the contracts would have probably still gone through," I said. "You needed to make sure we got on the right track. So you told me about the tapes and hearing that rumbling and all that. Of course, you'd already cleaned it out. But not without leaving the one recording that might point us in the right direction. What I'm wondering is whether Neal Watkins is hiding out in Florida or Canada, or is he sucking mud in the Jersey swamps. Too big a coincidence that he started out as a researcher down the hall from you. You had to have planted him there."

"You make me sound like a gangster," Waterhouse said with a hint of a smile.

"Nah. I've met gangsters. You're something else."

"And what is that?"

"Someone who enjoys pulling the strings of the people pulling the strings."

This time her smile was more than a hint; it was almost cheerful. "What a wonderful turn of phrase," she said.

Then she uncrossed her legs, casually smoothed out the creases on her skirt, and stood.

"You have no evidence, of course." It was a statement, not a question.

"We do not," Ms. Pentecost admitted.

Waterhouse turned toward the door but stopped when my boss held up a hand.

"One thing puzzles me," Ms. P said. "You could easily have avoided my notice. By directing me at Belestrade, while remaining in her orbit, you almost assured that we would eventually come into contact."

Waterhouse gave her head a cock, as if giving Ms. P the point.

"Even today, you must have suspected why I called you here," my boss said. "So why come at all? If not to confess?"

Again, Waterhouse took her time answering. Like she was working out something in her head.

"I think . . . I hope," she said, "that we could become friends."

Whatever Ms. P was expecting, it wasn't that.

"Or at least allies," Waterhouse added. "We have so much in common. Women striving to change the world for the better."

Ms. Pentecost jerked up ramrod straight, good eye blazing fire.

"I bring criminals to justice. You blackmail and rob and murder, and justify it using your own twisted moral code," she declared. "We are far from alike."

Waterhouse nodded, like she was considering a question from one of her lecture-hall students. "Perhaps," she said. "Perhaps not." She glanced down at me. "How is Becca doing, by the way? Moving on, I hope?"

My throat went dry and I let my fingers curl around the butt of my gun.

"It's quite all right, Miss Parker," Waterhouse said. "Becca's secret is safe with me. I'm merely pointing out that there is often a vast gulf between what is the law and what is right. And that everyone in this room understands that. The only difference, currently, is how far each of us is willing to go to see justice done."

She took out her glasses and slipped them on, like she was donning a costume.

"This has been illuminating. Seeing you work," she said. "You are, by far, one of the most interesting people I've ever had the pleasure of meeting. Both of you are."

She nodded at the book sitting open on Ms. Pentecost's desk.

"I hope you read it," she said. "On the surface, it examines our inability to grapple with our own mortality and how that can be used to control us."

"And beneath the surface?" Ms. P asked.

"You might say it's about strings and the people who pull them. Who have been pulling them for a very long time, and how it is long past time for some strings to be cut," she said. "Good day, Ms. Pentecost. Miss Parker."

With that as her exit line, she walked out. I stayed in my seat and listened for the sound of the front door. Then I got up and checked. She was gone. I drew the dead bolt and went back to the office.

"What now?" I asked. "Give Lazenby a call?"

"And tell him what?" Ms. P asked. "That a professor of cultural anthropology is responsible, directly or indirectly, for a number of crimes, some of which are not even recorded as crimes? Our credit with the NYPD does not stretch so far."

"I guess we start a file box on Waterhouse," I said. "Or whatever her real name is."

Ms. P nodded. "We will need to keep a close eye on her."

She reached for her cane and stood. She hadn't had a bad day in a while, but she was using the cane more regularly. And the shadows under her eyes had never quite gone away.

"You think she'll keep at it?" I asked. "Even knowing we know?"

"I think she enjoys being discovered," Ms. P said. "As you noted, she comes alive when she's in front of an audience."

She walked to the kitchen to see what Mrs. Campbell was preparing for lunch.

———

As I type this out, the smell of fresh-baked bread is wafting in from the kitchen. These days, kneading the dough fires up Mrs. Campbell's arthritis and she has to soak her hands in ice water for an hour after making a batch. But she still refuses my help when I offer it.

Stubborn old woman.

I can hear her singing softly to herself. It's a hymn I don't recognize. The light coming in through the windows is starting to dim. I'll have to turn on the lamps soon.

The big desk is empty. Mrs. Campbell says I should start using it, but I can't bring myself to. At least not tonight.

Maybe tomorrow. Maybe never.

I'm stubborn, too.

Back when I started, I talked about invisible costs. I wondered how my ledger would be weighted at the end of the day—in the red or in the black.

All of this, and I still don't know.

What I do know is that I started this story with a piece of advice wrapped in a lesson: The trick is knowing when to let go.

There's a flip side to that coin. These days the lesson I try to take to heart is one Ms. P never said out loud but lived every day of her life: Hold on tight to what you can while you can. There's not a better world out there. There never will be.

Unless we make it.

WILLOWJEAN PARKER

LEAD INVESTIGATOR

PENTECOST AND PARKER INVESTIGATIONS

NEW YORK CITY

A C K N O W L E D G M E N T S

There were so very many people involved in getting this book from my head to your hands. Special thanks go out to:

My agent, Darley Anderson, whose faith and enthusiasm in this novel were spectacular. The exemplary work he and his team did is the reason you're holding it now.

My editors, Bill Thomas and Margo Shickmanter, who provided an exceptional debut experience. They helped make this book the best it could be and ensured I didn't trip over my feet the first time out. They were assisted by a battalion of talented people, including Carolyn Williams, Maria Massey, Maria Carella, Peggy Samedi, Mike Windsor, Elena Hershey, Hannah Engler, Aja Pollock, and a host of others. And if you're holding the U.S. edition, three cheers for illustrator Rui Ricardo's work on the cover.

Game-master Austin Auclair, who was kind enough to beta-read for me and who test-drove the mystery. Eventually I will stump you.

My dear friend and co-conspirator, Melissa Hmelnicky, who has always been one of my most passionate cheerleaders and whose love of Lillian and Will gave me hope that others would feel the same.

And most importantly, my wife, Jessica, who has been my first reader, first supporter, and first love for many years. Who after reading an early draft said she'd love to see more of Will emotionally processing things, which is a contender for best note I've ever gotten. If you enjoyed this book, I think you'll agree. She regularly provides me with examples of how to be a better writer and a better person, and this novel wouldn't exist without her.

About the Author

Stephen Spotswood is an award-winning playwright, journalist, and educator. As a journalist, he has spent much of the last two decades writing about the aftermath of the wars in Iraq and Afghanistan and the struggles of wounded veterans. His dramatic work has been widely produced across the United States. He makes his home in Washington, D.C., with his wife, young-adult author Jessica Spotswood.